PRAISE FOR *THE NATURALIST*

"[A] smoothly written suspense novel from Thriller Award finalist Mayne . . . The action builds to [an] . . . exciting confrontation between Cray and his foe, and scientific detail lends verisimilitude."

—*Publishers Weekly*

"*The Naturalist* is a suspenseful, tense, and wholly entertaining story . . . Compliments to Andrew Mayne for the brilliant first entry in a fascinating new series."

—*New York Journal of Books*

"An engrossing mix of science, speculation, and suspense, *The Naturalist* will suck you in."

—*Omnivoracious*

"A tour de force of a thriller."

—*Gumshoe Review*

"Mayne is a natural storyteller, and once you start this one, you may find yourself staying up late to finish it . . . It employs everything that makes good thrillers really good . . . The creep factor is high, and the killer, once revealed, will make your skin crawl."

—*Criminal Element*

"If you enjoy the TV channel Investigation Discovery or shows like *Forensic Files*, then Andrew Mayne's *The Naturalist* is the perfect read for you!"

—*The Suspense Is Thrilling Me*

THE GIRL BENEATH THE SEA

OTHER TITLES BY ANDREW MAYNE

THE NATURALIST SERIES

The Naturalist
Looking Glass
Murder Theory
Dark Pattern

JESSICA BLACKWOOD SERIES

Angel Killer
Black Fall
Name of the Devil

THE CHRONOLOGICAL MAN SERIES

The Monster in the Mist
The Martian Emperor

OTHER FICTION TITLES

Station Breaker
Public Enemy Zero
Hollywood Pharaohs
Knight School
The Grendel's Shadow

NONFICTION

The Cure for Writer's Block
How to Write a Novella in 24 Hours

THE GIRL BENEATH THE SEA

ANDREW MAYNE

This is a work of fiction. Names, characters, organizations, places, events, and incidents are either products of the author's imagination or are used fictitiously. Any resemblance to actual persons, living or dead, or actual events is purely coincidental.

Published by Thomas & Mercer, Seattle

www.apub.com

ISBN-13: 9781542009577
ISBN-10: 154200957X

Cover design by Shasti O'Leary Soudant

Printed in the United States of America

THE GIRL BENEATH THE SEA

CHAPTER ONE

SHALLOW WATER

Something else is in the water.

Never dive alone. Dad's words ring through my head as something splashes above me. My hand goes to the knife strapped to my leg. I take long breaths through my regulator and try to stop myself from fidgeting.

If I'm already being hunted by something, it won't really matter. Avoiding sudden movements is a way not to surprise an alligator or crocodile that hasn't noticed you. If they have . . . it won't make a difference.

I didn't see any large reptiles on the bank of the canal when I dived in, but that doesn't mean one couldn't have slipped past my attention.

Unfortunately, I can't see more than a few feet in front of me because of the murkiness of the water and all the sediment my shovel has kicked up from the bottom. The only wildlife I've observed so far is a curious turtle that quickly bobbed the other way once she spotted me.

An alligator in this canal wouldn't be unusual. I've been around them my whole life. I don't have any special fear of the toothy reptiles, only a healthy respect. As a teenager knee-boarding up and down the 84 Canal behind my boyfriend's boat, I saw them all the time. They'd watch from the banks with their greenish-yellow eyes like bitter old men remembering the days before the rambunctious kids moved into their neighborhood. The gators had a good run, spending millions of years here in Florida as the peninsula rose from the ocean floor, sank back, and rose again, over and over, outlasting the saber-toothed cats, ground sloths, elephants, and camels that all called Florida home at one time or another.

When people think of Florida, they tend to visualize the beaches, the blue-hairs, and the Everglades—forgetting the long history of the region. That's why I'm fifteen feet underwater in an unusually deep depression in a canal that feeds into the Intracoastal Waterway. Somewhere below the muck I'm probing with my shovel, there's a story to be told.

Until the splash, I was looking for rocks and fossil fragments to bring back to my PhD adviser as a favor. On the wall of her office at South Florida University is a map of the region with little Post-it notes marking potentially interesting paleontological and archaeological locations. This is one of them.

She got excited when I told her I dived for the police department and could help her investigate some of those sites—which basically meant me bringing her plastic bags of unusual things I found.

In a hole like this, you could find dinosaur fossils, mammoth bones—try to imagine those massive creatures roaming across the Sunshine State—or even ancient human remains. The Tequesta people spent two millennia in this area, and we still know very little about them. The fact that the Spaniards forcibly resettled many of them to Cuba didn't exactly help preserve their culture.

I remind myself that I might be risking my own extinction if I'm not careful. I take the knife out of the sheath, hold it in front of me, and pull my legs in so there's less to chomp on. In my other hand, I raise my shovel as a second weapon.

Although exceedingly rare, human deaths from alligators have increased as both of our numbers have gone up. *If* there's an alligator in the water, 99.999 percent of the time it couldn't care less. Millions of people come within feet of them every year without a problem.

Of course, millions of people don't go diving in remote water holes in which an alligator might feel a little more territorial. Also, millions of people don't sit on the floor of the canal like a large grouper waiting to be eaten . . .

Then there's the growing population of crocodiles, which are much more aggressive. Add to that the even more ferocious *Nile* crocodiles now swimming around out here too. Not to mention the increasing numbers of invasive giant pythons . . .

It's underwater *Jurassic Park* down here.

I slowly turn my head and scan the water around me, ready to stab the eyes and snout of anything that emerges through the murk. I could be less than two yards away from a twenty-foot alligator and not even know it.

I exhale a big burst of bubbles, letting anything nearby know I'm here. It's better to surprise something from far away than accidentally step on it.

Satisfied that I'm not about to be attacked in the next half second, I decide it's time to surface and head for the bank.

I kick and swim for the shining surface, working my fins until my head pokes above the water.

I half expect to see an alligator floating a few yards away watching me with a lazy expression. Instead, I'm greeted by a green canal still rippling from my own waves.

It's when I turn toward shore that I feel my heart stop.

I've swum close to alligators hundreds of times. I've seen more sharks than I can count.

The sight that greets me isn't the first time I've seen something like this . . . but never so unexpectedly.

The splash I heard wasn't an alligator slipping into the water.

It wasn't a crocodile or a slithering snake.

It was a body.

A human body.

A dead body.

Dumped into the canal while I was underwater.

CHAPTER TWO
COASTLINE

"You were diving alone?" a detective named Levine asks me.

"Yeah," I reply, glancing at the body under the tarp by the canal.

"That doesn't seem very safe," he scolds before walking away to confer with his colleagues.

No. It's not. Dad taught me everything about diving. First and foremost was to never dive alone. Sure, *he* did it. And I did it, but you weren't supposed to. And Nadia wasn't supposed to cancel on me today either.

She's got a good heart, but my Brazilian friend is a little on the flaky side when it comes to morning appointments. I had drinks with her last night, and she'd begged me to go out dancing. I declined. My daughter, Jackie, was with her father at his parents' mansion in Miami Beach, and I decided to binge *Jane Eyre* on Netflix and then get a full night's rest.

Of course, I ended up texting with Jackie until past midnight as she relayed the latest outlandish things her grandmother said.

Jackie . . . Jackie deserves a mother who isn't so stupid. A mother who isn't standing fifty feet away from a corpse she bumbled into.

Palm Beach Deputy Macon, a middle-aged man with a kindly demeanor, tries to keep me distracted while various men wearing khaki pants and polo shirts with different department logos take turns looking at the body.

Some of them take photos. Others compare the body to images on their phones.

"That's six," I note as another vehicle pulls up with yet another cadre of cops from some agency or department.

"What's that?" asks Macon. He'd been asking me what school my daughter goes to when Detective Levine walked over to tell me that diving alone was dumb.

Yep. Got it. Maybe I should make a sign and wear it?

I point to the SUV behind Macon as two men get out. "Miami-Dade PD," I explain. "No markings, and the rims look like something a drug dealer would have, which means the vehicle was probably a seizure. So I'm guessing they're narcotics."

Macon turns around to glance at the two men dressed in light pants and loose-fitting silk shirts. Both of them have their badges out on lanyards. Undercover cops.

"Huh," Macon replies. "You said you're a part-time police officer? You looking to go full somewhere?"

The undercovers walk over to Detective Levine, who responded after Macon called it in.

"No. I'm working on my doctorate in archaeology. I prefer my bodies to be long dead." I regret the joke immediately. It's fine for hanging out with friends over beers. Here, maybe not so professional.

Macon gives me a half smile. "So, you dive mostly? Just for your department?"

"They loan me out a lot. Lauderdale Shores has the highest number of canals and waterways per capita of any city in America," I reply, giving our rote response. We're a tiny community that most police departments barely know exists. "We also have three bridges and a mile of canal in a high-trafficking zone. It was cheaper to put me on the payroll than keep hiring me freelance to pull guns and evidence out of the water."

"So I guess this isn't your first body."

"Sadly, no." Macon's a nice enough man, and I decide to give him a fuller answer. "Remember that small jet crash six years ago in the Everglades? That was my first."

"Mercy. Eight people died, right? That had to have been horrible."

"The worst part was the jet fuel and the gators and snakes. I had to wear a dry suit. It was hot that summer." I omit the part where I passed out from dehydration and the only thing that saved me was inflating my buoyancy compensator at the last minute.

I'd pulled a dozen more bodies from the water since then. Some only hours dead, others in such advanced stages of decomposition that I had to wrap them in plastic so parts didn't fall off.

Today's body is the latest addition to that morbid list—if you don't count the people I rescued lifeguarding and spotting dive excursions. They'd all lived.

But today, I could tell the moment I saw her that she'd been killed recently. Maybe within hours.

Her. It's the first time I've thought of the body as anything more than a body.

After dragging her to shore, I'd torn off my dive gear and tried mouth-to-mouth in case there was hope. The coldness of her lips told me it was too late. But I had to try.

Grandpa Jack used to tell stories about men being pulled into the boat who seemed like goners, only to be revived after a heroic bout of CPR. He had lots of stories like that. Fighting off pirates, giant squid, hammerheads with vendettas. Some were probably even true.

The woman I'd pulled from the water today looked to be about twenty-three. She was wearing denim shorts and a T-shirt and had a smattering of post-millennial tattoos and hair dyed dark red.

The most distinguishing mark on her was the angry red gash across her neck.

Her throat was so badly crushed I could hear a faint wheeze as I tried to force air into her lungs. But I'd kept trying anyway.

It's what I would have wanted if it had been my . . .

Don't go there, Sloan. Don't go there.

The detective in charge, Ruiz, walks over to us. He's got a stocky build, a thick head of hair with silver streaks, and a goatee. We'd spoken briefly when he first came to the scene.

"Do you have an ID on her?" I ask.

Ruiz squints at me for a moment, then recognition dawns on him. "Right. You're the deputy for Lauderdale Shores?"

"Yes." I'd explained this to him a half hour ago.

"Did you know her?" he asks.

Suddenly he sounds like a cop talking to a person of interest. Something weird is going on here.

"I don't believe so. Have you identified her?"

He ignores my question. "What do you mean you don't believe so?"

I count to three and spare him the legendary McPherson temper. "She doesn't look familiar."

Ruiz nods and jots a note on a pad. "And you were underwater when it happened?"

You want to cop me? I'll cop you back. "When what happened?"

He gives me an incredulous look. "You were underwater when the girl was killed?"

"How would I know that?" This is frustrating. It's not what you'd normally ask a witness. It's what you'd ask a potential suspect.

Macon is watching us closely, sensing the tension. He tries to defuse the situation. "McPherson's the one that pulled the bodies from that plane crash in the Everglades we all had to respond to."

"I know who she is," Ruiz replies dryly.

I almost sensed a *what* in his response, implying that he knows my family history—including about my uncle Karl, currently serving time for a drug-trafficking-related parole violation.

I point to the body and ask again, "Do you know who she is?"

"No, we don't. Not yet."

I nod at the cops scattered around the scene. "I've pulled my share of bodies from the water. I've never seen . . ." I count all the jackets now on the scene. "DEA, Customs, FBI, BSO, PBSO, and Miami-Dade all show up for one. That's a little unusual. Don't you think?"

Something changes in his demeanor. I wouldn't quite call it relaxing, but his focus shifts slightly. "Yeah. It's odd. The field examiner took a temperature reading. She estimates the victim died about seventy minutes ago."

He watches the expression on my face as my body turns as cold as the victim's.

She wasn't only dumped here . . . I was in the water when she was killed. Perhaps in this exact spot.

"You okay?" asks Ruiz.

"I'm managing."

His tone softens slightly. "There's nothing you could have done. If they'd seen you, they would have just taken her somewhere else to kill her." He adds, "I don't think you were ever in any danger."

My attention goes to the knife still strapped to my leg. "I wasn't worried about me."

Ruiz turns to Macon. "Will you get a copy of her driver's license and contact information?"

"Do we need the suit?" Macon asks, pointing to my dive suit, which I forgot I'm still wearing.

"I think we're okay," Ruiz replies.

This comes as a relief. If he thought I'd killed the woman, he'd want it as evidence.

"Where are you parked?" asks Macon.

I point to my Explorer on the side of the road behind a row of bushes. "There."

He glances at the truck, then back to the water, probably noticing what I did: it's not visible from the road.

Ruiz returns to the other cops while Macon walks me to my truck.

"Let's be careful," he says, pointing to a muddy patch.

Forensic techs are already cordoning off the area so they can try to get footprints and tire tracks. Hopefully it'll be enough to find the killer if they already have leads. Hopefully.

At my Explorer, Macon waits while I rummage through my backpack. Half the contents are already spilled on the floor. I'd dumped it out when I raced back to get my phone to call 911.

"Here you go," I say as I pull my wallet from the pile, then freeze.

Something is wrong.

"McPherson?" Macon asks. "You okay?"

I turn my wallet toward him so he can see the spot where I keep my driver's license.

It's empty.

"Shit . . . ," he says. "You don't seem like the kind of person to forget that."

I shake my head.

No, I'm not.

Macon shouts to the group of detectives. "Ruiz!"

He comes running over to us. "What's up?"

I show him my empty wallet. His cop brain figures it out quickly. "He took your license."

I nod.

The killer knows who I am.

The killer knows where I live.

CHAPTER THREE
DOCK LINE

When I think of my father, I think of sharks, and oddly enough, it relaxes me. Right now, he's sitting on the stern of his boat with a concerned look on his face, and I'm the one trying to calm him.

My earliest memories are of Dad teaching me to swim. My most vivid is my first time snorkeling in the ocean.

I was six, and we were paddling over a shallow wreck, the *Copenhagen*, off the coast of Pompano Beach. I was still adjusting to the taste of salt water and the burning sensation it made in my nose when I didn't clear it properly while my older brothers free dived down to touch the ship's rusted anchor.

That's when I saw the hammerhead shark. My mind's eye remembers it being twenty feet long. In reality it was probably less than half that.

I'd seen more schools of beautiful fish than I could count, but this was something else . . . something alien.

I wasn't sure how I was supposed to react. My brothers had been teasing me, calling me Shark Bait. Sharks were scary and mysterious. I looked to Dad to see how I should respond.

He had a broad smile on his face and gave me the okay sign.

I smiled back. From then on, I never feared sharks or anything else in the water. Respected them, yes, but did not fear. If Dad wasn't worried, then I didn't need to be.

Of course, I hadn't been thinking about the scar on his leg left by an angry bull shark. Or the dotted welts on his forearm from a sea anemone. They seemed more like tattoos than physical proof that the ocean isn't a petting zoo.

Being a cop and a student on a college campus that doesn't have a criminal-justice program, I'm looked upon as a bit of a curiosity. I'm often asked if my father was law enforcement as well.

Usually, I simply answer, "No." If they don't recognize my last name, then explaining that Dad's a treasure hunter who spent our last dime in his crazy pursuit is more effort than it's worth.

I'd hold a grudge against Dad like my brothers do if I didn't love him so much.

I'll never forget the look Harris, my oldest brother, gave Dad when his Mustang was repossessed because we could no longer afford the car payments. The fury, the hate.

I was only nine, but the expression on my dad's face broke my heart. He was a lousy businessman, and his quixotic ambitions caused us plenty of suffering, but never for a moment did I doubt how much he loved us.

Money came and went, but Dad showered us with love.

I realized that I cared more about the people around me than about going to private school in North Miami or living in a house with more rooms than extended relatives. All that mattered was my family and the water.

After leaving the crime scene, I drove straight over to talk to Dad. He was sitting with Robbie Jr., my thirteen-year-old nephew, in the tiny kitchen on his boat, repairing a sonar system—one of the ways he makes money nowadays.

Robbie bolted around the table to give me a hug while Dad looked up from a circuit board and asked if I was the one who'd pulled the body from the water. I was confused until I saw the small television perched on the counter with the volume muted. Local news had been teasing a six o'clock report about a possible murder victim found in Palm Beach.

Dad and I went up on deck, and I gave him a quick summary while Robbie worked belowdecks.

The lights of the Fort Lauderdale skyline twinkle in the background as Dad peels the label from his beer bottle, something I've seen him do a thousand times when he's stressed. It's a habit I picked up too.

Some of my best memories were made on the stern of one of Dad's boats talking to him while the waves gently rocked us.

His boat, the appropriately named *Fortune's Fool*, is docked off the Intracoastal behind a large, one-story house that belongs to Freddie Kleinman, a physician who owns a chain of medical clinics. He's an old friend of Dad's who helps him by investing small sums in expeditions and letting Dad dock here rent-free when he can't afford the marina.

"You were in the water when the girl was killed?" Dad asks.

"Yeah. I was about fifteen feet down."

"In a canal?" Leave it to my father to get hung up on a hydrological detail.

"It's an old sinkhole that got absorbed by an oxbow."

He nods. "How did Nadia react?"

I still haven't told him the part about not having my dive partner there or the fact that my driver's license is missing. "I was alone."

His face turns cross. "What have I told you about doing that?"

I point to the row of oxygen cylinders and the single regulator near his legs. "You do it."

"That's different," he says. "You're . . . you're a mother."

I laugh. "And you're a father. And a grandfather."

"It's not the same." He pauses for a moment. "You're all grown."

"Uh-huh. *That's it.* Great comeback." I flick my bottle cap at him.

He catches it midair. It's a family game I learned before I could talk. He makes a theatrical sigh. "My daughter the solo-diving police officer who pulls corpses and assault rifles from the water. If I'd known having daughters would be this stressful, I'd have only had sons."

"Daughters aren't all bad," I reply, thinking of Jackie.

"The runt? She's too smart for her own good." *Runt* is his pet name for her. It's a joke because she's the tallest girl in her class and can outrun the boys.

"Hard to believe she's a McPherson," I add.

"Even harder to believe who her father is," Dad shoots back.

My father and Jackie's father, Run—aka Scott, his given name—have what you'd call a complicated relationship. Half the time Dad's dive buddies with Run; the other half he's harping on him for not making me an honest woman—even though the choice wasn't his.

Dad's worried look returns. "So, they killed this girl while you were underwater?"

"Yep."

"And they don't know who she is?"

"Nope. Although . . ." I stop myself.

"What?"

It's been nagging at me since I pulled her from the water. "There's something familiar about her. And not like someone I just saw once. Like she was a friend of a friend."

"That's depressing," Dad replies. "No idea who?"

I shake my head. "I'm sure they'll ID her soon. I'll ask around tomorrow at the office."

I know he's imagining if this had happened to me. It's instinctive. I'm not sure if I should tell him the other part. My stomach's in knots, but that's the reason I came here.

"There's something else you should know . . ."

"Last time you told me that, you were pregnant."

I remember his reaction—the same broad smile he gave me when we saw the hammerhead. Putting me at ease. Mom, on the other hand, was ready to kill Run and then drive me and his dead body to the justice of the peace.

"Whoever killed this woman knows who I am," I say flatly.

He cocks his head. "Because of the police report?"

"No. Because he went into my truck and stole my driver's license."

Dad's face turns vacant as he tries to process this. "Why?"

"I don't know. In case I saw something. It's not a big deal. It's just a thing."

This is hitting him hard. "But he has to know you're a cop by now, right?"

"Probably."

Dad looks at the loose hoodie I'm wearing. "You have your gun on you?"

"Yep." I took it out of the lockbox in my truck, and I've kept it near me since I left the crime scene. I don't feel as though I'm in immediate danger, but it seemed like the smart thing to do.

"It's going to be fine," I say, mostly trying to assure myself.

"Are you positive he took it?"

I nod. "Right now, a forensic tech is dusting my truck for prints. I got a ride here from a friend at the Broward Sheriff's Office."

"BSO? I thought this was in Palm Beach?"

"It was. There were a lot of cops there." I shake my head. "Something weird going on. Nobody would tell me anything."

I think that has me more worried than anything else.

"I need a favor, Dad." This is the part that kills me. "I'm going to ask Run if he can take Jackie for a few more days. I'd like you to keep an eye on her too."

This week is my turn, but we've always been pretty relaxed about it, mostly going along with what Jackie wants.

Dad's eyes narrow as he realizes what's been tearing me up. It's not only that I might have a psychopath after me.

It's that the address on my license is my daughter's address too.

CHAPTER FOUR

CHIEF

Police Chief Katherine Roche motions me into a chair in her office, then shuts the door behind us. I can tell this is going to be serious. When she closes the door, it usually means someone's going to get chewed out or fired.

I think I'm on safe ground in that regard. The last person she let go, Stephen Halperin, was a chronic alcoholic who refused treatment. Chief Kate, as we call her, went above and beyond to try to keep him in line, but his addiction was too severe. I also secretly suspect he had a problem taking orders from a Haitian American woman with a Queens accent.

Through the window by the door, I catch a glance of Carla Esmeralda pretending to type a report as she gives me an arched eyebrow. She knows something, but she's not about to clue me in on anything.

Chief Kate takes her chair and stares at me for a moment. Photos of her two sons flank her from the bookshelf. Daniel is an aircraft mechanic at Fort Lauderdale–Hollywood Airport, and Arnold is working on a graduate degree in international finance in New York.

Chief Kate and her husband, a retired postal worker, are rightly proud of their children, and I sometimes feel like a part of the extended

Roche family when she sticks her neck out for me—even going so far as to argue before the Lauderdale Shores City Council that my position is essential, as questionable as that sometimes seems.

"So you decided to go looking for bodies in your off-duty hours?" she asks.

"Not exactly. I was trying to get some extra credit with my archaeology professor. Paleo-Indian stuff," I reply.

"You thought about bringing doughnuts to class instead?"

"Fair point."

"Well?" she asks after a long moment waiting for me to add details.

"Well . . . I don't know anything else," I reply, not sure where she wants me to take the conversation. I called her from the crime scene yesterday and told her what happened.

"Anybody come talk to you?" she asks.

It's only nine a.m., so it seems a little odd that she'd be asking that. "No. Not yet. I expect I'll get asked to go back up to Palm Beach and make a statement."

"I expect," she replies but draws the sentence out a bit, implying something.

I turn back over my shoulder. Carla is still pretending to work on her report while keeping an eye on our conversation. Something is definitely going on.

"Chief? Is there something I should know?"

"How's that archaeology thing going?" she asks.

"Good . . ." *What's she getting at?*

"Kind of like being a cop? Looking for clues, asking questions?"

"Um, yeah . . ." I sit up in my seat, paying close attention, as if someone's going to pop out of a filing cabinet with an explanation.

"Where do archaeologists make most of their interesting finds?"

"Er, the ground?"

Chief Kate's starting to make me question my own sanity.

"Yes, but where?"

"Trash piles. Midden heaps. That kind of thing."

"Right," she says eagerly. "The trash." Her gaze flicks briefly to her plastic wastebasket.

It takes me a little longer to realize I should take a look. At first glance I don't understand what she's going on about, but then I see it: two empty Starbucks coffee cups.

The trash is taken out each night by Octavio, our custodian. We all get our coffee from Dunkin' Donuts or Lester's Diner—which means that the chief had at least two visitors before I got here . . . visitors who probably told her not to tell me why they were here. Which could mean they were anything from district attorneys to feds.

Knowing Chief Kate, she told them she'd do whatever she damned well pleased but settled for not offering up the information. Meaning, she wouldn't lie to me if I asked.

So I ask. "Have any visitors?"

"Funny you should ask that," she says with an eye roll. "I had two DEA agents up from Miami pay a visit. They asked a lot of questions about you."

"And the murder?"

"Yes. Specifically, they wanted to know if you knew the woman." She pauses for a beat, waiting for me to jump in.

"I was up all night asking that same question." I leave out the part about keeping my gun under my pillow, worrying that every rock of my houseboat was the killer stepping on board to finish me off.

"And?"

I shrug. "Someone vaguely familiar, like a waitress you say hello to, then forget. DEA?" I add after thinking about that part. "Why is the Drug Enforcement Agency interested in the murder of a Jane Doe where there were no drugs on the scene?" I answer my own question: "Because they think it may have been drug related due to the way she was killed." This sinks in. "So the DEA thinks this is some kind of drug hit? A hit man with a similar MO?"

"That's the worrisome part, Sloan. They asked me about you for thirty minutes. The killer never came up."

"Whoa." My pulse starts to race. "They don't think *I* did it?"

"I have no idea what they think other than they were suspicious about you being there at the exact time of the homicide." Her voice trails off a bit, suggesting that she's a little curious about that too.

"Well, I didn't know I needed to coordinate my dives with narco-murder dumping schedules." No laugh from the chief. "They really didn't say anything about a killer?" I ask. This is hard for me to accept.

"Nope. I suspect that he may be a known person to them, or at least they have a strong suspicion of who he could be."

I think this over. "So they're wondering why a police diver was already in the same water."

"Basically. I told them you were good people, all that. Which of course just made them suspicious of me."

I throw a small shrug at the bullpen, where Carla's still watching. "And her?"

"They talked to her too. I overheard them asking if you had any boyfriends or trips to exotic locations."

"Don't I wish," I groan. "So now what?"

"If you are into something you shouldn't be, now is the perfect time to skip the country with your Colombian drug-dealer boyfriend."

"And if I'm not?"

"Just keep doing what you're doing. They're chasing down leads—let them chase. It probably won't go beyond them asking some more questions before they move on."

"Still, though," I say. "What about the killer?" I hesitate for a moment, weighing whether to tell Kate about the driver's license. For some reason I feel ashamed about that, but after a moment of introspection, reason wins out over irrational guilt, and I fill her in on that tiny detail.

"Yikes," she replies. "And I'm sure you're mostly worried about Jackie."

My stomach twists. "Yeah. I asked Run to take her for a few more days. I said I had some work stuff."

She nods. I can tell she's taking this seriously, because she doesn't use the opportunity to give me a jab about Run, whom she jokingly refers to as "that trust-fund redneck of yours."

"If it helps, Walter and I are happy to have her over. In the meantime, I'll call over to Biscayne and BSO and make sure they send some patrols by the house and her school."

I want to say that she doesn't need to go to so much trouble, but the protective mother voice that appeared in my head the moment I first looked in Jackie's eyes convinces me otherwise.

"Thank you."

"Of course. We look out for our own. Speaking of which, you're headed to Miami Beach, right?"

I'd nearly forgotten. It was in an email this morning. I'm supposed to do a dive for Miami-Dade police. Someone tossed a gun into the canal three days ago. Their divers couldn't find it, and Chief Kate offered me out as a favor.

"Yeah," I reply. "I need to get my gear."

"Be careful. Watch out for mermen with bad intentions."

"Thanks," I say, getting up.

"Oh . . ." She hesitates for a moment. "You should know, the dive you're heading to?"

I nod.

"Detective Alameda mentioned that Miami-Dade brought in a consultant on the case. George Solar. I think you know him."

Ice goes through my veins at the sound of that name. I know exactly who George Solar is: he's the cop that sent Uncle Karl to prison and nearly put my father there too.

Growing up in a family full of sailors, we had no fouler curse word than the name of George Solar.

"I thought he retired," I say calmly. Rumor had it he was forced out after some kind of internal affairs scandal.

"He did. They brought him in to consult."

"Interesting," I reply, failing to hide my anger.

CHAPTER FIVE

Muck

The Seventy-Ninth Street Causeway is a low bridge that connects the middle of Miami Beach to the mainland. The small islands that dot the route are a mix of commercial real estate and suburbs. A half mile to the west of where I'm standing is the Pelican Harbor Seabird Sanctuary, where I once thought about working after a middle school field trip.

Watching rescuers pull a fishhook from one of the enormously beaked pelicans made me realize that these creatures weren't just the fat buzzards of the sea I'd always thought them to be.

That notion changed a week later when a pelican gulped a mackerel I'd been reeling in after snapping my rod.

Nothing teaches you the laws of nature like a bird swooping in and eating your lunch. I bear no ill will toward the big birds, but I still harbor a slight grudge.

I've had porpoises steal bait off my hook, but they at least pop out of the water and throw you a playful taunt, which somehow makes the theft more tolerable. Pelicans are simply an ungrateful mouth on wings. Of course, I never tell my daughter, Jackie, that.

No pelicans in sight, and I'm already in my wet suit checking my tanks when Miami-Dade Lieutenant Cardiff and Officer Swanson pull up in an SUV. Both are wearing khakis and department polo shirts.

It's nice to be at a crime scene where I'm not the center of attention. Each day is something new and different as a police recovery diver who gets loaned to different departments. It's hard to keep track of all the faces, and the cases themselves tend to run together—which is why I'd probably make a horrible detective. My skill is finding things in the water.

I know this pair of detectives fairly well. Cardiff has what we refer to as the SICM—Standard-Issue Cop Mustache—while Swanson is clean shaven. I've pulled evidence, mainly guns, out of the water for them before. I think Swanson has a thing for me, but he's too much of a straight arrow ever to say anything. Cardiff, on the other hand, throws the kind of glances that creep me out.

"McPherson," says Cardiff, greeting me.

Today there's something different about the way he's staring at me. Not the usual leer. More hesitant, almost suspicious. I reach into my gear bag and feel an unfamiliar object and pull it out. It's a handheld radio. I must have forgotten to give this back on a dive working with another department. I shove it back in, reminding myself to call around tomorrow and find out whom I boosted it from.

"Hello, gentlemen," I say. "I read the report. But can you give me the CliffsNotes?"

Swanson pulls a map out of his case and lays it on the hood of their truck. "I was finishing up a call here at about ten p.m. when I saw a late-model Mercedes drive by real fast with no lights. I decided to follow, and when I got to the next light, he saw me and gunned it through the intersection. I chased him over the causeway but lost him in traffic. A patrol unit found the car ten minutes later in a CVS parking lot."

"Any camera footage?" I ask.

"Parking lot. Not very good. Hispanic male between twenty and fifty," he replies.

"Half of Miami," mutters Cardiff. "Five minutes before Swanson saw the car, a witness put it at a shootout in the parking lot of the Carolina Bar."

"Any other witnesses?"

"Only the waitress in the bar. The suspect and the victim all fled. We got some blood, but that's all."

"What makes you think the gun was tossed here?" I stare down the length of the bridge. It's a good two hundred feet long. We have fairly accurate estimates for how far a gun is likely to be thrown, but that still leaves me a mighty wide search area.

"Because we didn't find it in the car," Cardiff replies. He kicks a toe at my underwater magnetometer. "We thought we'd send you out with that thing and you might find it."

"Didn't your diver try?"

"He spent about an hour," says Swanson.

"This same exact area?"

"Are you trying to avoid going in or what?" Cardiff growls impatiently.

"I'm just trying to keep my search pattern from being something larger than the county." This guy irritates me. Swanson I can handle.

They both look over my shoulder as an old blue pickup truck pulls onto the grass near the bridge entrance.

Damn. I'd almost forgotten about George Solar. I don't know if it shows in my face, but I can feel my blood pressure rising.

I continue to check my gear, making sure my breathing regulator gets a fifth look, a totally unnecessary inspection, and do my best to pretend that George Solar being here is no big deal. With DEA asking questions about me this morning and Solar showing up now, I can't help but feel a little paranoid.

"Need any help?" Swanson asks.

I glance up and give him a weak smile as I vent air from the regulator. "Nope. All good. Just checking."

I catch Solar's shadow as he walks over to us. There's something spooky about the perfectly still way he stands there watching me.

Watching . . . I remember his eyes most clearly. As we sat behind my uncle in the courtroom—I must've been thirteen at the time—George Solar occasionally glanced in our direction from the witness box. His dark-green eyes scanned each of us, trying to figure out how much we knew.

Nothing. That was the plain truth. I could recall a few arguments between Dad and Uncle Karl but not the context. Dad admitted to me later that he knew Karl had been running around with some people from Everglades City known for trafficking, and he wasn't happy about that. For his part, Karl had told his older brother to mind his own business.

Uncle Karl wasn't the first outlaw in the family. Great-Grandfather McPherson was a rumrunner, and it was a poorly held secret that his son had been involved with the trade of archaeological artifacts whose provenance was in some dispute. As serious as those crimes were, they sounded almost quaint compared to Uncle Karl getting arrested smuggling cocaine in the false bottom of a boat.

The family rallied around him, in no small part because the newspapers impugned us all with headlines about World-Famous Treasure-Hunting Family Fingered in Cocaine-Smuggling Plot.

It didn't matter that my uncle was the only one charged, or that when the son of the governor got busted for selling MDMA on campus around the same time, the matter was quickly dropped. There was no headline about the governor's mansion being a potential center for drug trafficking, even though it's a near certainty that his son was dealing while living there.

When I complained to Dad about the injustice, he explained that the rich and the powerful had better lawyers and could fight such accusations. It didn't seem fair, especially when I heard whispers around school about my family's involvement in Karl's crime.

To be honest, it wasn't as bad as it could have been. I was still going to private school at the time, and there were dozens of kids there with parents who made headlines for everything from Ponzi schemes to the overthrow of foreign governments.

Well, I can't pretend to inspect my gear forever, so I stand up, acknowledging the presence of George Solar.

He's older now. Grayer, more wrinkles, more weathered. The green eyes still sit behind tinted glasses, silently judging.

"McPherson," he says with a nod.

It sounds like something between a greeting and an accusation—as if he's just reestablished his label for me. McPherson: White-Trash Drug Smuggler.

"Mr. Solar," I reply. Probably a little too coolly.

"Ah, that's right, I forgot you two know each other," says Cardiff with restrained glee.

If Cardiff was waiting to see my reaction, he'll be disappointed. Instead, I throw it back in his face.

"It's good of you to come out of retirement to help Cardiff with his work."

"George is just here to advise," Cardiff responds, a little defensively.

Swanson jumps in. "I was thinking we should start the search at the far end of the causeway. The last diver was in a bit of a hurry. A few of the streetlights are out at that point, and that seems like the most probable spot for the gun to be tossed."

I notice that Solar's head tilts to the side a little as if he's about to say something, but he doesn't. That's the other thing I remember about George Solar—the way he used silence.

When Uncle Karl's attorney had him in the witness box, he took his time answering each question, sometimes creating long, drawn-out moments during which he simply stared at the attorney like a monkey in a cage.

This drove Uncle Karl's lawyer nuts, and he asked the judge on several occasions to make Solar answer the questions more quickly. The judge demurred.

At one point, Karl's attorney even called Solar out on it in front of the jury, saying he should answer the question before they fell asleep. Solar only stared and took his sweet time. I saw smiles in the jury box and felt a pang of frustration, realizing that Karl's lawyer might have lost the case right there by making them take sides. Between Uncle Karl and his sun-bleached surfer looks that screamed *rich-kid drug dealer* and the working-class Solar, who could have come straight out of a Tommy Lee Jones movie, it was no contest for the jurors. Solar was in control.

I hand Swanson a rope tied to a small inflatable raft with a dive flag and a line that will extend to the bottom of the waterway. The flag's to warn boaters I'm down there, and the line gives me something to keep my bearings underwater. These channels are pretty murky, and it's easy to find yourself fifty yards from where you thought you were searching.

"Let's start at the far end, like you said. But first I'm going to do a surface swim and look for anything shiny. Got it?"

Swanson nods and takes the line over to the railing on the causeway. I pull myself over the seawall and drop into the water next to the small raft while Cardiff and Solar watch from the causeway sidewalk above.

I pull my mask down, purge my regulator, and go under, putting them behind me.

Things are so much simpler underwater.

CHAPTER SIX

SHINER

In the two hundred feet from one end of the causeway to the other, nothing shines or gleams back at me. At the deepest part, the water is about fifteen feet deep. It's clearer than usual, and the sun is out, which means I can see about twelve feet.

Besides the fact that the gun—if there even is one—probably isn't chrome plated, there's the problem that the muck at the bottom is a thick haze barely penetrated by light. I didn't expect to see the gun from right below the surface, but it's always a good idea to get an overview of the area first.

Tossing a gun from the driver's seat means throwing it through an open passenger window and managing not to hit the guardrail. With a strong enough arm, the gun could be anywhere from right below the bridge to fifteen feet away or more.

I'd plotted a graph on a map showing the probable areas along the bridge. I've done this so many times I can create a search pattern with my eyes closed. The tricky part is if there's a strong current and sediment flow on the bottom.

Guns generally tend to stay where they land. Bags of cocaine, bodies, and cell phones drift. Although bodies have a habit of gassing up and floating to the surface, which makes them easier to recover, it's not always the case. Bullet and knife wounds can keep a corpse underwater.

One of the first things they teach you in forensic-diving classes is that there are exceptions to everything, but in 90 percent of the cases, follow the tables and rules of thumb.

I reach the end of the causeway and touch the seawall. Swanson's shadow is above me, still holding the line.

"No luck?"

"Nope. I'm going to go deeper and try the magnetometer."

I reach down to the cable at my belt and realize that the device is not attached. *Damn.* I turn back to the shore where I went in. It's not sitting there either.

I must have dropped it during my swim.

Not good.

Congratulations, expert police diver Sloan McPherson, you just lost a five-thousand-dollar piece of equipment while trying to conduct an evidence search.

"Everything okay?" asks Swanson.

I give him a thumbs-up. "I'm going to start here," I lie. What I'm really going to do is go to the bottom and quickly backtrack to the other side of the causeway to try to spot my bright-yellow metal detector before anyone realizes I dropped it.

Ace move, as my brothers liked to say any time you made a bold attempt to cover your ass.

I kick off from the seawall and keep my body close to the bottom of the channel in case a speedboat decides to rip through here and chop me in half.

While I have a cold relationship with pelicans, I've swum close to manatees and seen firsthand the scars on their backs from boat propellers. Other than seeing Jackie get hurt, nothing twists my heart like one of those big-eyed, gentle giants with a wound from a careless boater.

I skim along the bottom, creating eddy currents of muck like an airplane swooping over a dusty field. To the left I see the swish of a tail. It probably belongs to a grouper lurking in the shadow of the bridge. I've seen some pretty large ones in some of the out-of-the-way places I've dived. But I keep my mouth shut about the really large ones, the potential record breakers. The last thing I want is to tip off some trophy hunter.

I spot the yellow handle of the magnetometer sticking out of the sediment only a few feet from where I entered the water. A grimy layer of dirt covers the rubber controls, so I surface to clean it off.

At the same time that I pop my head out of the water, a small Boston Whaler glides by carrying a suntanned elderly woman and a little dog.

She doesn't see me but waves at someone over my head. That's when I spot the shadows of Cardiff and Solar on the rippling water. They're directly overhead on the causeway.

". . . there are no coincidences," Cardiff is saying. "Isn't that how it goes?"

I'm about to dive back in and mind my own business when I catch a reference to me.

"We're supposed to believe that she was just out randomly diving? Bullshit." Cardiff's shadow grows animated as he explains this to Solar. "You know her family. What they do. My money's on her and that Miller girl going out there because they had some inside info. Then one of Bonaventure's people caught up with them."

Miller. Why does that name ring a bell? And Bonaventure? I know that one. He's a Miami lawyer who reps drug dealers.

Cardiff thinks I'm tied up with them? I've half a mind to tell him to go fuck himself right now. Fortunately, the rational side of my brain keeps me from going all McPherson on him. I take a slow breath and put the regulator back in my mouth as I slip under the waves.

From beneath the surface, I can see Cardiff gesturing wildly as Solar stands perfectly still watching the water . . . staring at me.

How much does he know I overheard? How much should I care?

I don't know.

It seems like everyone knows more about what happened yesterday than I do—yet somehow, I'm allegedly at the center of this murder?

Only it's more than a murder. Bonaventure is a serious name. The shipment my uncle got busted for belonged to one of his clients. I distinctly recall Dad saying to my oldest brother that his biggest fear wasn't the feds; it was the people Karl owed money.

I suspect the reason he didn't plead to a lesser crime was because he knew if he did, there'd be a bill due when he got out of prison—one he couldn't hope to afford.

I swim back to the side, where Swanson is still waiting, and emerge from the water.

"Anything?" he asks.

I hold up the magnetometer. "I'm just getting it calibrated."

Out of the corner of my mask, I can see Solar still looking at me. That damn stare.

I look at the device meaningfully. "Okay," I tell Swanson. "I'm good. What I need you to do is move the line ten feet every five minutes. Okay? We'll stop at the midway point, and I'll grab a new tank."

"Got it."

I dive back to the bottom and drag the device just above the muck and feel the buzzing in the handle as it picks up various metallic objects.

There are dozens here. Aluminum cans, bottle caps, coat hangers, wire, you name it. I've done this enough times to know the familiar pulse of a large piece of metal; I only have to stick my knife into the muck a few times to pry out a rusted wheel rim and a metal fence post.

Halfway to the midpoint, I find an entire automobile bumper. Reluctantly, I call it out to Swanson so he can use a line to drag it to shore.

While it probably broke off years ago when a car collided with the guardrail, there's a chance it was in a hit-and-run and still bears a visible serial number.

I finally finish my sweep and climb out of the water where I started. Cardiff and Solar are talking to Swanson.

"Are you sure you didn't miss it?" asks Cardiff.

I ignore the stupidity of his question. "I did a thorough sweep in the most probable zone."

"What about the improbable ones?" he replies. "It seemed like you didn't clear the area directly below the guardrail and only did a narrow band."

"Those are the FBI tables," I answer as calmly as possible while unfastening my regulator from the tank.

"Well, this isn't the FBI. We don't quit until we find what we're looking for."

I think he's goading me into saying I have to go pick up my daughter or that I'm tired. Instead I vent the other tank and start attaching my regulator. "Who said anything about quitting? I'll do as wide a pattern as you want. I have three more tanks in the car. I can do this all day and night." I throw the last part out just to bait him. "It's overtime and a half for me."

Solar watches this exchange, then looks out at the causeway. "Swanson, you mentioned the driver was smoking a cigarette?"

"Yes. I believe so."

"And how do you know that?" he asks.

"I saw the sparks from the butt as he threw it out."

"Do you recall at what part of the bridge?" asks Solar.

"No, sir. I was still far back. Maybe in the middle."

Solar walks through the grass back up to the causeway and starts a slow pace down the sidewalk, staring at the concrete and into the water beneath the rail.

"If he finds the cigarette butt, I'll eat my own dick," Cardiff murmurs.

"I'll find you a teaspoon," I mumble before putting the regulator in my mouth and letting it vent.

Cardiff blinks, trying to figure out what I said. Swanson turns red.

Solar stops a third of the way across the causeway and shouts back to me. "McPherson, can you do a three-foot-wide sweep from here to about twenty feet out?"

I give him a thumbs-up. "Swanson, you got the line?"

I plunge back into the water, curious to see what Solar thinks he's found.

Over the years I've heard stories from other cops about the man. His ability to find evidence seemed almost supernatural. From the trial, I know for a fact that Uncle Karl went to great effort to conceal his cargo, but Solar somehow knew exactly where to tell the DEA search team to look.

Some said he's simply got a knack. Others said he had informants and might have been dirty himself.

Up until now I've chosen to believe the latter, because it makes Uncle Karl's conviction look more like a miscarriage of justice, but damned if I'm not curious to find out if it's the former.

CHAPTER SEVEN

THE KNACK

I find the gun four feet from the edge of my first search band. Right where Solar told me to look. It could have taken me ten hours to get this far, if at all. Instead, it only took four minutes.

I slide the gun into a pouch and place a weighted ribbon in the spot where I found it, then swim to the surface. Solar is leaning over the edge of the railing, still staring down at me.

Cardiff and Swanson look surprised.

"The cigarette butt," Cardiff blurts out. "I said I'd eat my dick if he found *that*."

Solar does a slow turn toward him with an expression I can only describe as contempt. Well, at least he hates everyone. That's good to know.

"How the hell?" asks Swanson as he lets the line go slack and the raft begins to drift.

Solar catches it. "Let's let Officer McPherson dry off first."

Officer McPherson? Did I just get a promotion from white-trash drug smuggler to possible human being?

I hate myself for how much this grudging nod of respect means to me. But it does mean something . . . How *do* assholes make us care what they think?

I swim over to the seawall, and Swanson gives me a hand up. After putting my gear back in the truck, I unzip my wet suit, causing a moment of panic as the cop doesn't know whether to keep staring or look away.

I'm wearing shorts and a Lauderdale Shores Police Department T-shirt underneath. When he realizes I'm not about to strip down to a G-string, he relaxes.

Shorts and a T-shirt are a lot warmer underwater than the bikini I wear for recreational diving, but it puts my male colleagues at ease when they realize I'm not about to parade around a crime scene like a French model in South Beach. Maybe it disappoints them too. Who knows?

I towel off and slip my aqua shoes back on. Solar and the others are standing by Cardiff's truck as he photographs the gun.

Even in the water, I could see that the serial number had been filed off. A clear sign that this gun belonged to a bad guy who was up to no good. I'm sure they already have a suspect in mind.

Cardiff sees that I'm all packed up. "All right, let's have the amazing Solar tell us how he pulled this out of his ass."

From out of nowhere I blurt, "Maybe he was the one driving the car."

Cardiff blinks, and Swanson's jaw drops. Solar stares at me and makes a slight nod.

"I'd say that would be the obvious answer," he replies. "But I have an alternative explanation for you." He looks at me, ignoring the others. "This way."

I follow him onto the causeway with Cardiff and Swanson behind me.

"Did you time it?" asks Cardiff. "From when the driver saw the bridge and decided to toss the gun?"

Solar says nothing and keeps walking.

Swanson puts a hand over his eyes and squints at the water. "Is it the way the light reflects this time of day?"

I keep my theory to myself, because it doesn't sound any better than theirs.

We reach the point where Solar told me to look, and he comes to a stop. "The cigarette."

Swanson stares at the ground around his feet. "I see a lot of them."

Solar doesn't even acknowledge the man. "Page six of the forensic report on the car."

"What about it?" asks Cardiff.

"Residues. You recall?"

"There weren't any. The steering wheel had been wiped too."

"And in the Carolina parking lot where they think the car was first parked?"

Cardiff shrugs. "Nada. I'm not following."

Solar turns to me. "Are you getting it?"

I think I am. "Ash. There were no ashes."

"None in the car. None where the car was parked," replies Solar.

"So the guy owned a fucking vape pen," Cardiff interjects, clearly pissed that this is going over his head.

"Or there was no cigarette," replies Solar.

"But I saw the sparks," Swanson insists.

I see it before Solar has to point it out to the others.

Jesus, this guy is clever.

It's obvious when you look for it. Right on top of the railing, there's a metal scuff mark where the gun struck, created a spark, then bounced into the water.

I tap the rail. It's steel. Most of them are aluminum and wouldn't make a spark when hit by the frame of a gun. This was an exception, the outlier.

Cardiff holds the gun next to the scrape on the railing.

"I'm surprised it didn't go off," Swanson says under his breath.

"So, you think this is Rodrigo's type of gun?" Cardiff asks Solar.

"Rodrigo?" I ask.

Cardiff realizes this is the first time he's mentioned the name in front of me. "Just a name."

Solar replies to me, ignoring Cardiff's attempt to downplay the name. "Rodrigo Mustano. He's the brother of a man I was after. Carmine Mustano, aka Mustang."

I get a chill. I've heard that name before. I think I even overheard my uncle mention it to my father when talking about the trial. Mustano was an enforcer for the cartels. He's probably killed dozens in the US and god knows how many in Bolivia and Colombia.

"Aren't there like a hundred warrants out for that guy?" I ask. "What's he doing back in South Florida?"

Cardiff stares at me for a long moment. "Right."

I turn to Swanson, trying to figure out what that's supposed to mean. He avoids eye contact. This has something to do with the conversation I overheard back on the bridge.

"Lately there have been a lot of undesirables spotted in South Florida," says Cardiff.

"Why?" I ask.

"That's the question," says Cardiff, echoing Solar. "Why indeed?"

There's a long silence, like when you're waiting for someone to confess. Cardiff is clearly under the delusion that I know something. Meanwhile, Solar is studying us.

"We might be able to get some prints off the shell casings in the magazine," Swanson suggests hopefully.

"We'll see." He eyes my gear by my truck. "You need any help?"

It's an insincere offer, and I treat it as such. "I'm good."

Cardiff looks over to Solar. "Can you help me out with some background? I'll buy you a beer."

"Sure you're good?" Solar asks me.

"Yep."

I can't tell if he's being genuine or wants another chance to inspect me like a bug under a magnifying glass.

Cardiff and Swanson drive off with Solar following in his pickup. I load my gear into the back of my SUV and make sure I didn't leave anything behind.

After I'm all packed up, I get inside and take long, slow breaths. For some reason, I thought that when I became a cop, it'd make me feel less uncomfortable when I was around police. Most of the time that's true, especially at the Lauderdale Shores station, but outside of that place, my family, not only my uncle, constitutes my reputation—and it's a mixed reputation at best.

I thought being a cop and a grown-up would mean that I would never have to feel intimidated again. The presence of George Solar proved otherwise.

I'd like to think that's the last time I'll have to deal with the man who helped ruin my childhood, but I have the sense to realize that won't be the case.

CHAPTER EIGHT
HOUSEBOAT

The sun is setting as I reach the marina and load my gear onto the cart I use to haul it back and forth from my houseboat. Most of the other boats have returned, and I spot the cars belonging to the other onboard residents. Like me, they prefer to live slightly apart from society. The towering condos and buildings reflect in the water all around us, but we remain detached.

When I take a step onto my houseboat, I feel the comforting sensation of the vessel giving way slightly to my mass. It's weird, I know. But living on a boat is like sleeping on a waterbed, if it's your thing. I think part of it is the contained environment. No matter how stressful the rest of the world is, no matter what your situation on land, on a boat with a radio, a good fishing rod, and some provisions, life is manageable. I can cast off at any moment and take my home with me, far away.

That's exactly what we did the day after my uncle was escorted from the courtroom and sent to spend the next five to ten years in prison. Instead of heading to our house, which was already under foreclosure, we went to the family boat and sailed to Bimini. We spent a week going around the Bahamian islands while Dad thought and Mom argued with him. Things were already over between them by then, but my brothers and I carried on, snorkeling, exploring, and occasionally taking our little raft to one of the superexclusive islands where celebrities pay tens of thousands of dollars a day to vacation. We even managed to find kids our own age and play with them.

That experience was imprinted permanently on me. Which is why I've never been able to live on land for long. Technically, my address is the apartment above the marina where the boat is docked, but the *Eclipse* is my home. Not that I'm terribly fond of this particular ship. The thing's barely seaworthy, but the *idea* of the boat is what's home for me.

I agreed to supervise the marina in exchange for the apartment when I got pregnant with Jackie. The owner, a man called Southie, for reasons I can only assume have something to do with his Boston accent, is a friendly snowbird who comes down here once a year to work on his old yacht. The rest of the time, a woman named Beth and her son do most of the work around the marina. They call me when something difficult needs to be fixed or someone has to be served an overdue-rent notice. That's not a part of the job I enjoy, but it's a price I'm willing to pay to give my daughter a fixed home of sorts.

It's that fixed address that was causing me so much stress yesterday. A day after my driver's license went missing, I feel a little bit more relaxed. If the killer wanted to stop me from talking to the investigators, he missed his chance. While I haven't made a formal statement in the Palm Beach station, they have all the critical details. To be honest with myself, I'm more concerned about the fact that the cops don't seem in any hurry to take my statement. On the surface this should be a good thing, but if the suspicion around me means what I think, they're only biding their time for a more intense grilling.

I hose down my gear and set it on the stern to dry off. By the time I've downed half my postdive beer, Jackie's ringing me on WhatsApp.

"Hey, Momma!" she says with a large grin.

The photos on the wall behind her are from Run's office. He must have taken her there after school. His boat-renovation company lies off Las Olas Drive a few miles from here. Typical Run . . . it's closer to restaurant row than the actual location where his work takes place.

"How you doing?" I ask, setting my beer down so it's out of the frame. I have one a day on average, but the admonishment from my daughter about it being "early" or "drinking alone" stings, even as playfully as it's intended.

"Dad wants to know if it's okay if we get takeout and watch *Back to the Future*. Is that okay? He said you could join us."

"Thanks, sweetie. Let me talk to him."

Run takes the phone from her. His blue, almost silver, eyes and tan face flash a warm smile—not that different from Jackie's, I'm noticing more and more lately.

He calls over to our daughter. "Hey, brat, give us a second, will ya? Official grown-up business."

"And who would the grown-ups be?" Jackie snaps back from off-screen.

"Scram," he says playfully. "Go terrorize Mr. Martinez in the gallery next door."

She throws a hug around his neck, then leaves the office. Run stares a moment at the phone, trying to figure out the interface.

"Just talk," I reply.

"What happened to old-fashioned phone calls?"

"Thanks for taking her for another day." Run's offer of takeout and a movie inevitably led to Jackie asking to spend the night at his place. Run, the clever manipulator, clearly figured this would give me an easy out if I needed him to watch her again.

"No problem. I'm just trying to maximize the time that she still thinks I'm cool."

"I don't think you'll ever have to worry about that."

Despite Run's failings in the relationship-with-me department, he's an exceptional dad and spends more time with Jackie than many married fathers would. At times I feel a little jealous that he gets to be the fun parent while I have to be the business parent.

"Ha. You have no idea how hard it is to compete with a cop mom."

Compete . . . He uses that word too. It's a crummy way to parent, but it's a reality.

"Anyway, I, uh, figured you were still processing what happened yesterday."

Processing? Is that what he thinks this is all about?

"I've seen more dead bodies than you've seen naked ones. I'm not processing," I respond a little too defensively.

"Sorry. You didn't give me a lot of details yesterday. I figured it was something more than work stuff."

"It is, and it isn't. Whoever killed that woman took my driver's license."

The words pass my lips before I can contain them. I really didn't want to tell this to Run. There's a side to him that few people ever see. Once you understand what lies beneath that happy-go-lucky charm, it's hard to look at him the same.

I saw it when we were dating in high school and Seth Kwan made a drunken grab for my breasts at a kegger. I gave him a black eye, but Run pummeled the shit out of the kid until his whole face was black-and-blue. A small crowd gathered, watching Run land blow after blow. Some tried to pull him off; others rooted him on.

A few years later, I was pregnant, and some teenager in a Camaro almost ran us off the road. Run chased him into a parking lot. The kid pulled over and got out of his car, ripping his shirt off in some kind of alpha display.

Run grabbed the blackjack he kept under the seat, exited the car, and clipped the kid in the temple, knocking him out cold.

We left him there in the parking lot, unconscious. Run was steaming mad for ten minutes. Then it vanished, and he was asking where I wanted to go for dinner.

Once you see that side to someone, you never forget it's there, waiting to erupt.

Run's face turns a little red, and he looks in the direction he sent Jackie. I can tell that he's trying to figure out what he's supposed to say. Does he yell at me for not telling him? Does he make some macho statement about protecting her?

To his credit, he handles it differently than I expected.

In a calm voice, he replies, "Tell me what I can do."

It takes me a moment to get over this response. Is this a sign of a maturing Run? Or has he learned how to be more calculating?

"Watch her for a few more days. Keep an eye on her."

"What if she asks?"

I'm about to say she won't, then remember she's not six anymore. I wish I could be up front with her, but knowing Jackie, if she thought I was in some kind of trouble, she'd Uber herself here in a heartbeat to protect her mother.

"I'll tell her it's work, and I'll explain later."

Run laughs. "Explain later. That one always works."

"Explain what?" Jackie asks from out of frame.

Run doesn't miss a beat. "Explain the meaning of minding your own beeswax. Why aren't you bothering Mr. Martinez?"

"He was showing some people a painting that looked like a rainbow threw up on a dolphin," she replies.

"And?"

"I told them that. He got pissed and asked me to leave."

Run stares at me with a wry smile. "I wonder who that reminds me of."

The first time Run's mother showed me her art collection, I asked if she bought the pieces from the local art college. It did not go over well.

She called me a philistine, and I excitedly brought up an article I'd read about the excavation of Tel Qasile, the port city founded by the actual Philistines. She was not impressed and started calling me "that weird girl" behind my back.

I watch the bluish-purple sky as the sun finishes setting and streetlamps start to turn on around the marina and surrounding streets. Just beyond the small fence that separates the marina parking lot from the street, I notice a parked SUV in a no-parking zone.

I scan the seawall to see if there are any fishermen nearby, then realize that there's someone in the truck. I catch the glint of light on glass as he lowers something. I instinctively reach into the console by my feet.

Run calls out to me. "Sloan?"

"Just a second." I set the phone down, pull out the night-vision goggles I keep on board, and step down into the cabin.

Keeping my head down low and my IR illuminator off, I look back at the truck and see the bright glow of an infrared light as someone watches me back.

"Everything okay?" Runs asks.

I step back out onto the deck, pretending I didn't see what I just saw.

"Let me call you back," I say, forcing a smile and ending the call.

Beer bottle in one hand, phone in the other, I stroll toward the marina office, pretending not to notice that I'm being watched.

The moment I pass a row of lockboxes on the dock, I put the phone in my pocket and replace it with the gun from my waistband.

CHAPTER NINE

THE KEY

I was twelve the first time I had to threaten someone with real violence. We'd taken our boat to Hammerhead Key on the west coast of Florida so Dad could chase down a legend about a sunken rumrunner that allegedly went down with a full hold of cargo.

My oldest brother, Harris, was back on the boat while Robbie and I took the little Zodiac raft around the tiny islands.

We'd been speeding across sandbars and goofing off when I took us through a thick patch of kelp and fishing line that fouled the propeller. Robbie climbed out of the boat and used a rusty bait knife to try to cut the line.

That's when we were approached by the two men in the beat-up Boston Whaler. I could spot the out-of-season lobster traps sitting under a tarp.

The fact that they were poachers didn't faze me as much as the way they looked at me. Both were naked to the waist, wearing ragged cutoffs and the kind of unhealthy suntan that you only see on the homeless. Theirs was the only other boat we'd seen all day.

"Need some help?" the older man asked as they approached.

"We're okay," I replied.

Robbie popped his head out of the water and held on to the side of the raft, catching his breath. "I almost got it."

The look on the men's faces changed a little when they realized I wasn't alone—*disappointed* was the only way I could describe it.

They exchanged glances. The younger one spoke up. "Why don't we pull you into shore?" He started to reach out for our boat.

Robbie, although two years older, looked to me for direction on how to handle the situation.

"Our parents' boat is that way." I pointed to an island in the distance.

"Can you radio them?" asked the older man.

"We don't have a radio," Robbie answered before realizing he shouldn't have said that.

"Our dad's coming here anyway," I interjected.

They looked at the sandbars around us that their own boat could barely get over and immediately knew I was lying.

"We can't leave you out here," said the older man. "It wouldn't be right."

"We're okay," I insisted.

They ignored us, and the younger man reached into our boat, grabbed the mooring line, tossed it to the other, then climbed into our raft and watched me for a moment. I sat there, frozen, not sure if I was supposed to be a good girl and let the adults handle the situation or make a protest.

"I almost got it," Robbie replied.

The younger man looked at the motor and could see the prop was still fouled. "Sure you do. Why don't you get into our boat and go get help with my dad while I stay here and try to fix it?" He turned to me and asked, "How old are you?"

I'd always been quick-tempered but never violent—except when it came to slugging my brothers. I acted on fear and impulse. Robbie had dropped the knife back in the Zodiac when he came up for air. I grabbed it from the deck and held it in front of me.

"Get out of our fucking boat or I'll cut your balls off. Then my dad'll come back and make you eat them! He's killed people. He likes it."

The older man let out a loud laugh from their boat while the younger one stared at the blade, trying to decide if I was serious.

I glared at him, not wavering an inch.

"Come on, Christian," said the other man. "Let's save your cojones for another day."

The younger man backed away and returned to the other boat. In my terror, I didn't move a muscle, but it must have looked like steely resolve.

They pushed off and motored away, leaving Robbie and me alone.

Once they were gone from view, Robbie finally spoke. "You said the *F* word."

He clearly didn't understand the severity of the situation. When we got back to the boat, I tried telling Dad what happened, but he thought it was all a misunderstanding. No doubt he was too mortified to accept what I was suggesting—that his daughter was almost raped or worse while he'd been elsewhere.

As a parent, I can understand that kind of willful ignorance to the severity of situations our children find themselves in. My experience on the sandbar, and others that would come later, taught me that there are bad people out there who want to do bad things to you.

I knew this before I pulled my first body out of a canal.

I also know from family lore that some of the bad actors out there were people I'm related to. It might be why I have my own mean streak.

I could have stopped Run when he kicked the shit out of Kwan. I could have told him not to get out of the car when that kid cut him off, but I didn't.

I wanted to hurt them too.

As I pass the lockboxes on the dock, my right hand keeps the gun close enough to my hip that the shape won't stand out unless someone's looking closely.

From the SUV's vantage point, there'll be a blind spot when I pass by the marina office. Right before I reach it, I ditch the beer bottle in a trash can, then make a beeline for the far edge of the building.

To the driver it should look like I'm heading into the office. As I get closer, the motion-activated light kicks on, illuminating the parking lot and creating a shadow image of me. *Oops.* My gun's visible in my shadow silhouette. I bring it tighter to my body, hoping the watcher didn't catch it.

At the point I should be entering the office, I instead run around the building, climb over the fence, and slip through a line of shrubs that separates our lot from the public landing next door.

I reach the edge and peer at the SUV. It's still there. I can only assume he's watching the office, waiting for me to leave.

That is, if I'm not making a big something out of nothing.

No, you're not. He was watching you with night vision. There's no innocent excuse for that.

The SUV doesn't belong to the Lauderdale Shores fleet, nor is it owned by anyone who works there. So I can be fairly certain that this isn't someone Chief Kate assigned to look after me.

A car passes the truck and heads in my direction, creating a distraction. I cross the street the moment it moves past and walk along the side of the street opposite the truck.

When I get to a position parallel to the driver's seat, I look through the open passenger window.

The man is still watching the building through his goggles, facing away from me. He probably noticed the lights didn't go on in the office and is realizing that something's up.

I take a step toward the truck and point my gun at the back of his head.

CHAPTER TEN
BAIT

The hardest part about being a cop is pulling your gun on someone and knowing that only millimeters separate them from death. A car backfiring, a sneeze, even a nervous tic can turn a routine stop into a fatal encounter. And in this tweet-first, ignore-the-facts-later culture, even doing the right thing can ruin a reputation and earn widespread shaming from people who know less than nothing about what it means to be a police officer in a pulse-racing, life-or-death situation.

I'm thankful that I'm a part-timer with Lauderdale Shores, where I experience aggressive encounters only once or twice a month. In some cities, cops suffer them hourly.

I don't have to announce my presence. The man behind the wheel knows I'm there by the time I have my gun pointed at the back of his head.

To someone watching this from afar, it might look like I'm overreacting. But I can't take the chance that he'll pull a gun from his lap faster than I can draw my own. I have to take the upper hand while I still can.

He catches me out of the corner of his eye. "Put the gun away, bitch."

He's in his late thirties: Hispanic or Mediterranean.

"Hands on the wheel. Police."

The man does a slow turn. He's got a slight grin on his face. "I'm going to start my car and leave."

"No. You're going to stay here until I call for backup."

"Backup? As far as I'm concerned, you're just some crazy bitch who pulled a gun on me." He reaches for the ignition.

What am I supposed to do now? Shooting him is a ridiculous thought, and I have no cause to place him under arrest.

This is the gray zone.

I need to stall him for a few seconds.

"Stop. Don't turn that ignition or . . ."

I leave it open-ended. He's cocky and wants to hear what I'm going to say, since he's now sure that I won't pull the trigger.

"Or what?" He leans his left elbow on the steering wheel and stares back at me, challenging me to do something.

I pull my phone out of my pocket and raise it up to my face.

"Why don't you call this one in, little sister."

The flash from my phone's camera momentarily blinds him. He responds by swiping his left hand in my direction.

I keep my finger light on the trigger. It's a ridiculous position for him to try to throw a punch from. Instead, it tells me that he really, really doesn't want his photo taken.

"Fuck you," he growls, leaning back and keying the ignition.

He slams the SUV into reverse, almost clipping me with the rearview mirror, then swings out into the street and races off.

I snap a photo of the retreating car, getting the license plate in case anyone questions my memory.

Before his taillights have turned the corner, I'm calling Captain Mercer's personal cell phone. He's the on-duty Fort Lauderdale police captain.

"Hey, McPherson," he says after half a ring. "Find a missing shopping cart in the canal and the ladies at Shores can't get it out by themselves?"

Mercer loves to refer to us as "the ladies at Shores" because our chief is a woman. He also loves to act like a misogynistic asshole, but it's mostly show. His wife is former air force and his daughter's at the Coast Guard Academy, and he couldn't be prouder.

"You heard about that body I found yesterday?"

"Shit, that was you. What's up?"

"Long story short, I was in the water when the victim was killed, and the perp may have stolen my driver's license from my vehicle. Just now I caught some creep watching me at the marina with night vision."

He's a quick study and doesn't need any more details. "You stop him?"

"Yeah, but he called my bluff and drove off. Can I give you a plate and a picture of him?"

"Go for it."

I read him the license plate number, then text him both photos.

"On it. Want me to send a patrol car by?"

I want to answer no out of pride, but having a marked car roll through the area would definitely discourage my watcher if he decided to loop back for another visit.

"Yeah, that would help. I'm going to call Chief Kate and tell her what's up. I'll be on my boat with the shotgun across my knees."

"I'll have someone by in five. Don't shoot any of my people," he replies, half in jest.

"Then tell 'em to take their shoes off before stepping aboard."

Mercer gives a cackle and hangs up. I head back to the boat, keeping my eyes on the road around me. I don't want to be halfway back to the marina and find out that my watcher's waiting around the bend, ready to run me down.

I make it back to the gate and can see all the way down the street to the stoplight. I think he's well and truly gone.

Something about the way he acted when I took his photo has me thinking. My phone starts to ring before I can give it any more thought.

"You okay?" asks Run.

"Yeah, fine," I reply.

"Last time you said that, you were on the way to the hospital to give birth to the squirt."

"Florida State was playing that day. I'd never have heard the end of it if I made you miss the game. Anyhow, I've got another call coming in. Everything is chill."

"Liar," he replies.

Got me.

But I can't have him racing over to play my savior. I need him with Jackie.

I text Run: Just keep your eyes on our girl.

He replies with the one word I need to hear: Understood.

❧

I'm sitting on my stern, drinking my second beer for the night. To avoid looking totally unprofessional, I've tucked my gun back into my waistband. The shotgun is within arm's reach, just inside the belowdecks entrance. If anyone comes walking down the dock, I can have that drawn on them before they reach the plank.

When I spot an SUV pull into the parking lot, I start to reach for it until I realize that it's Captain Mercer himself.

He spots me and raises his hands in mock surrender. I hold my own up in return.

"I wasn't expecting *you* to show," I say as he approaches the stern.

"I couldn't take the guilt of you shooting one of my guys if they mucked up your deck." He eyes the boat and then his shoes.

"Come aboard." I point to the scratched wooden deck with a shrug.

He joins me and takes a seat on the bait well.

"We ran the car."

"And?"

"Lease. Biscayne Shipping."

"What the hell is that?" I ask.

He shrugs. "No listing. Just the name of the holder of the credit card."

"That's not very helpful. I'll ask Chief to run a credit search."

"No need," Mercer replies. "I already shared the photo with a couple of people in the department."

"And?"

"One of them recognized the driver right away."

I say it before he has a chance to. "Let me guess, DEA?"

"Yep. If I'm not supposed to tell you that, then DEA should have bothered telling me so. But they didn't. Any chance they were just looking out for you after what happened?"

"It's not a DEA case, as far as I know. And if that's looking out for me, I'd rather be on my own."

He ponders this, thinking about the implications. "You talked to a lawyer?"

I shake my head. "I don't need to. If they think I know something, they're not only barking up the wrong tree, they're in the wrong forest."

"Think they're watching you because of your asshole uncle?" he asks bluntly.

I'd like to defend my uncle but, technically, Mercer is right. My uncle is an asshole. "Maybe."

"Rough." Mercer stands and leans against the railing. "So, how well did you know Stacey Miller?"

I feel my heart skip a beat.

"Stacey Miller?" he says. "The girl you found."

Damn. Stacey. Winston Miller's little daughter. I hadn't seen her in years. She used to hang around her dad's boatyard. That's why I didn't recognize her. The last time I saw her, she was maybe thirteen. I could have run into her at a festival or an art-in-the-park since then, but she would've been one face in a hundred.

Oh, Stacey. I remember how you loved feeding those miserable ducks by the boat ramp. Treated them like your pets. You even named them.

"You didn't know? Sorry. Uh, are you okay?"

"Yeah." I take a swig of my beer. "Holy shit."

"So, you knew her?"

"Sort of. I never thought much about her, to be honest. I didn't even realize it was her when I pulled her out of the water."

I can see the father in Captain Mercer's eyes as he takes this in. "She had a rough life. A half dozen agencies have called up in the last twenty-four hours, asking about her."

"Asking what?" I reply.

"Who she hung out with. Boyfriends. Arrest records. Reputation."

"Anyone ask about me?"

Mercer takes his time to respond, which tells me everything I need to know. I see now why it seemed implausible that I didn't know Stacey Miller. Her dad patched up our boats, and everyone on the water knew Winston. Hell, *I* wouldn't have believed me if I claimed I didn't know who she was. No wonder it seems like I'm covering something up.

The questions come at me in a rush:

Why would anyone think I'd lie about knowing Stacey?

What the hell did she get herself into?

And, most of all, how did Stacey end up in the same canal at the exact same time as my dive?

What are the odds of that?

I feel a cold finger touch my soul.

What if Stacey came to the canal looking for me?

CHAPTER ELEVEN

LURE

Dad is sitting at the bar in the back of the Crab Pot restaurant, talking to a younger man with a watch that cost more than my boat. He's tan, well coiffed, and wears khakis under a navy Burberry shirt. I can't remember the name of the watch, but it's not a Rolex or something you use to impress people who don't have money. It's the kind of watch you have to be really into watches or ultrarich to understand how valuable it is.

When Dad told me to meet him here, I should have realized he was working. The bar at the Crab Pot has an "authentic" local vibe, but the locals stopped going here years ago when the yachties started showing up and prices skyrocketed.

Dad's "business" is talking wealthy people into a charter—if they're lucky. Or investing in his next treasure hunt if they're not so fortunate.

Dad looks up and waves me over. "Hey! There's Sloan!"

I walk over, give Dad a peck on the cheek, and greet his victim with a smile.

"This is Jeff Green. He's visiting from California. I was just telling him about the *Atocha*'s stern castle."

Green shakes my hand. "Your dad says that Mel Fisher didn't find everything he was looking for."

Ugh. This again. "The stern castle is where they think the Muzo emeralds were held."

"Muzo what?" he asks.

"Emeralds, worth over a billion dollars," Dad interjects.

"Those are the emeralds the Spanish conquered and subjugated the Muzo people for. If anyone finds them, they'll probably be tied up in court for years," I reply, harshing Dad's pitch.

"Did I mention my daughter is working on her PhD in archaeology?" Dad responds.

"Did he also mention that I'm a cop?" I shoot back.

Green smiles, trying to make sense of the exchange. "Interesting. Anyone else in the family in law enforcement?"

"Nope," I reply. "Pirates all the way back. I hate to interrupt, but I need to borrow my father. He can talk you out of a small fortune later if you like."

Dad gives me a frustrated look.

"I'll say this, though," I add, feeling a little bad. "He's an honest man. He'll never try to convince you of something he hasn't convinced himself of."

Green nods to my father. "Robert, I'd like to hear more about this later. Specifically, some of the advancements in millimeter radar. That might make uncovering the wreck easier."

After he leaves for another part of the restaurant, I shake my head in disbelief.

Dad gives me a wry grin. "The best salesman lets them sell to themselves."

"You should have gone into politics," I reply.

Dad holds up his hand for the bartender, an older woman named Cassie. "Two Ghost Castles. My daughter is buying."

"Stacey Miller," I say to him after the beers are placed in front of us, looking for any reaction.

Dad just blinks. "Who is she?"

I believe him. Not that I was suspicious. "Winston Miller's little girl. Remember her?"

"The one that used to feed those ugly ducks at the boatyard?"

"Her. Only she's older now. And dead."

His eyes narrow for a moment, then he gets it. "The girl in the canal? The one you found?"

"The one who was murdered while I was diving just a few feet away. That was Stacey Miller. I didn't recognize her because it's been years." I add the last part defensively. I haven't even begun to assess my guilt for not realizing that was her.

From an adult's perspective, I realize now she was a sad little girl. Her dad kept her in the boatyard almost all the time, and the only friends she had were the people who stopped by. A visit from my brothers and me always got her excited, although she was a bit socially awkward.

"Do they know who did it?" Dad asks.

"No. Or if they do, nobody's telling me. I have people watching me because they think I might know something."

Dad thinks about this. "Do you?"

"No!" I say a little too loudly, getting attention from other people in the lounge. "I don't. The other important question is, why was she there at the canal when I was?"

I look at Dad. He looks at me.

"Okay," I say, "what do you know about her?"

"Me? I barely remember her. You're the cop."

I found a handful of legal encounters on Stacey's official record: a couple of arrests for possession, one conviction that sounded like a plea bargain down from intent to distribute cocaine, and two DUIs that were dismissed. Out of curiosity I looked up her attorney. It turned out to be an expensive firm in Miami, which means she had someone with money paying her legal bills.

I keep it simple for Dad. "She's had some troubles, but nothing like this. What about Winston?"

"I haven't talked to him in a while. Maybe a couple years?"

I didn't know the man like Dad did, except that he worked on our boats and had a temper and a drinking problem. As a kid you don't see things as clearly. "Do you have any contact information for him? It looks like he sold the boatyard a while back."

Dad takes out his phone. "Let me see the number I have for him. Winston was always having financial problems and changing his phone. Don't get me wrong, Sloan. He's brilliant. He used to work for the navy before he had the yard. He freelanced for builders up in Newport News."

"Patching boats?" I reply.

"No. Building them. Specialty craft. Torpedoes. Remotely Operated Vehicles. A lot of secret stuff too. I know he worked with a contractor that did stuff with Naval Special Operations, but his drinking got in the way. Got worse when the wife died. Lost him his security clearance."

I never knew this side of him. I just knew that he was the guy you took your boat to, told him how much money you had to spend, and let him figure a way to make it work. He was clever, I'll give him that. His boatyard was filled with random junk you'd never expect to see. There were old RVs he'd buy for cheap to salvage the septic systems . . . even airplane parts.

I took Winston's cleverness for granted when I was a kid. I thought all boatbuilders were that resourceful.

Dad sends me Winston's contact information, and I save it to my phone.

"Did Stacey stay in the business?" I ask.

"I think she may have worked around the office, but she never got into the mechanical side, if that's what you're asking. I think she hated boats." He shakes his head. "Sad. Just sad."

I dial Winston's number. A moment later I get a mailbox-full message.

"Anything?" asks Dad.

"No. Let me try texting."

A second after I get a notice that my message can't be sent through.

It looks like he's off the grid. Did this happen before or after Stacey was found dead?

"Nothing," I tell my father. "Know anybody who would have talked to Winston recently?"

Dad stares down at his beer and starts to peel away the label. "Nope."

Nope is Dad's tell for when he's lying.

"Nope? Or no?"

Dad grimaces. "I haven't talked to him . . ."

"Pop. This is a serious situation. Talk." I put just enough edge into my voice.

He reluctantly answers, "Karl."

"*Uncle Karl?* Were they . . . ?" My words trail off at the suggestion that Winston may have been involved with my uncle in some kind of trafficking activity.

Karl's currently serving a three-year sentence for a parole violation. The first time out, he seemed clean, but he started working boat charters that took him outside his probation area. His first probation officer let that slide as long as Karl took him on the occasional charter. It was a great scheme until he ran into a coast guard inspection that happened to include a DEA agent on board who ran my uncle's record and realized that he was about ten miles farther out than he was officially allowed.

Things have been pretty rough for Karl ever since.

I was hoping to avoid this, but it seems I have no choice. I send a text message to a friend in the US Marshals Service.

"Who are you texting?"

"I'm seeing if I can go talk to Uncle Karl," I reply.

"That takes weeks to arrange. Why not just call him?"

"He has a harder time lying to me face-to-face." A message bubble appears on my phone. "I can get in to see him at FCI tomorrow," I tell Dad.

"Sometimes I forget that you really are a cop," he says.

"Hopefully Uncle Karl forgets that too."

CHAPTER TWELVE

HARDTACK

The Federal Correctional Institution in Miami is a minimum-security prison intended for nonviolent offenders with a low probability of attempting to escape—which means it resembles something between the prisons we see on television and an inner-city high school. Its alumni include Panamanian dictator Manuel Noriega and boy-band producer Lou Pearlman, who served time for a Ponzi scheme.

The part that movies generally fail to get about prisons is their antiseptic, bureaucratic feel. The jails and prisons I've visited have felt more like college admissions offices than gritty, ironclad, Gothic castles. Maybe it's different up north. But down here they remind me of public schools with cots.

Ben Simmons, the US marshal who helped arrange the visit, ushers Uncle Karl into an office. I could have gone through the warden, but it's easier to keep the conversation private this way.

"I'll be outside answering calls," Simmons explains. "If you need anything, let me know." He leaves the door open a crack to be safe.

"What's up, Catfish?" Uncle Karl greets me with a warm hug.

Man, he's lost weight. He still has his dark tan, but his eyes seem strangely sunken. Either he's having a health problem, or he's using something. I decide to shelve that conversation for another day.

He's uncuffed, as is typical around here. I motion for him to have a seat. "You have enough in your account?"

Prisoners are allowed to buy extra food and snacks with a prison account.

"I'm good," he replies. "Someone's been looking after that."

That someone is me. I check his balance periodically to make sure he has enough. I haven't told him, and I'm not sure if he suspects. Despite my anger toward the man, I can't forget he's the one who'd bring me cookies when I was sick and stick up for me when my brothers teased me too much.

"Stacey Miller," I say flatly.

The look on his face says a lot. He knows she's dead, but what else does he know?

"When was the last time you talked to her?" I ask.

"Is this an official visit? Is Lauderdale Shores part of some kind of interagency narcotics group now?" he jokes at my department's expense.

"It's a personal matter. I pulled her body out of the water two days ago."

His face goes pale. "I didn't know you still do that kind of thing."

"I do. But this one was more freelance."

"Freelance?"

I don't elaborate. "What do you know about her?"

"Nothing. I never talked to her much," he replies.

"That's it? That's all you have to say?"

"I haven't talked to her in at least a couple years. Why?"

I ignore his question. "What about her dad? What can you tell me about Winston Miller?"

"He worked on our boats. You remember. He had some trouble a couple years ago. We lost touch."

"Dad says you still talk to him," I reply.

"Not since . . . Not for years."

"Not since when?"

"Not since I went to jail the first time. I lost touch with everyone. Nobody wants to talk to a con."

I roll my eyes. "Enough of the pity-party bullshit."

"When did you become such a hard-ass?"

"I'm a McPherson. It's in the DNA. But apparently it skips a generation."

"Touché."

"Not since . . . ?" I repeat his words back to him.

"What?"

"You said, 'Not since,' then fed me some bullshit about you losing touch because of prison. But that's not what you meant to say."

He shrugs. "Who knows why he stopped talking to me?"

It's more of a delaying tactic than a response.

"*Did* he stop? I remember the trial. The odd part was where they said you built the compartments on the boat for hauling cocaine. I remember thinking to myself how impressed I was that you kept that mechanical side of you so well hidden. But charts and currents were your thing, not fiberglass and epoxy."

Uncle Karl remains silent. His eyes flick to the open door, where Marshal Simmons waits on the other side.

"So, Winston made the compartments." I say it as a statement, not a question.

Uncle Karl doesn't say anything, which tells me enough.

"Did he do it for other people?"

Karl is clearly uneasy. I've touched a nerve. He's probably wondering if I'm wearing a wire for some kind of sting.

"I'm just asking questions," I explain. "I'm your niece. Not the police."

"In a US marshal's office," he says in a lowered voice. "With the door open."

I turn to the door and shout, "Hey, Simmons, my uncle just told me he plans to escape and join ISIS."

"Tell him to wear sunscreen," he replies from the other side.

"He doesn't care about a case from more than a decade ago. Nobody does."

"Tell that to the judge that sent me here."

"Tell that to the dumb ass that keeps violating parole."

Anger flashes across his face. "It's not easy being treated like a convict. Especially for something that half the people around you are guilty of."

I lose my temper. "It's not easy being the niece of a convict and getting treated like one even though you never did the things you say everybody else did."

"Yeah, well, you certainly benefited from it," he mumbles.

"What's that supposed to mean?"

He glowers at me but stays silent.

"What are you trying to say?" Is he claiming his ill-gotten gains supported Dad and us?

I feel gut punched as I realize that . . . of course . . . Karl wasn't smuggling for the first time when he got caught. *Shit.* How naive can I be?

The investors he helped find for the family business . . . the shares he bought. *Damn.*

Dad may not have known, but he probably suspected. *Goddamn it. Focus, Sloan. Worry about the past later. Right now we stay focused.*

"Winston. Tell me about him."

Karl looks off to the side, ignoring me. "I'll talk to my niece. But not the cop."

"You asshole. Fine. What do you want to talk about?"

"Did you come in here and treat me like family and tell me how Jackie was doing or did you just treat me like a suspect?"

Not a hint of humor or tenderness. He's seriously angry. Well, screw him and his self-pity.

"Jackie? My daughter, your grandniece, is staying with her father because I'm too scared to let her come home after whoever murdered Stacey Miller stole my driver's license. She's great. Thanks for asking. I'll tell her she can come home once I figure out why the daughter of her uncle's drug-smuggling partner was killed a few feet away from her mom. Then it'll all be great. We'll bake you a fucking cake."

Uncle Karl's eye twitches for a second, then he drops his head into his hands. I brace myself for his temper and a barrage of grief.

Instead he quietly says, "I'm so fucking stupid. I'm so, so fucking stupid."

"What do you know?"

He inhales and sits up, wiping his eyes. "I don't know why anyone would be after you. I swear."

"What about Stacey? Is there a reason she would have come looking for me?"

Karl thinks about this. "She probably knew you were a cop."

"She probably knew a lot of cops," I reply.

"Yeah, but I think she looked up to you."

"Me? She hardly even knew me."

"You don't know how people see you from afar. I talked about you. Believe it or not, I was proud of you. I even put your academy graduation photo on my cell wall."

"That must have gone over well."

"You'd be surprised. Guys congratulated me." He wipes his eyes. "Don't get mad. But I told them you were my daughter."

"What?" I'm not mad, but I thought Karl would've been embarrassed to have a cop daughter.

"You're your mom and dad's kid through and through, but I like to think some of the good stuff came from Uncle Karl. It . . . it makes me feel like one percent less of an asshole. Maybe Stacey heard me talking about you. I did it a lot." He shrugs, then says, "Maybe . . . Oh, I don't know."

"Maybe what?"

"Maybe she got into trouble and figured she could go to you because of that."

"What kind of trouble?"

Uncle Karl glances at the door and lowers his voice. "The Mendez money."

Mendez is the name of a cartel that's been making the news in the last year or so, since the feds arrested a South Florida attorney trying to lock down their money.

Jason Bonaventure. That's the attorney they arrested. That's who Cardiff was talking about with Solar.

As I recall, the charges were dropped, and Bonaventure filed a huge lawsuit. His Palm Beach island estate was all over the news because the feds were digging holes and trying to search for records or something.

"What *about* the Mendez money?" I ask.

"It's missing. Over half a billion dollars. You might remember, the feds were trying really hard to find it. A week ago, one of Bonaventure's attorneys serving time in here got a visit from some lawyer from Colombia."

"And?"

Karl shrugs. "I don't know. It was a big deal to some of the folks in here. They say there are more cartel captains in Miami right now than in South America. Something's up."

"Something? What does that mean?"

"The money's still missing."

"It was already missing. That's why Bonaventure went free."

"I'm not talking about the feds looking for it. I'm talking about the cartel. Now they're going ballistic."

"What does Stacey have to do with all this?"

"Maybe she overheard something. Have you talked to her father?"

"No. I can't even get a text through."

Karl lowers his head. "That means they already got him."

"Got him? Like he's dead?"

"That's probably why they went after Stacey. They thought she knew something."

"And she came looking for me."

He nods. "Catfish . . . you need to take Jackie and get out of here. If these people think you have *anything* to do with this . . ." His voice trails off, and his eyes drift toward the small window near the top of the wall. "Damn it."

"I can't just run."

"Do it for Jackie. Forget your McPherson pride."

My anxiety starts to build. "These people have private jets and attorneys around the world. Where would I go? What would I do?"

He makes a violent shrug as he thinks about my predicament. "And you *can't* go to the cops."

"What? It's not like we have *your* reputation," I reply.

He shakes his head. "You don't understand. The Mendez cartel is deep. The reason Bonaventure got away was because he was tipped off."

"Someone in law enforcement?"

"Someone? A lot of someones. Assholes like George Solar and all the other crooks."

I don't mention that I saw Solar yesterday. I'm still hoping I can get some useful intel out of my uncle.

"So, you think Winston is dead."

"Definitely."

"Anybody else I could talk to?"

"They would have gotten to everyone by now," he replies.

"That's not good enough. I need a name. Someone who knows Winston."

He thinks about this for a moment. "Raul Tiago."

"Who is that?"

"Peruvian kid. He worked for Winston. I think he and Stacey were . . . um, seeing each other. Chances are he's dead or back in Peru. If not, maybe him."

That's the thinnest of leads. I came here hoping for a simple answer, and now it turns out things are far more complicated and dire than I realized.

I've gone from worrying about a lone psychopath coming after me to an entire cartel with thousands of hired guns and cops.

I should have stayed underwater.

CHAPTER THIRTEEN

LIGHTHOUSE

After an awkward goodbye with my uncle, I go back to my car and check for messages. The Palm Beach Sheriff's Office still hasn't asked me to come in and make a statement. That's either sloppy or odd.

I could call them, but that would be asking for trouble. I'm also at the point where I think I might need an attorney if they want to question me. I've heard too many whispers about me already to believe I'll be given a fair shake.

It doesn't matter if I had nothing to do with Stacey's murder other than discovering her body. A good prosecutor will find something to hang a case on. Did I have my dive tanks properly stored in my truck? Have I been keeping proper track of my personal versus professional tank refills? Did I use a federally funded magnetometer for personal purposes? Did I keep all the appropriate records? The list goes on.

I need a moment of normalcy and decide to text Jackie.

How's it going?

A minute later she replies.

VG gonna drop by house with Dad and get some clothes ltr k?

Okay. I'll be home in a couple of hours. Love you.

Love you more.

Those three little words make me relax and feel a little glow inside. In telling me that she's picking up some clothes, Jackie's made it clear she knows I need a few more days and Run is on board with this.

We make a good team, for a fractured family unit that was never really a whole family.

If only Run . . .

Stop it.

I check my email and see that Nadine Baltimore, my supervising professor, has asked for a checkup on the canal site she asked me to take a look at.

Clearly, she hasn't been following the news. Nadine spends most of her time in the lab separating pieces of linen from dredged-up mud and very little time paying attention to anything that happened in the last couple of centuries.

I decide to give her a call.

"Hey, Sloan," she says in a monotone manner. She probably has her earbuds in as she stares into a microscope at a specimen.

"What are you looking at?"

"Could be a baby's leg or a parrot thigh bone."

"Really?"

"Of course not. The parrot bone would be smaller and more porous. But that's what it looks like on first glance."

Nadine has an odd habit of giving you her stream-of-consciousness thinking when you ask her a less-than-direct question.

"Find anything in the canal?" she asks.

"Yeah. A body."

"Really?" she replies with an excited change of tone.

"Um. A recent one."

"Classic? Postclassic?"

"This week."

"What?" she replies.

"The person was killed and dumped while I was in the water."

"Oh my god. At my canal spot?"

"Yeah. Long story short, it's a murder scene."

"Well, that's inconvenient. Did you find anything before you found the body? Why are you laughing?"

God bless Nadine. She's not going to let something like a tragic murder and ensuing homicide investigation get in the way of science. I think this is why I called her in the first place.

"No, I didn't."

"Oh. Will you be able to go back and have a look? It's a really interesting area. From the aerial photos, it looks like the bend on that stretch was only recently connected to the canal and was a pond for a long time before that. I'll bet anything that just below the muck there's a clay layer that'll yield something."

"I'll see what I can do."

"Thank you. Anything else?"

"You get a chance to look at the paper I wrote?"

"Yes. Your spelling is atrocious, and your references were mismatched."

"Oh . . ."

"I submitted it to the *Journal of Underwater Archaeology*."

"Wait? What?"

"I cleaned up the errors. Other than that, it was good. A little dry, but good."

I'm confused. "You submitted it? Coauthored?"

It's pretty common for professors to slap their name on their grad students' work to increase their publication count.

"No. Of course not. I was looking at the academic calendar and realized that you needed to have a paper published this semester. I decided to go ahead and submit it."

"Thank you."

"It'll run. I know the reviewer who's handling it. They're looking for something like this. So, congratulations."

That's Nadine for you. One moment she's a thousand years away, aloof to your worldly problems, then at three a.m. she remembers something and saves your ass. Part of my education is being paid for by an obscure scholarship she discovered that was funded by a philanthropist who made his fortune selling dive gear to the navy.

"You're the best," I reply.

"Then get me some sediment. The boys over in the genomics lab say they've got a multichannel sequencer they want to test out on something unusual."

That sounds more like a musical instrument to me than a piece of scientific equipment, but I don't admit my ignorance.

"Wonderful."

After we hang up, I momentarily contemplate sneaking back into the crime scene to get Nadine those samples, then think better of it.

I make it back to the harbor an hour after sunset. When I turn the corner on the dock, I see the light is on in the bow cabin, Jackie's room. She must've just arrived.

A smile comes to my face.

She'll love the news about my paper getting published. Run won't know if this is on par with having your Little League photo in the local newspaper or the Nobel Prize, but he'll suggest we all go out to dinner and celebrate.

I wish I could accept, but the less time I'm around them right now, the safer it is for Jackie.

I set foot on my boat, and my brain tells me something is wrong. I just can't quite figure out what that is.

The cabin door is wide open, and the only light is coming from Jackie's room.

"Jackie?"

No answer.

She could be listening to her phone with her earbuds in.

"Babe?"

I move past our galley, down the tiny hallway that leads to the bathroom on the left and my cabin on the right.

When I push the door to Jackie's cabin open, I spot a man dressed in black kneeling on the floor next to her bed.

And he isn't Run.

CHAPTER FOURTEEN

QUARTERDECK

Survival or maternal instincts kick in—take your pick. The man begins to stand, his right hand going behind his back. Before he can draw, I give him a side kick to the exposed ribs, slamming him back against the narrow bed.

The narrow *empty* bed . . .

My hand reaches for my own gun, tucked into the waist of my jeans. As I raise it, the man glances over my shoulder.

I duck, but not quickly enough to avoid a partial blow to the back of my neck that sends a shock down my spine and makes me see stars.

I wheel around, gun extended toward my unseen attacker.

Another man, this one a tall white guy with receding hair, is blocking the small passage. He lands a right hook to my jaw. My knees buckle, and I feel the gun being pried from my hands by the first man.

BANG.

I fire a round before he twists the barrel back so far that I have to let go or break a finger.

"Fuck!" he curses over the ringing in my ears.

I hope I hit him, but I'm afraid I only singed him.

"Get down!" says his partner, grabbing at my hair.

I throw a punch with my left, straight at his balls. He turns, avoiding the worst of the blow, but he's unbalanced and has to brace himself on the door frame.

I surge past him, trying to squeeze through the small space between his body and the wall. The other man grabs at my calf, sharp fingernails clawing into the muscle.

I kick back, hit something, and push forward.

"Jackie!" I scream, my first words since seeing the man at her bed.

There's no answer. I grab the door to the head and slam it open, blocking the tall man for a moment.

The bathroom is empty.

A long arm reaches through the space between the door and the wall and grabs my neck.

I kick the door backward, breaking the hinge and stopping him for a moment.

"Jackie?" I yell as I pull open the door to my cabin. Even though it's dark, it only takes me a second to see that she's not inside.

There are a half dozen places she could hide, but I'm praying she's not on the boat.

I take two steps up the small stairs that connect to the galley and living room, making my way to the cabin door.

As I reach the last step, a hand grabs my foot and pulls me back.

"Just kill the bitch already."

Ice runs through my veins. I have seconds.

My fingers grasp the edge of a cabinet as they try to pull me back down the steps. My grip slips on the slick varnish and drops until it finds a brass handle.

I yank the drawer open, hoping I can grasp the inside and pull myself away from them and make it off the boat.

Hands grab both my legs and attempt to yank me down the steps. I hold on to the drawer, but it rips free, the contents spilling onto the deck.

I want to scream but stop myself. You don't scream underwater. You handle the situation.

"Get her gun and grab a pillow," one man says to the other.

One pair of hands lets go. The other is still pulling me back.

I claw at the carpet, my fingers grasping at the first aid kit, fishing hooks, and other random items from the drawer.

I touch something wooden. Sense memory and recognition flood my head.

It's the haft of a fileting knife.

The man behind me gives me another strong tug, trying to pull me into the hallway.

I let him drag me down the stairs, unsheathing the knife as he tries to improve his grip.

Twisting and slashing, I cut into the space where I assume his head would be.

"FUCK!" he roars as blood spatters on me.

I see his thigh in the dim light and stab into it, then twist and rip.

"FUUUCK!" His scream ends with a whimper as he falls back into the other man.

I scramble on knees, gain my feet, and shoot up the stairs.

BANG. Someone fires, the noise even louder than the first gunshot.

I make it out the door and onto the deck. There's a loud scramble from behind as one of the pair continues his pursuit.

The long dock stretches in front of me. While it appears like the safe path, it's not. They'd have a clear shot and could drop me before I make it to land.

I dive over the edge. Don't even look. Just throw myself into the water, hands first, and swim.

A barnacle-covered dock pole scrapes my back as I slide past it.

When I feel the upswell of the water on the bottom, I open my eyes and see the silhouettes of the other boats in the moonlight.

I swim for the farthest one, *Permanent Vacation*, a fifty-foot Gulfstar sailboat that belongs to a man named Ed Acosta, a retired Pennsylvania schoolteacher and full-time pothead.

He keeps his boat anchored in the bay, away from the docks. I swim hard for it in hopes of keeping my pursuers as far back as possible.

I spend a half minute swimming and go all the way under the big boat's keel to the small platform on the back.

I try to make as little noise as possible when I emerge.

"Ed?" I whisper as I slide onto the deck.

I can smell the scent of his weed. The interior is glowing from a television set.

"Ed . . . ?"

"Hello?"

His shaved head pokes out from his cabin. "Sloan? Rent due?"

"No. Call 911."

"You hurt?" He starts to walk toward me.

"No. Stay down!" I scan the dock for my boat and see it rocking as someone steps onto the deck. "Call 911!"

"I don't have a phone."

I spot the outline of a man scanning the other boats from the deck of mine.

I duck and gesture for Ed to do the same.

"Seriously. Get down, now! Then radio it in."

CHAPTER FIFTEEN

SHORELINE

From Ed's boat I make a frantic call to Run, telling him to stay clear of the harbor. He knows from the tone of my voice not to ask any questions. There's been a lot of that lately.

After that I call Captain Mercer at Fort Lauderdale while still keeping my head down low so I can't be seen.

"Two men were on my boat. Armed. May still be there," I say curtly.

"You okay?" he asks.

"Yes. I'm on another boat."

"We've got units on the way. I'll be over in a couple. Can you give me a description?"

I spurt out a few details mechanically, hardly even processing what I'm saying. Poor Ed, who only wanted to spend the evening getting high, is crouched at the base of the stairs with his radio microphone in his hand, watching me, waiting to see what happens next.

When I peek back over the edge, my boat is rocking again. My assailants probably just stepped off.

I have a momentary panic attack, afraid that they might decide to take another marina resident hostage, then remember that I'm the only one currently moored to my pier.

A bright light splashes over me and blinds me as it bounces off the white deck. I squint up at the police helicopter and point at my boat.

The spotlight turns to my craft, and the chopper begins a search pattern.

Red and blue lights appear in the parking lot, followed by the deafening roar of one of Fort Lauderdale's marine-unit boats as it pulls up behind us.

I wave my arms in the air, letting them know I'm here. The boat pulls up alongside, and the spotlight tilts away.

I recognize the driver as Becky Vendable. I don't know her well, but we've spoken a few times.

"You okay?" she shouts.

I give her a thumbs-up.

She speaks into the radio attached to her vest, then nods to me. "Patrol units are looking for a car that just left the area."

She nods to two police officers running down the dock toward my boat. One of them stops and aims his light at the deck. I can't hear what he says or see what he's looking at, but he only spends a moment before moving ahead.

The officers reach the edge of my boat's pier and kneel behind a dock locker.

Over the din of the helicopter and boats, I can't make out their words, but they seem to be hailing my boat and telling whoever's in there to surrender.

This goes on for what feels like a million years until four more police officers join them on the dock and provide cover.

I glance over and see that Becky Vendable has a shotgun resting on the console, trained on the bow of my boat. *Hmm.* That won't be too useful at that range, especially with her own officers in between, but I keep my mouth shut.

A few minutes later, a police officer emerges from belowdecks and gives the all-clear sign.

"McPherson, hop aboard," shouts Vendable.

I step into her boat.

Vendable takes us to an empty slip two piers over. I help her tie off, then climb up to the deck. At least six more patrol cars are in the parking lot. The helicopter veers off, probably in pursuit of the vehicle they spotted leaving.

When I get to the end of the pier, Captain Mercer is waiting for me.

I get ready for the billionth "Are you okay?" of the night.

Instead, he shakes his head and says, "What the hell?"

"You know what I know," I reply.

"Are you sure?" He motions me over to the end of my dock. It's being taped off as the other boats are searched.

Mercer aims his light at the wooden planks that run one hundred yards to the end of the pier. A long red smear stretches the entire distance, starting at my boat. Every few feet you can see partial footprints, as if someone were being half carried.

That's a lot of blood.

"What'd he look like?" asks Mercer.

"Who?"

"The dead man."

The dead man?

I get Mercer's point. There's no way someone could survive that much blood loss unless there was an ER at the end of the parking lot. Which there isn't. And chances are, these men were not heading for the nearest hospital.

I got him good. Artery. *Shit.* Not the gunshot, I'm pretty sure. It was my little stab and twist that sealed his fate.

Mercer must see the look on my face. "Serves the asshole right. Good job."

I know he's trying to make me feel better, so I nod. He doesn't have all the facts. Hell, I could have just stabbed Run in a domestic dispute and made up the whole story. That'd be dumb and fall apart in two seconds, but it's not the point. He trusts me.

"Were they waiting for you?" asks Mercer.

"No . . . I don't think so. I think they were looking for something."

His eyes drift from the dock to me. "What was that?"

"I have no idea."

"Then how do you know they were looking for something?"

I give him a cross look. "They sure as hell weren't there to steal Jackie's sticker album, were they?" I sigh and pull wet hair away from my eyes. "Sorry."

"Easy, officer. I'm just trying to get some clarity."

Unfortunately, that's in short supply right now.

"When can I go back aboard?" I ask.

"Seriously? It's a bloodbath in there. Easier to scrap it after we're done."

His face registers how much hearing this hurts me. Mercer's used to talking to other cops about little-people problems behind their backs. His brain still didn't fully comprehend that this happened in my home.

"Write down a list of what you need, and I'll have someone get it for you. Okay? You have a place to stay?"

"I'm fine."

"All right. Let's let forensics have what you're wearing and get you into something dry, then down to the station to make a statement."

CHAPTER SIXTEEN

Portside

"Are you sure it wasn't a misunderstanding?" asks the FBI agent sitting across the conference room table.

He's in his late thirties with jet-black hair showing the first signs of gray at the temples. He has Hispanic or Mediterranean features but no trace of an accent, Miami or otherwise. He was introduced to me as Special Agent Maris by Detective Carbone, the Fort Lauderdale plainclothes in charge of the case—although calling it a case at this point may be wishful thinking on my part.

In the last hour, I've gone from certain death at the hands of two unknown assailants to convincing these idiots that it wasn't a misunderstanding. Next thing you know, they'll be questioning if it actually happened.

"Miss McPherson, other than the blood, we're having trouble finding any forensic evidence," says Carbone.

Spoke too soon.

I take a deep, long breath that probably sounds like a wheeze. I'm trying really hard not to let my temper get the best of me. I take another breath.

"Could we get you a glass of water?" asks Maris.

I give him a gaze that could freeze an ocean.

One more breath. "You mean no other forensic evidence besides the gallons of blood and the bullet holes?"

Carbone makes a little throat-clearing sound. "Well, yes. There are bullet holes in the hull of the boat. Forensics is pulling the slugs."

"Yeah, that little detail. Of course, what do *I* know?"

"We're not questioning your recollection of events," says Maris, even though that's exactly what he's doing.

I'm still trying to figure out what the hell an FBI agent is doing here. Carbone would only say that he'd been working with him on cases. That seems unusual.

The only thing that makes sense is that I'm one of those cases and Maris thought he could get a chance to see me up close, overlooking the fact that I'd find that highly suspicious. Or maybe he doesn't care.

It's also apparent they don't care all that much about what happened to me. While my friends at Fort Lauderdale went out of their way in responding, Carbone, the detective assigned to this, is no friend of mine—or of my contacts here.

This all feels wrong. Why are they acting as if this is all no big deal?

If this were some kind of conspiracy and these two clowns knew my assailants, that would make some sense, but they had no trouble sharing my descriptions of the assailants with other agencies. And as far as I know, the blood from my boat and the dock is on its way to a legit forensics lab to be ID'd.

That's hardly how you cover up for someone. That plus the way Agent Maris keeps looking up at the camera in the corner, as if he has friends watching remotely.

I should have asked for a lawyer. Run's family knows all kinds of fancy attorneys who'd be running circles around these jokers. But nope.

Here I am. I thought I'd be talking to friendly faces, not trying to convince someone what happened, happened.

"Any other details, Miss McPherson?" asks Carbone—like he's inquiring if I want breadsticks with my order.

"Officer," I answer.

"Actually, it's detective," he replies.

"No. I'm Officer McPherson. Not Miss McPherson."

Maris looks up at the camera and makes a little smirk.

"I understand," I say instead of answering his question. My petty display served its purpose.

"What do you understand?" asks Carbone.

"Why you think this is bullshit. Why you're not taking what happened seriously."

"Of course we take you seriously," says Maris.

"There you go," I reply, "with your clever wordplay." I point to the camera. "The show you're putting on for whoever's watching." I turn to the camera. "You think I made this up?"

"Why would you think that?" Maris asks in a condescending tone.

"Because you think I know more about the dead woman I found than I do. Because you think I'm somehow at the center of this whole lost-drug-money thing."

"What drug money?" Maris responds unconvincingly.

"Right. Right." I sigh. "So, the way I look at it, you're already convinced that I'm implicated in all this. But when I call the cops claiming I was attacked by people looking for something, it didn't exactly fit your presumed-guilty theory . . . unless I made the whole thing up in the hopes of making myself look like a victim. Right? Because why else would a crooked cop at the center of a drug investigation bring even more attention to herself? Unless it's just some dumb, desperate attempt to divert the attention from something else."

A good five seconds of silence follows, which I take as a sign that I put my finger on it. Maris checks a message on his phone. Probably his friends on the other end texting him a question.

"Did you just call yourself crooked?"

"Unbelievable." I stand and head for the exit.

"We didn't say you could leave," says Detective Carbone.

It's the kind of cop power move you try on an idiot. I was never under arrest. I can leave any time I want.

I step through the door, take two steps into the hallway, and notice there's another conference room right across from us. I wonder who's in there.

Don't do it, Sloan . . .

I do it.

I open the door and see five men and a woman sitting around a table with a television at the far end showing the conference room I just left.

They're in the middle of a heated discussion. I only recognize one man from Fort Lauderdale.

They all turn to look at me, faces frozen in surprise.

"Hello. I'm Officer Sloan McPherson. If you have any questions you'd like to ask me, please let me know. Of course, you'll have to go through my attorney from now on, but I'm happy to assist your investigation in any way I can to get its head out of its ass."

I turn around and feel their eyes burning through the back of my head as I walk away.

As I walk down the hallway, I hear someone shouting after me. "McPherson!"

I ignore him and keep going, too afraid to find out what'll happen if I stop.

He catches up with me and touches my arm. I jerk it away and spin around to face him.

He's shorter than me, bald, and wearing a suit. He doesn't look like a cop.

"I'm with the district attorney's office. My name is L Ferguson."

"L?"

"Long story. Anyway, I want to apologize for what happened back there. I told them to take you seriously, but . . ."

"They already made up their minds."

He makes a pinched face. "Um, yeah. Sort of. You know how cops are, and their gut instincts."

"Right. Well, while they're following their gut, Stacey Miller's killer is still out there. Nothing's stopped. Nothing's changed. And they're worried about *me*?"

"We'd love to be able to formally talk to you. Maybe clear some things up."

"*Now* you're telling me this? Are you for real? Two men just tried to murder me, and I have to go through that clown show? Talk to my attorney." I start down the hall.

"Who's your attorney?" asks Ferguson.

I don't have one. I'm tempted to fire off a sarcastic remark, but instead I reply, "I'll let you know."

I walk through the double doors, into the lobby, and leave the station.

I sure showed them, I think to myself as I realize I'm in downtown Fort Lauderdale with no wallet, no phone charger, no ride, and people out there that want to kill me.

Ace move, Sloan.

I stand on the sidewalk, trying to decide if I want to walk to the marina or swallow my pride and go back inside and ask to use a phone—and pray that I can remember an actual phone number.

I feel a tingle on my neck as I realize a man in a pickup truck is watching me from across the parking lot. It's dark out, and all I can see is his shadow, but he's definitely staring at me.

The truck's engine roars to life, and the vehicle creeps toward me slowly. I take a step back toward the station, suddenly deciding it'd be much safer inside.

The truck does a loop, bringing the driver's side closest to me. The window rolls down, and a voice calls out, "Need a ride?"

My heart does a backflip when I realize who it is.

George frickin' Solar.

CHAPTER SEVENTEEN

SANDBAR

In my family, George Solar falls somewhere between Adolf Hitler and Charles Manson. He's the crooked cop who took my uncle down while managing to avoid going to prison for his own misdeeds.

And what exactly were those misdeeds? I ask myself as I stare at the open window and the man inside.

Rumors. Lots of rumors. There were stories that he'd taken kickbacks but avoided jail time by ratting out his fellow officers. Some said that rival drug dealers gave Solar tips on their competition, and he looked the other way in exchange.

Of course, stories and rumors are far more abundant than the truth around here. Like the new one about the niece of a convicted drug dealer in the middle of a big narco conspiracy faking an attack on herself . . .

"Are you here to murder me?" I ask casually.

"That wasn't on my calendar."

"Well, if you're hoping to find out where all that drug money is, I don't know."

"Of course you don't," he replies.

"What makes you so sure?"

"Because you wouldn't be anywhere near here right now. You'd be off on your little dinghy or whatever, sailing into the sunset."

"Huh. What if I knew something but not how to get to it?"

"You wouldn't call the police when someone else came looking for it."

"All right. So why the hell are you here? You know I really don't have any idea where the money is."

"If I was after money, I would have done a lot of things differently in life. For better or worse, I chose my own path."

"Right."

He nods. "So you've heard the rumors about me."

"A few. I also remember sitting in court watching you give testimony that sent my uncle away."

"And do you remember me saying anything you knew not to be true?"

"I was a kid. I don't know what I knew."

"But your uncle told you I was crooked."

"Are you?"

"I'd like to say I have a clean conscience, but that wouldn't be true. I maybe came down hard on some people that I didn't need to be so hard on."

"Like my uncle."

Solar laughs. "Definitely *not* your uncle. Do you know how much coke he got past us before we stumbled onto his routine?"

"How much?"

Solar hesitates—he didn't expect me to take him up on his rhetorical question. "Um, I don't have the exact number . . . but a lot. A whole hell of a lot. We were kicking ourselves that we only got to convict him for a fraction."

I suspected as much, but Solar's not winning any points with me. *Yeah, I get it, my uncle's a scumbag, but that doesn't lessen the pain, including that of associating with you now.*

"Is there something you need?" I ask.

"Me? I'm here about you." He nods to the police station. "How'd that go? What did they think of your story?"

My alarm bells start to ring. "What do you know?"

What *could* he? The incident only happened a little more than an hour ago.

"I talk to people. They tell me things. That was quite a mess back in the marina. Is that where you're headed now?"

There's no way they'll let me back on the boat, not that I should stay there if I want to stay alive. I was hoping to get some clothes from the storage closet in the marina office and decide what to do next then.

I'd go stay with Mom or Dad, but that would put them in danger. The other problem is what to do about Jackie. I still have to figure out how to keep her safe. It's beyond frustrating to accept that being in the same place as her is no way to protect my baby.

I'm going to have to fill Run in on the details and see to it that he has someone keeping an eye on her.

And for how long?

How long will my life be turned upside down like this?

"How about we go get a cup of coffee and compare notes?" offers Solar.

"What's your part in all this?" I ask.

"Just an interested observer." His green eyes seem calm and sincere.

"That doesn't sound suspicious at all." I glance down at my dead phone. "My friend is on his way to pick me up. Maybe another time."

I say that with all the insincerity I can muster.

"Right," says Solar. "Just one more question before I go. You armed? Or did they take your gun away from you for evidence?"

This makes my gut twist. I glance around to remind myself we're still in front of a police station.

Solar opens his glove box.

I think about diving back to the doors of the station, but I'm frozen.

Solar pulls out a pistol and sticks it out the window, butt first.

I stare at the Glock for a moment, trying to understand what just took place.

"Hold on to this until you get yours back."

I take the gun from him robotically. Is this a trick? Was this a murder weapon in some other crime, and I'm being framed? What the hell is Solar's game?

He sees my hesitation. "You have to make up your own mind about me. In the meantime, I don't want to see you get killed. I know not all McPhersons are crooks."

"Thanks," I say weakly, tucking the gun into the waistband of my still-drying jeans.

"The offer for coffee is still open. Let me know."

I watch Solar drive off, still trying figure his angle in all this.

Everything he said and did seemed sincere. But he's a smart man. Acting sincere and building my trust is exactly the smartest approach to get to me.

He's supposed to be retired. He has no official business in this as far as I know—which only leaves unofficial business. And right now, the primary unofficial business I'm aware of is finding the missing cartel money.

Solar doesn't seem like that kind of person, but a few hundred million dollars can bring about drastic personality changes.

I'm just realizing how much that affected my uncle—or was he always that way?

CHAPTER EIGHTEEN

SEASIDE

I can't fall asleep on the marina office couch, so I text Run a redacted update and decide to get an early start . . . on what? I know what I'm after: whoever killed Stacey Miller. But what do you call it when an off-duty police officer starts investigating a case in which she's a suspect?

Suspicious.

Whatever. It's clear to me that the powers that be are not acting in my best interests. You could easily make the case for the opposite. Rather than wait for the next couple of prowlers to climb aboard my boat in search of a treasure map or whatever—or, worse, threaten Jackie—the sooner I can resolve this, the better.

At first, I worried that meddling would make me look suspicious. *Well, dollface, too late for that.* Now I'm afraid *not* meddling could make me dead.

So, despite the best advice from everyone around me, I'm going to stick my nose wherever I can think to stick it. Trouble is going to find me either way. There's no doubt about that.

Ocean Tech Yard is Winston Miller's old boatyard. It's the only place I clearly remember seeing Stacey as a girl, other than some possible run-in at the Elbo Room or maybe the mall.

I pull over on the strip of gravel between the highway and the fence surrounding Winston's boatyard on the side away from the canal.

The two big sheet-metal buildings still stand alongside various boat lifts, supports, and other leftover equipment. The dilapidated dock remains, too, although it looks like it's on the verge of collapsing.

Beyond that, it's a ghost town. I grasp the fence and peer through, as if making visual contact will somehow cause the past to come alive again.

In a way, it does.

I remember our boat at the time, the *Sea Castle*, propped up on supports as Winston worked on the hull and outfitted it with a variety of gadgets like radar, side-scanning sonar, and even an underwater camera.

Dad got a Japanese television station to help pay for the refit in exchange for the television rights and part of any recovered bounty as we explored the Bermuda Triangle for lost treasure.

It was a bit of a con on Dad's part. He knew it wouldn't be hard to find something out there. The Bermuda Triangle is huge and filled with shipwrecks—like any other heavily traveled shipping route.

But with Japanese viewers, it made for great television—at least in theory. The network loved the idea of this seafaring family out in the remote ocean—remote for Japan—chasing down ghost ships and pirate plunder.

What was supposed to be a three-week trip ended up lasting only five days when the producer, the son of the head of the network, got incredibly seasick and decided that we should fake the whole thing off the coast of Fort Lauderdale while he supervised from the penthouse of the Yankee Clipper hotel and busied himself with local prostitutes.

This was fine by us. It was already a BS expedition to begin with and mostly a way for Dad to get someone else to pay for the refit of the *Sea Castle*.

We ended up shooting a bunch of stuff at night, faking some wreckage and getting shots of my brothers and me running around the deck, pointing at nothing and shrieking. We had a blast—and no idea how it would all be edited together.

Three months later we got a VHS tape from the producer and viewed the final result. It was the most bizarre thing we'd ever seen. My brothers and I loved it.

In the "documentary," we were attacked by ghosts in the middle of a storm after finding lost pirate-ship treasure, only to have it vanish the next day. Or something along those lines. We never had anyone translate it for us. All we know for certain is the special-effects spirits swirling around the deck looked like they had been lifted from some other movie.

The show was a bit of a ratings hit, and there was talk of another until the producer got involved in some scandal back in Japan.

It was during this period that I first met Stacey and the ugly ducks she used to feed by the dock.

The ducks are now gone. I suspect even they know the dock is a death trap.

"You looking to lease?" asks a woman from behind me.

I turn around and see a familiar face—Angie Woodward. She's the Jamaican woman who ran the paint store in the warehouse next to the yard.

I look over and see the paint store is still there.

"Hey, Ms. Woodward!"

She recognizes me and returns a big smile. "Well, if it isn't the Sea Monkey."

Sea Monkey was yet another of my brothers' nicknames for me. We'd scrounge for quarters and go spend them in the gumball machines in Angie's store, filling ourselves with Boston Baked Beans, Mike & Ikes, and M&Ms. I try to smile back without wincing.

"Come here to have a look around?" she asks.

"Sort of. How long has it been empty?"

"Winston got rid of most of his stuff right before the bankruptcy. I think he worked something out with the owners, though. He still comes by and gets equipment."

"Really?" My heart races. "When was the last time you saw him?"

Angie thinks for a moment. "A few weeks, I guess. Maybe more."

"Oh." I'd been hoping it was more recent than that—like this morning. Meaning there's a chance that Winston isn't dead like his daughter. "And Stacey?"

Angie's face changes. "You heard?"

"Yeah." I don't tell her how. "When was the last time you saw her?"

"A couple of years. Winston mentioned her now and then, but I never saw her. Her boyfriend came around here sometimes with Winston. Raymond, I think?"

"Raul?"

"Yeah. Raul. Nice guy. Quiet." She walks over to the padlock on the gate and produces a key from her pocket. "Have a look around, if you like." She points up to the tall boat-storage building across the water near a skyscraper filled with condos. "Who knows how long before it all changes."

"Thanks," I reply as I step through the gate. Even more memories begin to surface.

"Just lock up," she calls after me before walking away.

I walk across the cracked asphalt, trying to understand how the place could have shrunk over the years.

When I was ten, it seemed so much bigger. Of course, I was smaller, and there was a lot more going on here back then.

I walk over to the dock and give the rotten wood a wary glance. Stacey would sit here and feed her ducks pieces of bread as they quacked and jostled around her feet.

We thought Stacey a little odd. In retrospect, I can only imagine how lonely she must have been. Back then it seemed weird how she'd tag along with us and try to insert herself into our play.

I remember Harris teasing Robbie that Stacey was his girlfriend. In response, Stacey grabbed Robbie's hand and grinned. She also liked telling us "secrets" to try to win our friendship. It was little-kid stuff. Like how her dad had a lady friend or how nobody was allowed in the secret building out back.

Harris claimed the building was a painting booth and had dangerous fumes. Stacey insisted otherwise.

We tried peeking in through a window once and saw only a bunch of tools. Winston caught us looking, grabbed Stacey by the arm, and dragged her around the corner and gave her a spanking.

We all felt guilty as she sobbed, but the moment her dad went back to the other warehouse, Stacey turned the tears off and went back to her annoying self.

The secret building . . . I hadn't recalled it until now. I'd always assumed it was just a huge paint booth, like Harris said.

I walk to the back of the yard and spot the large metal building. The roll-up door and entrance remain as I remember them.

Out of curiosity, I try the door handle, and it opens. The morning sun streaks in through a window, the same one we peeked through long ago, illuminating part of the interior.

The acrid smell that hits my nostrils tells me that Harris wasn't kidding about it being used for painting. But that doesn't appear to be the only thing it was used for.

Rows of benches line the walls, and massive chains hang overhead. The kind you use to lift engine blocks. This workshop looks a lot like the other one in the yard.

Maybe this is where Winston fitted out drug boats?

The realization hits hard. Stacey was right about this being a secret.

I poke my light around the benches, looking for anything suspicious—not exactly sure what "suspicious" would look like, other than, well, suspicious.

I spot a wastebasket in the corner with some newspapers stuffed into it.

They're from last year. Not exactly incriminating, but from after the time Winston was supposedly evicted.

At the bottom there's a car magazine, *AutoSport*. Raul's name is on the label, but the address isn't the boatyard's.

Interesting.

CHAPTER NINETEEN

Shore Leave

Jackie steals a french fry from Run's plate and dips it into my barbecue sauce. We're sitting at a picnic table inside Tom Jenkins BBQ, a favorite of ours since Run and I were teenagers. It's a small place with a line that frequently goes out the door.

I keep a wary eye on the entrance, studying every face that comes inside. Run notices this but doesn't say anything. He can tell what's going through my mind.

Meeting him and Jackie here felt like a horrible idea, but my daughter was starting to get worried, and we're still trying to pretend everything is okay.

The story we told her is that I have a case requiring me to work odd hours. It feels wrong lying to her—especially when she could be vulnerable too—but there's no easy way to explain to your kid that there are people out there that may want to kill her mother and go through her daughter if they have to.

For his part, Run's been keeping a careful eye on Jackie. Two tables over sits Raymond Gunther, a friend of Run's from way back. Run's family hires him occasionally as security for their various businesses.

Gunther "conveniently" showed up at the restaurant, as far as Jackie's concerned. He's actually been shadowing Run and Jackie every time they leave the house, and he'll be parked across the street when she goes to school on Monday.

I don't know what it's costing Run to have Gunther do this, but I'm not in a position to make much of an argument. Jackie is as much his daughter as she is mine. I get it. I've decided to do everything I can to put a stop to this; so has he.

Run grabs a piece of okra from Jackie's plate and pops it into his mouth. "*Mmm* . . . Retaliation." He garbles the word between bites.

"Remaliation?" Jackie mocks him. "Mom must have done your homework back then."

"Hardly," he replies. "I had perfect grades."

"Perfect Cs," I say.

"Yeah. They were all Cs. Perfect."

"So, did you guys, like, study together?" asks Jackie.

"All the time," Run replies, suppressing a tiny grin. What he doesn't say is that we used homework as an excuse to go out on the boat, make out, party, and do all the things a couple of horny free spirits do when they're young and immortal.

Jackie uses another stolen fry to trace a circle in the sauce on her plate. "Do . . . do you ever miss it?"

She's getting old enough to realize our dysfunctional family dysfunctions in a weird way. When she was younger, she just assumed it was normal that Mom and Dad lived separate lives and made time for the kid. Now she sees that we're not like divorced couples and not even technically a couple.

That's not to say Run and I haven't hooked up every now and then, but we only do it with the full understanding that it's a casual thing.

I'll admit that I feel a twinge of jealousy when I see him out with another woman, but I'm free to do the same. But I've turned down a lot of guys because they simply don't hold my interest like Run. I'd rather spend a long evening in the bathtub thinking of old times than have some awkward, desperate fling I know I'll regret. Which I've done more than once.

Run looks up at me, waiting for my answer. The solution to the mystery of why Mom and Dad get along so well with each other—even have a kid together—but stay apart.

Jackie's asked me similarly probing questions recently, like if I've ever been mad at Run or if he's ever been really mad at me—trying, I assume, to figure out if one of us cheated on the other.

"I miss a lot of things about being young," I reply.

Jackie rolls her eyes at my answer. "Right. Like nickel movies and riding your dinosaur to school."

"Did you just call me a cavewoman?" I reply. "The penalty for that is half a hush puppy." I take a bite from one of hers.

"I was thinking . . . ," Run says after a few moments of silence.

"I'm proud of you, Daddy. Keep it up," Jackie replies.

Run puts his hand in front of her face. "I was thinking about getting you a muzzle. But I was also thinking maybe we all take a vacation." He hastily adds, "I'd get us some rooms, and we could go somewhere. Maybe skiing. Maybe Australia?" He gives me a hesitant glance, already afraid of the repercussions of saying something like this in front of Jackie.

"Oh my god! Australia?" she blurts out excitedly.

I have to measure my tone. Run is suggesting that we run away for a while. Although that may not be the worst idea, Jackie doesn't realize for how long he means. And then there's the fact that my problem could follow us there or be waiting when I get back.

"I have my work," I reply. "Maybe a father-daughter trip wouldn't be a bad idea."

"What? No," Jackie cries. "We should go together! Like . . . like a family. You two can get separate rooms and pretend you don't like each other and then go touch each other's butts when I'm not around."

"Jackie!" I say.

Run covers his grin and faces away.

Touching butts has been the family phrase for *sex* since Jackie was in kindergarten and came home trying to explain the pornographic act one of her classmates had seen on the internet. Hearing the term still gets a smirk from Run and me. We're too savvy to Jackie's tricks to issue a denial.

"I've got work, hon," I reply.

"When will that be done?" she asks.

"I don't know . . ." I'm struggling here. What do I tell my daughter?

"That sucks." She crosses her arms, sits back, and fumes. "Why can't we be normal?"

Gut punch.

Run is about to say something, but she interrupts him. "I can't figure out which of you is more selfish." She stares at me. "But I think I know now."

"Jackie . . . ," I protest. "We're here with you now."

"Oh yeah? Maybe I'd like to see both of you at the breakfast table. Maybe I'd like to fall asleep on the couch watching a movie between you guys. Maybe I'd like to have a mom and dad who love each other." She tries to hold back her tears.

"We do love each other," says Run.

Jackie points to me. "I want to hear her say it."

Damn. Once again, I'm reminded that growing older means finding new ways to experience pain.

"I love your father," I reply.

"My father? My father? Oh, do you mean the man sitting across the table from you? Why can't you just look at him and say, 'I love you'?"

Run puts his arm around her. "Baby, it's complicated. Sometimes people just aren't meant to spend their whole lives together."

"Is that what you really think?" She glares at me. "If Mom asked you to try being together, what would you say?"

Run makes a half laugh, trying to think of how to answer the question.

It seems my daughter has learned ninja-level manipulation tactics. I want to blame that on time spent with Run's mother.

"Things are complicated," I reply.

"The *C* word. Your favorite excuse. Dad loves you. I know he goes out with other women and all, but did you know you're the last one he . . . touched butts with? I heard him tell Uncle Gunther that. He loves you. But you don't love him. I get it."

"Jackie . . ." I'm at a loss for words. I want to tell her how I really feel about Run. I want her to understand that our situation's more about how I feel about myself. Run is perfect in his way. Me . . . ? I . . . I'm just trash that floated into his path.

I've always wondered if Run only stuck around because I got pregnant. The reason I turned down his hasty marriage proposal was because I hated the way it looked—like I got knocked up to trap him.

That's what his mother thinks every time she looks at me. That's what Run's yachtie friends say behind my back.

It's what I secretly think about myself.

I knew I'd never be able to hold on to him, so I did the next best thing—got us drunk, fooled around to the point we didn't know how to spell *condom*, much less use one, and got pregnant so he could never really leave my life.

I don't think that's *really* why it happened, but I can't convince myself it's not at least partially true.

I got pregnant so he wouldn't leave, and I refused to marry him because I couldn't admit to myself why I did it.

Ten years of denial, and now it has a face. A beautiful face covered in tears, looking at me, begging me to tell the truth: I love Run.

CHAPTER TWENTY

Shoals

Raul Tiago's address from the magazine label leads to a one-story white box in an older part of North Miami. The lawn is well kept, and a small row of stunted palm trees lines the circular driveway. Although his car is missing from the carport, there's no pile of newspapers or leaflets by the door to suggest there's a decomposing body inside.

On the way over, I stopped at a Wendy's, texted with Jackie, and did a little internet sleuthing. I found five Raul Tiagos in South Florida. None of them had this address.

Oddly, one of the addresses was in downtown Fort Lauderdale, fairly close to the marina. If I had to guess, I would have pegged that one for his place, not this house.

It's possible that he had two homes—which also makes it possible that the police went to the other one and not this one . . . which means I could be about to find a decomposing body after all.

I have no plans to break and enter. But I've smelled enough decomposing flesh to get a pretty good idea if a dead human is nearby. The trick is to walk around the house and smell the air-conditioning vents, pet doors, window seals, or anywhere else air escapes. I took a whole seminar on this subject. That was a fun experience. Our inspector, a retired forensic specialist, had all kinds of samples in plastic containers for us to smell. Some things can never be undone.

My nose twitches a little when I approach the front door and get a whiff of a semisweet scent. The door is open a few inches behind a screen door, and I feel a slight gut flutter at the thought of pushing it all the way open and seeing Raul's body.

After what happened in the canal and on my own boat, I'm fairly certain I haven't seen my last dead body.

"Hello?" I call out before pulling open the screen door.

From somewhere inside there's the noise of a television and rapid-fire Spanish. To my out-of-practice ear, it sounds like a telenovela.

"Anyone there?"

Footsteps.

I pull my hand back from the handle, suddenly concerned I've startled Raul's murderer. What if it's one of the men from the boat?

The door opens, and I'm greeted by a short Hispanic woman in a house gown.

"Hello?" she says, eyeing me suspiciously.

Okay, probably not an assassin, but don't be too sure.

"I'm looking for Raul," I reply.

"He doesn't live here."

Tremendous apprehension laces her voice. I have a feeling I'm not the first person to come around asking about him.

"I'm a friend of Stacey's."

"Oh . . ." Her face softens, and she opens the door a little wider. "I'm so sorry."

"Me too. Could I come inside and talk to you for a moment?"

She still seems wary and looks past my shoulder, then studies me a little more closely.

"She and I grew up together. My family used to have our boat worked on at her father's boatyard."

This seems to be the credential she was looking for. She opens the door and gestures me inside her living room.

Two new navy-blue couches fill the room, along with a glass coffee table and a television unit supporting a massive flat screen.

She excuses herself to go turn off the television in the kitchen, then comes back and sits down on the sofa next to me, placing two water bottles on the table.

Clearly there's a little money here. Hers or Raul's?

I make a point of looking around. "This is a very nice place."

"Thank you," she replies.

"Does your son live here too?"

She gives me a confused glance. "My son? You mean Raul? He's my nephew."

Oh. Interesting. It's entirely possible the police never even talked to her.

"I haven't seen him since they found Stacey. Have you? He must be devastated."

"He's away on work," she replies, a little too automatically.

"I see. I'd like to talk to him."

"Maybe you should call him?" She's on full alert now. Something I said triggered it.

I have to lie. "There's no answer."

If I were a better cop, I'd have figured out a way to get his number through Stacey's phone records or something like that. But I'm not.

I decide to try another approach. "Miss . . . ?"

"Carolina," she replies.

"I didn't know Raul. I knew Stacey. I'm the one who found her body. I think she was trying to tell me something right before she was killed. But I don't know what. I'm afraid for Raul . . . and I'm afraid for myself. Two men tried to kill me last night."

She puts her hand to her heart like a good Catholic, and her eyes go wide. I don't think she was expecting such frank honesty.

"You're not with the other people who came by asking about Raul."

"What other people? The police?"

She vigorously shakes her head. "Those men and that woman, they were not police."

Woman? "Who were they?"

"They said they were business friends of Raul. They wanted to know where he was." She points to the hallway. "They pushed their way in and searched everywhere."

"Did you call the police?"

"No, no. These people you don't call police on."

"When was this?"

"Two days ago."

"And you haven't heard from Raul in how long?"

"Five days."

"You have any idea where he is or how to reach him? Have you tried calling him?"

She looks at me like I'm stupid. "I've tried all his numbers. Nothing. But sometimes he's out of reach or doesn't get signal at the yard."

All his numbers? That's a little suspicious. "Is there one he uses more than others?"

"Yes. But that phone . . ." She stops, realizing she said something she shouldn't have.

"That phone? Is it here?"

She doesn't respond.

"Carolina, the men who killed Stacey may have been the ones that came for me. We need to stop them before they get to Raul." I try to say the last part convincingly, because I'm pretty sure he's dead.

"Okay," she replies. A minute later she returns with an older iPhone.

I press the button, and the screen asks for a thumbprint or a pass code. By the way she's looking at me, I can tell she knows what it is.

"Please," I say, holding it out to her.

She presses her third finger against the sensor, and the phone unlocks. Interesting. I bet she and Raul share some other secrets, like safe-deposit boxes and online accounts, but I don't push.

I open up his recent-calls list and use my phone to take a snapshot of the numbers. None of them have names, which is what you'd expect from someone who wanted to keep their contacts secret.

I notice an app for Bitcoin and other virtual currencies and open it up. The screen prompts me for a password, so I hand it to Carolina.

She stares at it for a moment, puzzled, then unlocks it. It shows a balance of about two hundred and twenty thousand dollars in various untraceable currencies. *Curious.*

I'm not sure what else to look for, then I remember something she said about not being able to reach him at the yard. Winston's boatyard was next to a cell tower. Why couldn't she reach him there? Why *would* she? That place has been effectively closed for years.

"You said that you had trouble reaching him at the yard? Which one is that?"

She shrugs. "He never told me where. He said it was a secret."

A secret boatyard? Is that where Winston and Raul were based when they retrieved equipment from Winston's old boatyard?

"What did he do there?" I ask.

Her eyes narrow a bit. "Raul worked on projects for the navy. Secret things."

Navy, my ass. Maybe the volunteer Bolivian navy.

"And you have no idea where this is?"

"No." She's trying to decide if she should take the phone back from me.

I cling to it, wondering if there are any other clues to be found. What about the Maps app?

I open it and look at the history of addresses.

Nothing.

Email?

I open the email app, and it asks me for a password. Carolina isn't offering one up.

I check text messages, but they've been wiped.

Okay, this is basically a burner phone.

I'm about to hand the phone back to her when one last idea hits me. I open the photo album, hoping to find some obvious landmarks. Maybe a sign that says **Secret Boatyard** next to a Waffle House I recognize.

No such luck. There're only a dozen or so photographs, and they're almost all sunsets or sunrises, the kind of thing Run used to send to me.

One photo shows the sun breaking through a group of mangroves. There's a canal in front of them with no seawall. I tap the photo, and it shows on a map where it was taken.

The location is southwest of Fort Lauderdale, a place I'm pretty sure there are no boatyards, only an RV storage lot and some tree nurseries.

Interesting.

As Carolina watches, I pull the location up in Google Maps and look at the satellite view.

Sure enough, tucked away from the canal and behind a dense forest of mangroves is a group of small warehouse buildings. They look like they were part of the nursery at one time.

I don't know when this image was captured, but I have a pretty good idea of what the buildings are being used for now.

It's the perfect location to work on drug boats, cars, and other clandestine ways of hiding contraband. It must be the secret boatyard.

I hand the phone back to Carolina. "Thank you."

CHAPTER TWENTY-ONE

Incursion

The frogs are chirping as the sun sets, casting a pink glow across the sky. I paddle my kayak slowly, watching the mangroves on either side. Occasionally I spot the headlights of a car as it goes down the road to my right. In the distance behind me, I can see the glow of the city. Ahead lies the setting sun and its mirrorlike reflection in the canal.

A turtle bobs its head up and swims along with me for a moment before diving back down. Under the twisted branches of the trees and shrubs lining the shore, soft splashing things crawl in and out of the water.

Although there's a perfectly good road leading to the mystery yard, it's also a small one-lane path that makes it pretty obvious someone is coming—and an easy place to get trapped.

The kayak seemed like a more sensible way to scope out the place. For starters, this is public water, so I'm not trespassing—as long as I don't leave the boat. Second, it's easier to explain my presence as a kayaker out for an evening trip than if I pull up to the yard looking suspicious.

At least that's my theory.

I have no idea what I'm going to find. Winston and Raul have to be long gone by now. What they left behind is the mystery.

I'm clinging to the idea that Winston and Raul used the site to install smuggler's compartments in fishing boats and pleasure craft.

If they did, those boats would probably need to be trailered in and out. I can't imagine anything floating through these canals with a keel more than a few feet deep.

Winston was a clever guy. It could be something else entirely.

But who knows? It could have been a drug storage and distribution site. Or perhaps there's no connection at all—maybe this place has nothing to do with anything and Raul took the pictures while exploring like me.

My doubts begin to fade when I spot the gentle slope of a concrete boat ramp leading out of the canal and into a gravel yard surrounded by a tall fence topped by barbed wire.

The fence even crosses the end of the ramp, with a large metal gate secured by a padlock.

An intimidating sign says, **PRIVATE PROPERTY. PATROLLED BY WESTGUARD SECURITY.**

What's even more intimidating is the eleven-foot alligator that has staked out the ramp as his personal resting spot. He doesn't budge as I drift closer.

I once knew an old trapper who lived out in the Everglades. He had a shack on stilts in which he kept his shotguns and other prized possessions. As a security measure, he used to throw dead chickens into the water to keep alligators around.

If one got too close to him, he'd have alligator meat for a month.

Unfortunately, I don't have any dead chickens to lure this one away, and he sure as hell does not look intimidated by a skinny broad in a rinky-dink kayak.

"Go away, beast!" I raise my voice at him, hoping it'll scare him.

The alligator doesn't move an inch. So much for that idea.

For a moment I wonder if he's even real. There's not much difference between a nonmoving fake alligator and one that's resting. Until it decides to move. Then things get deadly.

I could try to push him away with my paddle, but that would put me in close proximity to the creature. If he decided to charge me, the paddle would be as ineffective as a flyswatter versus a lion.

I bring the kayak sideways to the ramp so I can get out without having to step into the water. There's a better-than-even chance he'll ignore me and move away mopishly.

There's also a chance Jackie will see a news report about how some fishermen found my kayak and the partial remains of a stupid woman who got too close to an alligator.

"Okay, buddy. This is the way it's going to work: I'm getting out, and you can just chill. But if you decide to get a little bitey, I'm going to put a nine-millimeter round inside your teensy dinosaur brain and then turn you into a pair of sandals. *Comprende, amigo?*"

I point my gun—*Solar's gun*—at the alligator's head while my left hand steadies me against the edge of the ramp.

Being careful not to slip and either fall into the water, making myself extra vulnerable, or drop the gun and shoot myself—making Mr. Alligator's job all that much easier—I slowly move my weight onto the ramp, putting down first one foot, then the other.

Once I'm on solid ground, I realize that I forgot the rope.

"I'm still watching you," I tell the gator as I try to keep my gun on him while using my left toe to loop the rope. "Ha, got it."

I receive no applause for this feat, only more indifference. I'm okay with that.

I walk up the edge of the ramp in the direction of the alligator's thick tail. Reptilian eyes watch me.

This guy just doesn't care. Something tells me that Winston and Raul went out of their way to make him comfortable here and unafraid of people. *Chicken dinner every night?*

"I'm just going to tie this off." I loop the kayak's rope through the fence so it won't drift away.

With my gun still pointing in the general direction of the alligator, I move to the locked gate. Between it and the surrounding fence, the fence maker left a sizable gap. Useless for most trespassers, but there's enough space for me to squeeze through.

I pull myself through the fence and turn back to the ramp. The toothy doorman makes the sound of leather scraping pavement as he slides into the water.

"Seriously, dude? You waited until after?" The beast clearly wanted to show me that he was leaving on his own accord and was, like, totally not afraid of me.

I tuck the gun into my holster at the back of my jeans and flop my track jacket over the butt. If I get caught trespassing while wielding a weapon, I could get shot.

I survey the yard and realize that there's been a camera on a metal post watching the ramp the entire time. And it's not even an inconspicuous camera. A red recording light is shining brightly, making it perfectly apparent this place is under surveillance—or at least looks like it is.

When I was a little girl, some stores were too cheap to spring for security cameras and instead mounted fake plastic ones in the corner, always with bright-red lights and signs proclaiming **24-Hour Police Monitoring**.

I hope this camera's the same thing and that I'm not about to be attacked by guard dogs and private security guards rappelling down from helicopters.

I wait for a minute, inspecting the area and listening for the sound of anyone approaching.

Satisfied that I'm alone, with the exception of my pal floating somewhere near my kayak, I take a few more steps forward.

Passing through the line of trees, I face the two buildings I saw on the satellite map. But there's a lot more that didn't show in the imagery.

Aluminum trusses are scattered around, and there's something even odder—a large, aboveground pool.

It's the kind of thing you see in backyards in rural areas, about twenty feet long, ten feet wide, and a touch over five feet deep. An overhead lift on wheels is parked to the side, midway between the pool and the larger of the two metal buildings.

As I approach the pool warily, I smell a disgusting stench. Apparently, the pool boy's been a little lazy. The water is green and filled with leaves and branches.

Out of the corner of my eye, a headlight flashes. I abandon the pool and run to the building farthest from the road. I could have made it back to my kayak, but my curiosity's getting the better of me.

I slide behind the building and watch as headlights flood the area. It sounds like at least two large trucks.

Damn. I move deeper into the shadows behind the building and find a spot between two large metal drums, tucking myself between them.

Take it easy, Sloan. It's probably just some . . . whatever.

Doors open, and there's the sound of footsteps on gravel. I hear splashing followed by laughter.

It could be anyone. Don't panic.

One of the men steps in front of one truck's headlights and walks toward the fence along the ramp.

My blood turns to ice as I see his face.

It's the man from my boat.

The one I *didn't* kill.

CHAPTER TWENTY-TWO

Buoy

I press my back against the side of the building, willing myself completely flat. I'm in the shadows, true, but I don't know *how* in the shadows I really am. I decide that movement is worse than being visible.

The tall man walks up to the gate overlooking the ramp and peers down at the water. Did he see me on the kayak?

He's looking for the alligator, which means that he's been here before. Why? And why did he come back?

Someone else shouts to him, "Check the other one."

He turns around—his eyes go right past me as he walks over to the building I'm hiding behind. My knees buckle a little, and I panic for a moment, my left hand moving to my back to make sure the gun is still there. It feels nothing.

That's because it's still in your right hand, idiot.

The building vibrates as the roll-up door rises. The ramp is about a hundred feet away. I could try to run for it while they're inspecting the building . . .

I take a hesitant step forward, then spot a shadow of another man as he steps in front of the headlights. I hear the sound of a metal lighter, and my nose swears a moment later when it smells cigarette.

Damn it.

He's not moving.

Okay. What's plan B?

I look to my left and realize that the back of the building's shadowed by overhanging trees.

While waiting for the men to leave is an option, if one of them comes only a few feet around the side of the building, I'll be caught.

I decide it's better to make my way toward the back. Worst case, I can lose myself in the mangroves. Although that's easier said than done. They look incredibly dense from here. I'd probably only make it a few feet.

Shut up and do something, Sloan.

I start creeping back toward the trees. Each crushed blade of grass sounds like a crate of fine china being dropped onto pavement, but I keep moving.

The voices of the men carry as they talk while conducting their search. Boxes are moved around inside, and there's occasionally metal clanging.

Keep it up, boys. The louder you are, the quieter I am.

I reach the back of the building and take a slightly relaxed breath, then realize I'm inches away from a window. It's dirty, but I can see through it to the trucks parked out front.

The smoking man is a woman. Pretty, a few years older than me. She looks Hispanic and has a hard-looking face.

The tall man pushes some boxes back onto a counter and walks out of the building. Two other men join him. Neither is the man I stabbed. They're all dressed in work casual, not flashy like drug dealers. They could be cops, lawyers, reporters, schoolteachers, anyone.

"Nothing. Same as last time," says the tall man, his voice echoing around the empty yard.

"We were pretty thorough before," says another.

"Maybe he had it on him," the woman replies.

The tall man seems upset at this suggestion. "No fucking way."

"Check," insists the woman.

"You check," he protests.

She leans back against the hood of an SUV, takes a puff of her cigarette, and replies firmly, "Check it, Sewell."

Sewell? I lean in closer, trying to keep my body out of view of the window—as if my stupid head is invisible.

A thousand questions go through my head. What the hell are they looking for? Who is this woman? Who is this Sewell asshole?

"Jesus Christ," the man replies, then walks over to the aboveground pool. He kicks his foot around the edge until he finds something—a long pole with a hook.

He reaches the pole into the water and starts dredging the bottom.

WTF?

"Ugh," he says as the pole catches something. "Got it." He yells to the other man, "Don't just stand there."

"For fuck's sake. These are Varvatos shoes," he whines.

"They're going to be a dead man's shoes if you don't fucking help me."

The other man reaches into the pool and pulls something up. With the help of the tall man, they drag a body out of the water and flop it onto the ground. A metal weight belt makes a clanging sound as it hits the concrete.

In the harsh illumination of the headlights, the body looks pale blue. It's an older man with a beard dressed in a black shirt, utility vest, and pants covered in pockets.

It's Winston. I remember that vest, how he seemingly kept every tool in the world on him. When I was a kid, it was comical how he could pull anything from its pockets. He kind of reminded me of Doctor Who—if Doctor Who had been a foul-mouthed American with a short temper.

Both men start to rifle through Winston's vest and pants pockets, throwing Allen wrenches, screwdrivers, wire cutters, and other tools onto the ground. Part of me wants to shout at them to leave the poor man alone. But I'm days too late for that.

The tall man twists Winston's head so the neck is prominent. A red gash runs across the throat—exactly like the one on Stacey.

"Your friend is fucking brutal," he says to the woman.

She throws her cigarette to the side, kneels down, and starts looking at the tools. "You know what this shit is?"

"Yeah," says the other man. "Not what we're looking for."

"Keep going," she tells him.

The tall man undoes Winston's belt and pulls the pants off him and shakes them out. Small fasteners and parts clatter to the concrete. Some were probably tucked away there since the last century.

"That's all of it."

"Is it?" she asks.

"Shoot me now. I am not sticking my fingers up a dead man's asshole," he replies.

"He prefers them alive," says the other man.

"Fuck you. I'm already too far into this shit."

"Tell that to Eddie's wife," the other man responds.

"Fuck off."

Eddie. Is that the man I stabbed? These people don't seem terribly broken up about it. Of course, they clearly tend toward the sociopath end of the spectrum.

"Look around the buildings," the woman says. "Get flashlights."

Damn it.

The mangroves behind me are even thicker than I first thought. I might be able to lose myself a few yards in, but I'd make a hell of a racket doing it.

The men come back from the trucks with lights and start on either side of the buildings. My exit to the ramp is blocked. The only route left is straight between the two structures and the road. The problem is, I don't know where the woman is now. I could run right into her.

Damn it, Sloan.

Let's kick ourselves later. Right now I need to act. The beam from the other man's flashlight hits the trees in back of the far building and forces me to take action.

I bolt from my hiding spot and run around the corner, down the middle path. If I go fast enough, I might be able to make it past them before they know what the hell is going on.

Bam! My foot hits a bundle of aluminum pipes. Everyone had to have heard that. *Christ.*

"Could you make more noise?" says the other man.

"That wasn't me!" Sewell replies.

Fuck. Me.

I tear through between the buildings and bolt to the right, around the pool. The woman is standing near the first building, using the light on her phone to inspect plastic containers.

"Who the hell is that?" she shouts.

"There's some dude here!" replies the other man.

Dude? Screw you.

I duck behind the pool and keep my gun up.

"He's behind the pool," says the woman.

Screw you too.

"Let's wait here," says Sewell, clearly lying. I can hear his footsteps as he creeps around the pool.

"Hey, there. Come on out," says the other man. "We won't hurt you."

Sure. Like I didn't think anything of the body you just pulled out of the water.

I poke my head out to get a glance at the road. It's a long, narrow path. If I tried to run for it, they'd shoot me in the back at their leisure.

That leaves the canal as my only route out of here.

"Who's there?" asks Sewell. "Do you have a phone so we can call 911 for this guy?"

Does he think he's talking to a nine-year-old?

Okay. I still have a slight advantage; they have no idea who the hell I am or that I'm packing.

All right, Sloan. Time to put on the performance of your life. Too bad you used to make fun of the drama kids and say they all had daddy issues. Maybe they could have taught you something.

I try to sound like a teenager. "I . . . I was just looking for a place to sleep. My parents kicked me out."

Sewell laughs. "A fucking runaway."

Run away from this.

I fire my gun twice in the air, leap upright, and race around the pool. I take another shot at a pile of scrap so it'll make an even louder noise.

My sudden burst has the right effect. Sewell and the other man instinctively raise their arms to protect their heads. The woman dives behind her SUV.

I race past the headlights, aim my gun wildly behind me, and fire.

BANG! That shot's not mine. I duck as I reach the edge of the gate and start to slide through the gap.

BANG! A slug hits the fence and shoots sparks.

BANG! I fire blindly back at them for cover.

A second later, I'm through the fence and on the ramp. I don't even stop to see if the patrol gator is there. I just keep going until I hit the water and dive in.

BANG! Bang . . . The shots grow quieter as I swim deeper. Finally, I reach the bottom.

It's dark. I can't see anything, and I'm running out of air.

And, FML, that alligator's still down here somewhere.

CHAPTER TWENTY-THREE

Anchor

Beams of light dance around me as they use their flashlights to search the canal. The water is so murky, I can barely make out the glow; I hope they can't see me.

The world record for holding one's breath is twenty-four minutes. That's two minutes longer than a half-hour television show without commercials. That's also after breathing pure oxygen for thirty minutes beforehand.

The more relevant world record is holding one's breath without pure oxygen. Last I checked, that record is about twelve minutes. That's two more minutes than it took some guy to fly across the English Channel using a jet pack in a YouTube video Jackie showed me.

When I was her age, I practiced holding my breath with my brothers. I got better than them because I was willing to risk brain damage simply so they wouldn't outdo me. That probably cost me fifty points on my SATs.

I have no idea how long I'll need to hold my breath to be safe. I'm sure they're still up there. I'm also sure my reptilian friend is lurking nearby.

Ack! Something just slid past my leg. It was slimy and not bumpy.

Python?

Damn. Damn. Damn.

So, you jumped into the water and now you're clinging to a rock on the bottom. Was this your plan? Did you think you were going to sprout gills and be able to slip away and live happily ever after in Atlantis?

I should have stolen a car.

I should have gone for my kayak.

Which is still there . . . only a few yards away.

I'm not going to be able to wait them out.

This water is colder than I was expecting. My lungs are starting to scream. I didn't get a large enough intake of air.

It's all in your head, Sloan. You took a breath. Relax.

My heart is racing too fast. I won't be able to do twelve minutes. I won't even make my personal best of five.

I have to surface.

I need a . . .

BOOM! BOOM!

That sounded like a shotgun.

I can wait a little longer.

The lights vanish.

Now it's completely dark.

I get a second wind. I can stay a little longer.

No, I can't. I felt something again. Like a current. A large object is moving through the water.

Please be a friendly manatee to carry me away.

I know it's not.

I feel a choking sensation at the back of my throat. If I don't surface soon, my body will try to breathe water. That hasn't worked for more than a hundred million years.

Must. Breathe.

I hold my gun up in front of my face and decide to surface like a hero in one of the stupid movies my brothers used to love.

It's harder than it looks.

I kick to the surface, which isn't that far, and orient myself toward the ramp, ready to start firing at anything that moves.

I pop my head out, finger on the trigger as I train the pistol up the ramp.

Nobody's there.

This has to be a trick.

I scan the area behind the gate.

Empty.

Moving slowly, I pull myself up onto the ramp and squat with the muzzle aimed straight ahead.

Still nothing.

I stand and creep to the gate. The trucks are gone.

So is Winston's body.

They hauled ass out of here fast. Did they decide I was dead? I wasn't down there that long, was I? Did my superhuman breath-holding skills enable me to outlast them?

Don't be silly. It was three or four minutes, tops.

Something red glistens in the moonlight. Drops of blood trail from the gate back to where the trucks were parked.

Holy crap. I was shooting blindly for cover. I actually managed to wing one. What are the odds?

Too high.

Something else happened.

I hear a splash of water behind me. Not the kind an alligator makes sneaking up on you, but the kind a wave makes when it hits the hull of a boat.

That's how sharks find you. It's not the blood or the electrical signals you give off; it's the sound.

This sound tells me someone's behind me.

The fact that they haven't shot me yet means there's a reason I'm not dead. It's probably because they want whatever the other group was after. What happens when they realize I don't have it?

I could take a few more breaths and dive back underwater . . .

Yeah, that'll work. We'll just stay there. Have our mail sent to the bottom of the stinking canal. Jackie can make friends with all the little catfish.

I spin with my gun raised.

A bright spotlight blinds me. I have to squint and look away.

The light goes out, and I try to adjust to the dark and see who's there. At first all I can make out is a small fishing boat and a center console.

As my eyes adjust, a man resolves. He's got a shotgun on his hip and a completely neutral expression on his face.

I don't know if he's here to rescue me or kill me.

It's George frickin' Solar.

Again.

CHAPTER TWENTY-FOUR

STARBOARD

"I don't have it," I say preemptively.

Should I have said something cleverer? Hell, Jackie could have come up with something more convincing.

Solar's face reveals nothing. "I know. I'm also willing to bet you don't even know what *it* is." He lowers the shotgun and reaches down for his dock line. "Tie me off," he says, tossing it to me.

I grab the rope midair, then cast an anxious glance back at the boatyard. "Are they coming back?"

"Maybe. Maybe not. It looks like they dragged a body with them. My guess is they're afraid of someone coming back and looking around too closely."

"That body was Winston," I say. "This was his yard."

Solar hops down from the boat and checks my knot. "I was afraid it might be him. Here." He hands me his shotgun as he slides through the same gap I used between fence and gate.

I follow with the shotgun, still trying to figure out what's going on. "Uh, you want this back?" I ask.

"Hold on to it for a second." Solar picks up the pole Sewell used to search the pool and starts dredging the water.

"What are you looking for?"

"Another body. Tiago's. Who knows what else?"

Solar knows a lot more than he's telling me. He makes his way from one end of the water to the other, pushing branches out of the way and splashing water on his khaki shorts. "I used to clean pools when I was a teenager," he says. "I had to go back to that when I got fired from my first police department."

"Fired?" I'd heard he'd been let go in some kind of scandal. "And you still went back?"

More surprising, they took him back.

"Long story." Solar sets the pole down. "I don't think there's anyone here. What about this stuff?" He walks over to the scattered items from Winston's pockets.

"They didn't seem to find anything. Whatever *it* might be."

"I'm pretty sure they don't know."

"Who are they? How did you find this place?" I ask.

"Later." He picks up the components and inspects them one by one. "Is that anything?" he asks, holding up a small, cork-size plastic plug.

I take a closer look: there's a port on one end for some kind of electrical component. "I don't know. It's not a flash drive. It looks like some kind of marine electrical adapter or something."

He surveys the dockyard. "We should be going."

From the distance comes a police siren. "Somebody called the cops?"

"I did. Right after they spotted you."

"You were here the whole time?"

"I followed you."

"Me? What the hell? Why?"

"Because I figured you were going to do something stupid. And you didn't disappoint me."

"Screw you," I shoot back.

He ignores me and takes a last look at the area. "Any idea what Winston was doing out here?"

"I thought you had all the answers." I'm still pissed at the thought that he's been following me.

"You knew the man. You knew about this place."

"Barely. And I only know about this place because . . ." I stop myself from mentioning Carolina. ". . . I did some research. It seems like Winston was outfitting boats with secret compartments for smuggling."

Solar shakes his head. "He didn't need a place like this for that. Besides, you'd have to trailer boats in. Too inconvenient."

"What are you saying?" I ask.

He points to the crane and spare parts. "What are you seeing? Seems to me it would be easier to do this kind of work back in a marina. I don't get it. Nobody's been busted with a Winston Special in years."

"A Winston Special?" I ask as we slip back through the gate.

"That was the task force's name for boats he outfitted with secret compartments. Ask your uncle."

"I get it. I saw him two days ago." I look for Solar's reaction.

"I know."

Why am I not surprised? "Can you clear something up for me? Why the hell are you even here? Aren't you retired?"

"Just because the paycheck stops doesn't mean the job does."

"I get it. You're a nutjob. You fucked up in the past, and now you're easing your conscience? Or maybe you're after the money?"

"Believe whatever you want." He unties my kayak and fastens it to a cleat at the back of his boat.

"What are you doing?"

"Towing you."

"I'm not going with you."

Solar groans. "Fine." He hands me the plastic cork thing from Winston's pocket. "Then go find out what this is and let me know." He undoes my rope and tosses it back to me.

After stowing the shotgun, he revs his engine and nods to me. "Later."

He starts to back up his boat so he can turn around in the canal. From somewhere under the canopy of mangroves, something large slides into the water.

Seriously?

"Wait!" I call out to Solar.

He throws the boat into neutral. "What?"

"Let me tell my friend where I'm going." I want to see his reaction to me telling Run where I am. If he tries to shoot me, I'll take it as a bad sign.

"Great. But you don't know where you're going."

I look up from my iPhone as I text Run, Going somewhere with George Solar. Details later.

I look back to Solar. "Where *are* we going?"

"A friend's place," he replies.

"Uh, that sounds rapey."

Solar shakes his head and rolls his eyes. "For crying out loud. It's my girlfriend's place on the water. It's where I dock this boat."

Blue lights begin to splash treetops as a police car races down the road. Solar nods to the direction of the sound. "You want to wait for that? I'm sure they're going to have all kinds of questions for you."

"Um . . . no." I toss him back the rope to my kayak and hop aboard his boat.

Solar pulls us away from the ramp as a Broward Sheriff's Office car rolls into the shipyard. With the boat's running lights off, we're effectively invisible as we glide away.

Once we're back on the main canal, Solar throws me a beach towel from the center console.

I take it but can't help wondering why he's acting so helpful.

What is he up to?

CHAPTER TWENTY-FIVE

SEASIDE

Solar and I exchange few words as he navigates the canals to an older residential neighborhood in a suburb of Fort Lauderdale. We pass a marine-patrol boat, and I casually wave and receive one in return. It would seem the arriving police never saw us leave.

I'm still trying to figure George Solar out. His interest in the case is suspicious. Either he's after the money, or he's really a retired lawman vigilante trying to right unfinished business.

The latter I find hard to believe. Sure, I could be looked upon as a vigilante of sorts, but that's only because my life is on the line.

Or is it?

I started my own little side investigation when I realized I had a connection to Stacey. While my own personal safety is a factor, I'm also motivated by my own sense of justice—I guess. Or maybe it's my way of dealing with the fact that Stacey may have sought me out for help when she knew she was in trouble.

We reach a long wooden dock, where a pack of mutts of questionable breeding come yapping and barking at us as Solar ties off the boat. I step onto the dock and am surrounded by a mass of fur, sniffing and inspecting me.

"Don't mind the hounds," says Solar. "Cindy's into rescues."

The yard has been torn up by the marauding dogs, but the wooden deck and house are in nice condition. It's a large one-floor design with rows of windows and sliding glass doors overlooking a pool and expansive view.

"Nice place," I say. It's something you could afford on a cop salary if you got into real estate back in the 1980s. It would take me thirty years and ramen-only dinners to buy something like this.

"It's Cindy's. You'll like her. She's nosy like you." Solar pats the scrum of dog fur and sends them off chasing a tennis ball into the bushes.

We go through a sliding glass door into a kitchen with takeout boxes piling up in the trash. "We don't cook much," Solar explains as he leads me into a nicely furnished living room. Beige leather couches surround a large glass coffee table covered in books and magazines. The walls are lined with bookcases and framed newspaper articles.

I take a closer look. They're mostly investigative pieces on crime and corruption. The byline is Cynthia Trenton. She's been a South Florida crime reporter for decades. Pulitzers, Peabodys—whatever else they give good reporters, she's won them.

"Wait? Is your Cindy Cynthia Trenton?"

"Yep." Solar takes a seat in an armchair and places two beers on the table. "I framed those. She hates it."

"Huh. I never knew you two were a thing."

"It's not exactly a secret, but not exactly a thing we tell anyone." He emphasizes the last part to suggest I keep my mouth shut.

I drift through the different headlines, realizing the major stories Trenton has covered. One article catches my eye in particular.

SIX NEW RIVER POLICE OFFICERS ARRESTED FOR BRIBERY

The headline isn't that eye-catching, but the photos of the cops who were arrested are. A young George Solar's stern police graduation photo is in the middle.

I look back at Solar. He gives me a small nod. "Framed that one too."

"You guys have a weird relationship."

"It's complicated."

I recall Jackie chastising me for saying that about Run and me. "I can imagine." I stare at the couch next to Solar and realize I'm still wet. "Have another towel?"

"Yeah. Hold on." He grabs a towel from a hall closet and lays it on the couch. "When Cindy gets home, she can find you something."

I get a little nervous that the talk of the girlfriend and her being home soon is just a ploy to put me at ease. What if it's all a lie and she's really lying dead in another room?

Solar could be at the center of all this, and I just walked into his trap.

There's a loud knock, and I jump.

"Babe, we need to get this door fixed," a woman shouts from the front of the house.

"I'm on it," Solar shouts back. "We have company."

"I hope it's a carpenter," she replies.

"Better. A McPherson."

"That *is* interesting," says Cynthia Trenton as she enters the room. "Ooh, and my favorite one."

She's probably in her late fifties, but she looks younger. Dark skinned with a disarming smile, she makes me think of a Jamaican Meryl Streep.

My hand is wrapped in hers before I know it, and she gives me a firm shake. "Georgie's told me everything." She notices I'm wet. "Maybe not *everything*. Let me find you something. I used to be skinny once. I'll leave it on the guest-bathroom counter."

Cynthia disappears into the back of the house, leaving me alone again with George Solar. Or *Georgie*, as he's known around here.

I'm reasonably certain I'm not about to get murdered, unless this is an even more elaborate ruse than strictly necessary.

Naturally, Solar reads my mind. "Still think I'm here to kill you?"

"No," I reply with a little hesitation.

"But you don't trust me . . . That's fine. It's a good instinct. Saved my life a lot of times. We can work with that."

"What exactly *is* our work?"

"Getting ourselves out from underneath this pile of crap that's been dropped on us. Making it so you don't have to keep looking over your shoulder."

"And you? What's your part in this?"

"Unfinished business."

"That sounds ominous," I reply.

"You have no idea. No matter how messed up and corrupt you think things are, you have no idea."

"Enlighten me."

"This isn't just about a bunch of drug money that went missing. Reputations are at stake."

"Cops?"

"Feds. Others. People who intentionally did things and people who got caught up in things they didn't understand until too late."

I glance over at the article on the wall with his photo. "Like you."

"Ha. That's a story for another day. This is bigger—more complicated."

That word again: *complicated.*

"Okay. Explain."

"We'll start with the people back at the secret boatyard."

"They were cops? Right?"

"No."

"Cartel?"

"Nope."

"Then—"

"Let me explain," he interrupts to stop my interrupting. "DIA contractors."

"CIA?"

"Nope. DIA. Defense Intelligence Agency. They're kind of like the Pentagon's own CIA. You hardly ever hear about them in the news, which they prefer." He pauses, takes a breath, thinking. "This is oversimplified, but I'll paint the big picture for you. Historically, the DIA ignored drug trafficking because they were focused on armed conflict. The one exception was that they were actually helping facilitate poppy farmers in Afghanistan. They let the heroin business continue so they could stabilize the country's economy and bargain with the locals. Of course, this being the US government, that DIA division, called K-Group, did more than tell farmers it was okay. After some congressman raised the point that it seemed against our own interests to help the heroin trade only to have it show up in emergency rooms in the United States, K-Group decided to insist upon certain conditions in their little opiate business. Basically, better purity."

"That's insane," I reply.

"Ever check the back of a pack of cigarettes? Who makes sure that nicotine is the only thing killing you? The same people collecting a dollar on every pack. The same government that spends more money on advertising the lottery among low-income populations with poor math skills than promoting adult education." He pauses. "Damn, I'm sounding like Cindy.

"Anyway. I'm not pushing some grand conspiracy. It's just that people will do what they're incentivized to do. When K-Group was told to allow the sale of some heroin while making sure it was less deadly, that's what they did. Sort of. Only, ensuring purity doesn't make it less harmful. Worse, actually. Notice that heroin deaths are up five hundred percent since we invaded Afghanistan? Thank K-Group for part of that. Of course, the Taliban going into production overdrive, and later, ISIS, didn't help. Nor did K-Group's attempt to price them out of the market by lowering costs and supplying expert assistance. They even had Harvard economists making local-language manuals on cost pricing." Solar shakes his head. "On one end are you and me, trying to put drug dealers and gunrunners away. On the other are these assholes making our jobs harder."

"Like the CIA and the cocaine trade?" I ask. "I thought that was an exaggeration."

"It was. The CIA hired dirtbags to drop guns into South America. Those same dirtbags used their planes and contacts to bring cocaine back. It's not the same as saying the CIA controlled the drug trade, but it had the same effect.

"With K-Group, it was the government asking a bunch of contractors to make sure poppy farmers didn't help the Taliban. It ended up with people on the government payroll helping to build a better product and trafficking network. Perverse incentives, as Cindy calls them."

"Why the hell were they in South Florida? We're not a major heroin hub, are we?"

"I'm getting to that. Mission creep. K-Group actually started to wind down as it looked like they were a little too effective. Of course, part of the problem is that K-Group didn't want to shut down—certainly not the contractors and bankers they had working with them. Half of them were former government employees who left to start subcontracting businesses with K-Group. People made millions. They didn't want to stop."

"The American dream."

Solar nods. "Then, in the middle of closed-door congressional sessions deciding the program's fate, a miracle happened for K-Group. A miracle for them and a nightmare for the rest of us.

"DEA agents raided a cocaine-processing plant in Bolivia and found two things that freaked the hell out of them. One was a narco submarine better constructed than any they'd encountered before. The other thing is why K-Group received funding to keep doing what they'd done for heroin, now with the cocaine trade, all under the auspices of protecting our national security."

"What was the other thing?" I ask, taking his bait.

"A North Korean nuclear scientist."

"Wait? What?"

"Lee Yung-Un was actually a Chinese-trained engineer, but he also studied physics and shared his name with a North Korean involved in their weapons program. This made our intelligence community lose their shit. 'What if the North Koreans were going to use a narco submarine to smuggle in a nuclear bomb?' they asked. Why the hell the cartels would allow that, I have no idea. But they're not exactly known as stalwarts of sanity. Pablo Escobar himself tried to get ahold of a nuclear bomb as a bargaining chip. Either way, I'm pretty sure Yung-Un was in Bolivia to build a sub for cocaine, not bombs, but that was pretense enough. The government decided that it had to do something. Since they'd spent decades fighting a losing war on drugs, the new plan was to let K-Group take over a sector of the trade to keep tabs on it. They surmised a nuclear bomb in New York was a greater threat than a bunch of cocaine flowing into Miami."

"Holy crap," I reply. "I can't believe they allowed that."

"Well, they didn't, at first. Wiser heads in the intelligence community put a stop to it. So K-Group's funding was cut off. Only they didn't shut down. They didn't need the government's money. They were selling drugs. They *had* money. Billions. So instead they worked with a couple of cartels, listed their leaders as confidential informants, and kept things going."

"Okay. I get the big picture. Why the hell am I pulled into all of this?"

"Bonaventure, one of K-Group's lawyers and chief money launderers, was facing indictment by the FBI. He gave K-Group an ultimatum: shut down the federal investigation into him or he spills everything. Names, bank accounts. All of it.

"Remember back when he was under investigation and they were about to dig up his estate? K-Group got a friendly judge to grant an injunction. The FBI never found the money or his records.

"That's what everyone's after. That's why people are willing to kill you to find them."

Uncle Karl was underselling how bad this really is.

"So, what do we do?"

Solar holds his hands open wide. "I'm out of ideas at this point. That's why I followed you. I was hoping you had a plan."

CHAPTER TWENTY-SIX

HAILER

"So what the hell are they looking for?" I finally ask.

We've been sitting in Cynthia's living room without anything to say while I try to process all that Solar told me.

"Bonaventure's files, the money. I thought that was clear."

"Yeah, but what, exactly? Are they in a safe-deposit box? A U-Haul trailer? What were they looking for at the boatyard? And what did they expect to find on my boat?"

Solar shrugs. "Like I said, I'm not sure they even know."

"Crack team of spies, they are," I reply.

"In their defense, their expertise is money laundering and drug running. And most of them are K-Group contractors, not DIA employees." He thinks it over for a moment. "No. They know roughly what they're looking for."

"Fine. Whatever. Let's start with what *we* know—Winston was involved. What did he have to do with the missing money?"

"His role was building secret compartments for drug runners. Clearly, they must have used his services."

"Like you said, that yard didn't seem like the most practical location," I reply. "Winston did other stuff. I know he worked on cars too. Maybe he made a compartment on a truck?"

"Possibly. I'm not sure why that would involve you. Maybe his daughter was trying to tell you the location of something?"

"I haven't a clue." This is so frustrating. We're running in circles. I slap my damp jeans and realize I'm still holding on to the odd accessory we found from Winston's pocket. "What about this?" I set it on a copy of *The Atlantic* in the middle of the coffee table.

"Is it important?" he asks.

"I know boats, and I don't know what it is. Maybe it can tell us something about what Winston was up to."

"Should we take a photo and do an internet search?" asks Solar.

I'm surprised by the suggestion. "Okay." I take out my phone and upload the image to Google. It comes back with a hundred suggestions, from toilet valve to wine cork.

"Well, we tried," says Solar.

"Wait. I know someone we could ask. Les Albert. He's a local marine electronics guy. Everyone knows him. I'm sure he did some work with Winston. Electronics stuff."

"Have his number?" asks Solar.

"Better. I know where he is. The Straw Hut."

"The dive bar by the beach?"

"Yep."

Solar gets up and announces to Cynthia across the house, "The McPherson kid and I are going to a bar."

"Make sure she puts on something dry," she calls back.

❧

Twenty minutes later I'm riding shotgun in Solar's truck dressed in a pair of vintage jeans and a Police concert T-shirt.

"You go there on a date?" I ask, staring down at the shirt.

"What? Me and Cindy? I think they'd broken up by the time we met. Maybe. I don't know. But then again, I never followed music much. Any more personal questions?"

"Sorry," I say.

"I don't mean it like that. It's just that I have a few for you."

"Me? Like what?"

"How come you have a kid but you're not married?"

"Because it's not 1905. Women can vote now too."

He makes a groan. "I didn't mean it like that. It's just that you still seem close to your kid's father. That's all. I always wondered why you didn't marry."

I feel uncomfortable sitting next to him now. I have no idea who the heck he really is. "You always wondered? How does that not sound creepy? How long have you been into my business?"

"Ever since I looked across the courtroom and saw a little girl stare at me with murder in her eyes for tearing her family apart. I worried about what you were going to have to go through. I checked up on you," he replies. "I know that sounds bad."

"Maybe we don't do the personal thing?" I say. "My shit turned out all right. Thank you."

"Clearly," he mumbles.

Maybe I'm being too rough on the guy. What would I do in his situation? I've spent so long thinking of him as an enemy from the family's point of view, I never considered him from a cop's standpoint.

Yeah, I would be pretty torn up watching that happen to a kid. Hell, that was why Uncle Karl's attorney had me there. He wanted the jurors and the judge to feel bad for this kid in the hopes that they'd go easy on him.

I was a prop, I now realize. Damn it.

Besides my own father, is it possible Solar was the only other adult in the courtroom who cared about the effect the trial was having on me? Man, this is so . . . complicated.

"Sorry," I say after a long silence.

Solar may have followed me to the secret boatyard, but he also risked his life firing back at the K-Group cowboys. He could have waited, but he didn't. He was looking out for me—unless it's still some elaborate ruse.

Remember, Sloan. He got busted for corruption.

Maybe he's in this for the money or extortion, but I'm pretty sure he's not out to harm me—at least not directly.

If letting him get whatever K-Group's after is my way out of this, fine. If Jackie and I are safe, I don't care if he's just another crooked cop who thinks he has a conscience.

❧

Solar pulls into a parking space in the lot behind the Straw Hut, and we get out. I'm suddenly self-conscious of the fact that I'm dressed like a teenager at an eighties concert. Would it have killed us to throw my clothes in the dryer?

"What's the problem?" asks Solar.

I'm being ridiculous. "Nothing. I just realized I don't look very coplike." Disheveled hooker is more like it. Although George's extra pistol's still on me.

"That's a good thing," he replies.

He's dressed in the standard Florida male attire of shorts and a polo shirt, but his demeanor screams *cop*.

"And you?" I ask.

"Anybody I don't want to know I'm a cop already knows who I am. It doesn't make a difference what I wear." He gives me a long look. "Are you worried about this Albert guy?"

"Les? No. Let's go see what he says."

CHAPTER TWENTY-SEVEN

Trawl

Les Albert is sitting on a stool at the far corner of the rectangular bar. The Miami Hurricanes are playing the Tar Heels, and he's watching while sipping a beer. He's a large, barrel-chested man with a red-and-silver beard that flows over his neck and onto a pink Tommy Bahama shirt.

I've run into him a few times over the years, usually sitting at his same spot this time of night. When he sees me, he gives me a big grin. "Hey, Sloany!"

I walk over and give him a hug. "What's up, Mr. Albert?"

"Watching the game. Same as ever." He eyes George Solar. "We met before?"

"I think I questioned you a few times," Solar replies.

"Right. Right." He holds up his hands. "Still clean."

"Yeah, but your friends aren't."

"You're one to talk," Albert says with a half smile. "Can I buy you two a beer?"

I shake my head. "No, thanks."

"Sure," says Solar.

Albert motions for the woman behind the bar to bring us two Coronas. "What can I do for you? I take it this isn't a social visit."

"Uh, we were just in the neighborhood," I reply.

"She your trainee?" he asks Solar. "You need to work on that."

"I'm retired. She's too stubborn. You work with what you got."

"Too stubborn is right. Damn McPhersons," says Albert as he taps the neck of his Corona bottle against mine.

I take the component from my pocket and drop it on the bar. "What's that?"

He picks it up. "You tried googling it?"

"I stopped after one of the results said *butt plug*."

Albert drops the part on the counter. "I have no idea. Sorry."

"Really?"

I'd thought if anyone would know, it would be him.

"He knows," says Solar.

Albert shakes his head. "Afraid I don't."

"Take a guess," says Solar.

"It's really not my thing." Albert seems almost afraid.

"I thought you knew electronics," I reply.

"Not anymore. There's lots of new Chinese stuff out there. I'm retired."

"We found this in Winston Miller's pocket. He's dead, by the way," I explain.

Albert's eyes go wide as he stares at me. I can tell he's truly shocked.

"Oh, we didn't kill him. Someone else did. Maybe they were looking for this. We don't know. That's why I'm asking you what it is."

Albert turns to Solar. "Is that supposed to make me want to talk?"

Solar shrugs. "I don't know. I guess she thinks being honest will encourage you to be straightforward. Does it?"

"Hell, no. It scares the shit out of me. Winston's dead?"

"Come on, Albert. You knew he was involved in something," I reply.

"But you saw the body?"

"Yes."

"Fuck." He downs the rest of his beer. "Goddamn it."

"So, what is it?" I ask.

"Sloany, now is clearly not a good time to know anything about anything."

"Now is not a good time, period. I could tell you how my week started, pulling Winston's dead daughter out of the water. But all I really need to know is what this is."

Albert gives Solar a distrustful look. "You trust him?"

"No," I reply flatly. "But if you don't, then you can assume whatever you don't tell me here, he'll get out of you later with a knife at your liver."

"Jesus. Fine. It's a transceiver. You plug it into a radio."

"That's it?" I ask skeptically. "Just a run-of-the-mill radio part?"

Albert looks around the room, then lowers his voice. "It's military. More precisely, naval. Very low frequency, but it can handle data. Basically, a low-frequency modem."

"What good is that?" asks Solar.

I know where this is going. "Underwater, right? You could use this for an underwater radio?"

Albert nods. "Yep. Expensive. It uses a special kind of phased array to create a virtual antenna."

"A what?" replies Solar.

"It squeezes the big-ass antenna you'd need to make meter-size radio waves into a small package. Like I said, expensive."

"Do you know what it's for?"

"You mean what he was doing with it? Not a clue."

I push him. "And you have no idea what Winston's been up to?"

"Nope."

"I don't believe you."

"I do," says Solar. "If he did, he wouldn't be dumb enough to be hanging around here."

"Yeah, he would. He loves this place," I reply.

Albert shrugs and nods confirmation, clinking my bottle with his again.

Noticing the sheer number of people in the bar I've never seen before, I palm the transceiver and put it in my pocket. "We need to go. And, Albert, you should think about going back to the frozen north and visiting friends. People who knew Winston are going to be under a lot of scrutiny."

"Uh, okay," he replies.

I pull Solar out to the sidewalk outside the bar and nervously look over my shoulder.

"What's going on?" he asks.

"I think I know. Maybe. Or at least part of it. We need to go talk to my dad. He'll tell me if I'm crazy or not."

CHAPTER TWENTY-EIGHT

AFT

Dad sets a collection of charts on the table in the galley of his boat. He glances up at Solar. "Uh, that coffee warm enough for you?"

"It's fine. You're not much better at small talk than your daughter," Solar says.

"Yeah. It's just that I wasn't really expecting company," Dad says weakly. His eyes dart toward me. "Can we trust this asshole?"

"Mr. Solar is helping me figure out what's going on. It might all be a trick and he's just using me. I haven't figured it out yet. If I get murdered, make sure they know he's a suspect."

"You just blurt everything out there, don't you?" says Solar.

"My daughter's not a subtle person. She gets that from her mother."

We'd caught Dad on his couch playing sudoku on his iPad. To say he was surprised to see me with Solar was an understatement. I watched him keep an eye on his hidden gun, not sure at first whether I was George's hostage.

He mellowed a bit when I told him how Solar had helped me back at the secret boatyard.

"Okay." Dad points at the charts he gathered. "These are the tide and drainage charts for the canals west of the Intracoastal. A while back, a study was done about the feasibility of widening some of the canals and using them for barging materials to the industrial areas by Alligator Alley."

"What happened to that plan?" I ask.

"Environmentalists and logistics." He points at a group of canals west of Fort Lauderdale. "You get so much runoff soil from the Everglades deposited there in a storm that you could render the whole area unusable for anything with a draft of more than a couple feet. Although going north to south, there's actually some potential."

"But not here?" I point to Winston's secret boatyard.

Dad examines the numbers on the map. "This is the latest Army Corps of Engineers data. You'd barely be able to get *this* boat in there at high tide."

"There goes that theory," I reply.

"What theory?" asks Solar.

"It's stupid. I had a crazy idea. You mentioned that Winston wanting all that privacy was odd. I thought maybe because he was building a narco submarine."

"A submarine would never make it through here," replies Dad. "Maybe a small U-boat. But that would look kind of odd."

"It's a good thought, kid. That's the kind of thing Bonaventure would go for. It might also explain how he got rid of the records and the money."

"But it would never go down this canal," replies Dad. "Nothing you'd want to crew and send across the ocean, anyway."

"You could trailer it," I reply.

"Then why build it at a boatyard on the water?" asks Dad. "I've seen narco subs on the news. Those things are like World War II–size vessels."

"Yeah, I get it. It was just an idea." I set the transceiver on the table. "When we found out this could be used to radio underwater, I got excited."

"Low frequency?" asks Dad.

"Apparently very low, according to Les Albert," I explain.

"Interesting. Well, anyway. As you can see from the charts, the water's too shallow."

"Any chance it's deeper than that?" I turn to Solar. "Did you get a depth reading when you were out there?"

"I didn't pay attention. We could go back."

"Don't bother," says Dad. "A foot or two won't make enough difference for a manned submarine."

"Okay, next theory," I reply. "Maybe it's for finding some kind of anchored vault?"

"Or maybe it's just a random part Winston had in his pocket," says Solar. "I know you know the water, but maybe this doesn't involve it?"

He's right. As frustrating as it is to hear him say it. "Okay. What are alternative theories? A truck? A plane?"

"How much money did you say was missing?" asks Dad.

"It's about more than the money," replies Solar.

"I know. But what was the amount?"

"About a half-billion dollars," Solar says casually. "Give or take."

Dad whistles. "Still less than the *Atocha* stern castle."

This makes me laugh. "Oh, did we lose your attention? Is that not enough?"

"No. And legally you don't even get to keep it. Not that it matters," says Solar.

"I think I know a few maritime lawyers who might disagree," Dad replies.

"You're not allowed to keep illicit funds outside of reward."

"If it's in the water, it's salvage," says Dad.

"Not if it's drug money."

"That would take a court decision."

"All right, you old pirate," I snap at my father. "We're not exactly making a good impression here."

"Think I give a damn what kind of impression I give?" he retorts. "To him?"

"Uncle Karl broke the law and got busted. He went to jail. End of story. Solar is a cop. I'm a cop. We arrest people."

"You're a diver who works with the police department," says Dad.

"I have a badge. I carry a gun."

"So does a mall cop."

I slam my hand on the table. "Seriously? Is that what you think of me? Is that your assessment of my becoming a police officer? You think it's just a part-time gig like being a barista?"

"Isn't it?" asks Dad.

"No! I became a cop because I was tired of everyone thinking we were boat-trash, would-be pirates. I became a cop because Uncle Karl went to jail. I wanted . . . I wanted there to be at least one McPherson people knew wasn't crooked."

"Do you think I'm crooked?" asks Dad.

I turn to Solar. "Is he?"

"I stay out of family matters."

"No, Dad. I don't think you're crooked. But I think you get your priorities wrong sometimes."

"I see," he says quietly. "I'll be down below if you need me." He gets up and leaves us alone.

Damn it. I didn't mean to hurt him . . . *Wait. Don't do this. To hell with him for calling me a mall cop.*

Solar is leaning against a counter, watching me. "So, basically, I made you a cop?"

"Just shut up."

We go back over the maps, checking the depths of the canals. There just doesn't look like a practical way to get a submarine from the boatyard to the ocean or down the Intracoastal.

Solar is right. The radio antenna probably has nothing to do with the water. If not, then what?

Half an hour later, Dad walks up the stairs from his cabin and says, “One hundred and ten cubic feet.”

“What?”

“That’s how much space you’d need to fit five hundred million in cash. A hundred cubic feet, give or take.”

“What about the crew and air supply?” asks Solar.

Dad ignores the question and sets a piece of paper on the table in front of me. On it is a number: forty-four.

“What’s this?”

“It’s a filing box in the garage at your mother’s house. Go take a look at it.” He walks back down the steps into his cabin.

“Could you be a little vaguer?” I shout after him.

“You want to be a cop. Go be a cop. Hell, you already have people shooting at you.”

“Are things always this tense with the McPhersons?” asks Solar.

“You should see us when we *aren’t* getting along.”

CHAPTER TWENTY-NINE

CHARTS

Mom could give a damn that I showed up at her door with George Solar. In fact, she seemed almost overly polite when I explained who he was. She never cared much for Uncle Karl, especially after he got arrested. For her, that was one more warning sign that the McPhersons were a sinking stock.

She's a few inches shorter than me and still in great shape. Mom was more of a sportsman than Dad and loved to swim and scuba. Jackie possesses many of her characteristics. I'd say she's a good counterbalance to Run's mom, but they both have nasty streaks and love to talk shit about the other behind their back.

Mom's boyfriend, Hank, greeted us at the door and gave me one of his awkward hugs. He's a nice enough guy who works as a chef and a drummer.

If Mom was looking to trade up after the divorce, I'm not sure how well that worked out.

After I give her a brief, sanitized recap of recent events, she leads us to the garage, which is still filled with filing boxes and other mementos from our time at sea.

"This is what I got in the divorce," she says to Solar. "Lucky me. Most of it's notes that Robert was going to use for his book project. Still unwritten." She sighs.

"And you're still totally not bitter," I reply.

"I have a roof over my head. It's more than I can say for him. Still living on a boat."

"Yeah, those boat people. They're the worst."

"Oh, I don't mean you, dear. It's a phase. You're working out some kind of childhood trauma, I'm sure." She turns to Solar. "You know she tried to have herself emancipated as a minor? Legally separated? She wanted to divorce us first."

"That was a report for school, Mom. I've told you this a hundred times."

"Your brothers never gave me as much trouble as you," she replies.

"But they're not nearly as interesting."

This makes Mom smile, and she walks over and hugs me. "That's my little Sloan. Beating up the boys. Causing a fuss. Not taking any shit."

I glance over at Solar. "Have you ever seen this much dysfunction in one night?"

"Yeah, but it was on reality TV."

Mom lets go of me. "Oh, we almost did one of those. *Real Treasure Hunters of Miami* or *The Marauding McPhersons*. I forget." Shrug. "It never happened."

"Cable television's loss," Solar says dryly.

"All right, I'll let you dig through those," says Mom, without even asking what we're looking for.

After she leaves, Solar says, "Have you entertained the idea I may have done your uncle a favor?"

I start pulling boxes down. "It's crossed my mind."

A few minutes later, we find number forty-four. Inside is a collection of folders. Some of them are clipped articles about potential treasure locations. Others are magazine articles about new scientific gear and discoveries.

Dad was always looking for an angle, from an unexplored wreck to an improved way to detect sunken treasure. I divide the articles into piles as we pull them from the box.

We each take a pile, looking for some clue as to what Dad was hinting at. Nothing stands out until Solar pulls out a folder and whistles.

He shows me the label, which reads, OCEAN TECH YARD.

Winston's company.

Below it are two words printed in a futuristic font: Project Kraken.

"Oh snap!" I blurt out.

"You know what this is?"

"Yeah. It was some crazy thing Dad and Winston cooked up. It was a robotic explorer. Something they could just let run for months at a time searching the seafloor. They even talked some people into seed funding."

"What happened?"

"I think it was battery power or a sensor issue. Maybe both. This was the nineties. Batteries didn't last long enough. I don't think they could keep a computer running for long underwater. That's all different now. My daughter plays with stuff in school that could do it," I explain.

Solar spreads the contents of the folder on the floor of the garage. There are lots of electrical schematics and component-design diagrams. He unfolds a blueprint and lays it flat.

It shows a flat submarine that looks like a manta ray. Instead of being cylindrical, it's spread out, designed to skim along the bottom of the ocean.

Solar and I stare at the same number on the diagram—total height of the craft: thirty-six inches. Short enough to glide through the canals we've been looking at but large enough to carry significant cargo.

Solar reads the interior dimensions. "Pretty big inside for just one or two people."

"They wanted it to carry salvage to the surface. I wonder if Winston found a new purpose for it . . ."

Solar scrutinizes the image. "I'm confused. Where does the pilot go?"

"There is none. It's automated. Oh man!" I pull the transceiver from my pocket. "This!"

"That's a radio component. What good is a radio if there's nobody to talk to?"

"Very good if it's a modem. Remember what Albert said? This lets one computer talk to another. Data transmission."

"A remote control?" he asks.

"Or a way to load a new program." I stab the diagram with my finger. "Either way, I'll bet you anything this is what K-Group's looking for."

"An underwater narco drone . . ." Solar's voice goes quiet as he thinks it over. "This is serious."

"No kidding."

"I mean real, real serious. Narco subs are costly to build and operate. A fleet of these?"

"They can't cost more than a few million," I reply.

"And no pilot. I'd love to see one."

"There's one out there. Somewhere at the bottom of a canal." I add silently, *With a half-billion dollars inside . . .*

Jackie and I could go anywhere. Really anywhere. She might protest, but not so much if I bought her a pony farm in New Zealand.

Slow down, Sloan. We're the good guys . . . but what does that even mean anymore?

"I think I just saw your father in your eyes," says Solar.

"No shit," I say bluntly. "Before we decide to go rogue, we need to figure out where to look."

"If Bonaventure used this to smuggle the money and files, then our starting point is his estate. But that's being surveilled by the DIA."

"Hmm . . . But do they know what they're looking for?"

"Do we?" asks Solar. "Are you really positive that this Kraken's real?"

"No. But there's a quick way to find out."

CHAPTER THIRTY

RUMRUNNERS

All this talk of drug dealers got me thinking about the gangsters who used to smuggle booze through South Florida. With more than a thousand miles of coastline, Florida has always served as both an entry and an exit for illicit goods. Trying to stop it has been an ongoing effort for almost five hundred years.

For every naval innovation—faster boat, radar, airplane, satellite, what have you—smugglers have always been incentivized to outthink and outdesign law enforcement.

I had an economics professor who put it to our class bluntly: "When you restrict the supply of something, the price goes up. When the price goes up, you have more people working on more solutions to distribute the product. The market corrects for that."

According to him, the only two solutions that dramatically affect the price of an illegal commodity are decriminalizing it and easing restrictions or going the opposite direction and making sale and possession capital offenses. He claimed that educating the public on the dangers had only a nominal effect.

I'm not really sure where I stand. As a cop, I have to enforce a number of laws I don't agree with (and may have broken in my younger days). But I also recognize that I live in a democracy, and the laws we enforce are generally the ones everyone agrees on. Or at least this is my pat answer when I'm asked for my take on criminal matters.

A phrase you hear often in training and seminars is *use your discretion*. That gives us a lot of leeway in what we choose to enforce, for better or worse. I know for a fact that if we did as many drug searches of rich white schools as we do poor black ones, there'd be an outcry about our "lack of discretion." It's tricky on both sides. That's why I prefer the water.

Right now, I'm looking at a map of the south end of Palm Beach, where a small island called Turtle Isle perches by the mainland.

Solar and I are parked in a lot near the bridge that leads to the island, and we want to get our bearings straight so we know what we're looking for. Chances are, Bonaventure's estate is being watched by a lot of eyes. Even a swift drive-by is bound to get noticed.

"Turtle Isle has about twelve properties," says Solar. "Hard to keep track. Big ones get split into smaller ones. Two are owned by royalty—a German baron and a Saudi one as well. Some romance novelist owns another. A movie director and bankers or lawyers make up the rest."

"Must be nice," I reply.

"Maybe," says Solar. "The rich have their fair share of domestic squabbles, ungrateful kids, and opportunists preying upon them."

I don't point out how it's probably easier to deal with that when your biggest fear isn't losing the roof over your head. But I get what he's saying. When I went to private school, a rich family's divorce sounded like a civil war. Lines were drawn even in the cafeteria as stepkids sided against each other because trust funds were at stake.

I examine a printout from Google Maps, on which I've drawn a big red circle around Bonaventure's estate. I don't use the word *estate* lightly. There's a main house, several guesthouses, two pools, three hot tubs, a tennis court, a mini putting green, and a large boathouse next to a hundred-foot dock.

Bonaventure's boat, a ninety-footer cheekily named the *Good Fortune*, is currently docked in a marina in Miami.

"You sure there was nothing on the boat?" I ask.

"No. I'm not sure about anything in life. But DEA, FBI, and—I'm sure—a DIA search team have been all over it."

"Yeah, makes sense."

"DIA would have used antiterrorism stuff, military grade. Millimeter radar, X-rays, that new neutron thing. The boat was even up in dry dock with a robot arm loaded with sensors scanning the thing. Keep in mind that Bonaventure's smart. He knew the first thing they'd search is that boat."

"And where is he in all this?" I ask.

"Around. He's not under official investigation. He still goes back and forth between here and New York. LA. He doesn't leave the US, though, and he always has a security team with him."

"You'd think K-Group could get to him."

"They're afraid to kill him. They can't risk his files getting out. They'd rather get him into DIA custody and interrogate him."

Hmm. I nod.

"The reason he won't leave the United States is he's afraid he'll get hauled to some overseas black site."

"Rich-people problems," I reply.

Solar keys the ignition. "Ready?"

"I still think we should have used another car and worn a disguise."

Solar even has the windows rolled down.

He pulls us onto the bridge. "George Solar 101: if you know they're going to catch you doing a thing, don't try to hide. That confuses them and makes them think that maybe you're not doing a thing."

"Aren't we doing a thing?" I ask.

"Yep. And maybe they'll think we're just curious how Bonaventure lives. Who cares? If we used a rental car or one belonging to anyone we know, they'd trace it." He points to a traffic camera on a light post.

"That's not a Department of Transportation camera. That's a plate scanner. Right now, my registration and name are being added to a database with a time stamp. See the one ahead?" A camera is facing us on a traffic-signal pole. "That's taking photos of everyone driving onto the island. Facial recognition would see past a wig and sunglasses."

I get a case of the butterflies. "So DIA knows we're here?"

"Their computer does. It's not necessarily the same thing. They probably have it programmed to ping them whenever Bonaventure comes or goes. If he tries to sit in the back of a big SUV, there's a thermal profile for him—same thing Predator drones use to take out terrorists in their homes."

"Wonderful." It's one thing to know this technology exists; it's something else entirely to realize it's being used on you.

"If they have their act together, they probably have a database of persons of interest too. You'd be in there for sure."

"Delightful."

The main road on the island is a loop. On one side is the ocean view; the other is the bay side. While the ocean side has the better view, the bay side has the calmer waters and is where most of the houses with boat docks are located.

Bonaventure's parcel is at the tip, so it features a dock on the bay and an ocean view from the main house. I can't even imagine what it would be like to have that kind of money. This is Run's family's territory. I'm just happy if my boat doesn't have a leak.

The houses are all predictably immaculate and have perfectly manicured lawns. Some have fountains in front, others high fences.

When we get to Bonaventure's estate, I'm surprised that his fence is only two feet tall. It's more of a property divider. I'd been expecting a walled compound.

Instead, I can see clear across the estate to the ocean. Parts of it have stone walls and are shielded from the road, but the house itself and the cottages are out in the open.

You could almost go up and knock at the door if it weren't for the small guardhouse at the base of the main driveway. A stocky man in a polo shirt is sitting inside and watching as we drive by.

Solar waves to him, and the guard returns the gesture. Much to my horror, Solar stops the truck and rolls my window down.

"Is Jason around?" he asks.

The guard steps over to our vehicle. "Mr. Bonaventure isn't home today," he replies politely. "Shall I tell him you stopped by?"

"Yeah, tell him George Solar said hello."

The guard makes a note of this. "Yes, sir."

"Thank you." Solar gives him a grin, then pulls ahead to the far end of the loop and brings the truck to a stop.

"You're one ballsy man," I note.

"Did you get a good look?"

"At what? His clipboard?"

"George Solar 101: talk but see. He had a sidearm on his right side and another under his slacks on his ankle. Former cop. Which means he's paid a lot more than a regular security guard."

"Okay. That makes sense."

"Upper-right window over the side garage?"

"What?" I didn't even notice there was a side garage.

"The curtains were drawn partially, but there was a six-inch gap. A man with a telescope was watching from there."

"How the hell did you see that?" I resist the urge to turn back and look.

"Because Vernon, the ex-cop in the guardhouse, just turned around and looked at that window and flashed him an all-clear sign."

"No radio?"

"Would you trust a radio with DIA surveilling you?"

"Fair point. Anything else?"

"You tell me. Did you spot a secret submarine pen?"

He's serious.

"Um, no. They're usually on the water."

"Even secret ones?"

"Another fair point." I glance back at the dock and the boathouse. "I'd have to have a look from the water."

"All right, then. There's a boat-rental place ten minutes from here."

CHAPTER THIRTY-ONE

GROTTO

Solar makes a show of casting his fishing line into the water while I stare at Bonaventure's estate. At first I thought he was making a half-assed effort at being undercover, but then I realized he genuinely wanted to know if the fish were biting.

It's typical Florida weather: overcast skies to the south and bright sun to the north, each side seemingly flipping a coin to decide if it's going to rain or stay sunny here.

"What do you think?" asks Solar from the bow of the small boat.

"Your cast could use some work."

"I'm more of an inshore guy," he replies. "What about the place? Any James Bond villain chicanery going on?"

I was curious to get a look at the dock, but I see nothing suspicious about it. The seawall is made of large boulders and doesn't look like the ideal place to install a secret hatch or whatever.

A boathouse stands at the end of the dock, next to a small crane for lifting smaller boats out of the water. At the other end is a motorized boat cradle and a floating dock for kayaks and craft like ours. It looks like a thousand other waterfront properties in South Florida.

At one point, another guard dressed in the same maroon polo came out and walked around the grounds before going through a door in the back of the large garage area.

We figure that's their command center. If I were going to Jason Bourne this place, my first stop would be that garage entry, to knock them out or something. Thankfully that's not our job.

We're still trying to figure if there's some way Bonaventure could load or unload a Kraken-type craft here under watchful eyes. So far it seems questionable.

"What if it's under the dock while the larger ship is moored here?" asks Solar.

I try to estimate how much space there is under the dock. "I don't know. The waves are a little rough. I could see the thing getting banged up on the rocks. You might be able to do it under cover of loading a bigger boat, but that also seems like when there'd most likely be DEA and coast guard ships out there watching. Too risky."

"Yeah, I thought it was a dumb idea too. I just wanted to see what you thought."

I study the floating dock. "If that thing were hollow . . . maybe it could raise up underneath it? I don't know. The more I look at this place, the harder it seems for Bonaventure to use it to load and unload contraband."

"The sub may have been only for handling money shipments," says Solar.

"Why even bother? Why not Bitcoin it or something?"

"His South American partners prefer cash. Ever since the terrorism laws about money transfers, money laundering has been harder to get away with," he explains.

"What about the dark web and all that?"

"They're into that. For sure. But we're talking billions of dollars over time. Your street dealers get the cash; it moves upstream to Bonaventure, who has to figure out how to get it upstream to the cartel."

"I always wondered about that middle part, how it gets laundered."

"All kinds of ways. If you ever paid for a comedy show or a concert in an all-cash venue, there's a good chance your money got lumped in with drug money in the box office. You can clean a few million dollars a week doing that all over South Florida."

I never thought of that. Of course, I'm typically only retrieving evidence from underwater, not following a criminal enterprise's money chain.

"One day we'll take a little car ride and I'll show you where all the money goes. You'd be surprised how many hands are dirty—or at least don't ask questions. If you cut off all the drug money flowing into South Florida overnight, the economy would collapse in some cities. Hell, some countries would topple as well. The only thing keeping certain politicians in office in South and Central America is the payments from the drug trade. And the same could be said for here."

"Cheery thought."

"Here's another one for you. Nobody knows this, but right before Bonaventure got served a warrant, his people had been looking at a possible senatorial run. The cynic in me thinks that his opposition decided it was time to cut him off."

"You're pretty much all cynic." I eye the houses on the island. "I'm looking, but I don't see it. Maybe the transceiver was just that and not part of a robot narco sub?"

"What about the pool at the shipyard? Think Winston liked to go for laps?"

"Yeah, that . . . I don't know. But I'm not seeing where Bonaventure could park a sub here and not get spotted by the world. Maybe it was somewhere else? Some other property?"

"Could be . . ." Solar drags his words out a little, hesitating. "Let's just say I got a strong feeling money came through here."

"An informant?"

"An informed guess."

"Okay, but I'm still not seeing it."

"Maybe look at it differently," Solar suggests.

"Like with a drone?"

"Do you have one? I'm sure his people would love to see that flying over his estate."

"Not on me."

"But you could see a lot with one of those, right?"

"Yeah. I've played with my brother's. They're kind of cool. Our police department was thinking about getting one. Hold on . . . A lot of rich people live here." I nod at Turtle Isle.

"You think?"

"That means rich kids. Realtors . . ." I start typing on my phone.

Less than a minute later, I find more than a dozen YouTube videos of Turtle Isle taken by drones. I throw a towel over my head to block the sun as I scrub through the footage until I spot Bonaventure's estate.

"Uh, *that* doesn't look suspicious," grumbles Solar.

"It just looks like I'm changing film," I reply.

"Right. And don't forget to make sure your time machine has enough power."

"Quiet." I roll back a video and scrutinize the water a hundred yards up the island from Bonaventure's estate.

"Interesting . . ." The water is crystal clear blue except for one section where it's muddy, emanating from a narrow point—maybe a sewer or storm drain.

Solar pokes his head under the towel, startling me. "What have you got?"

"And *this* really doesn't look suspicious."

"They'll just assume we're doing drugs. No big deal."

I hold my phone up for him to see. "See the outflow? That could be something."

"Could be a sewer. It's also not connected to his property."

I drop our towel tent and stare at the area where the outflow occurs. "No . . . but who's to say how far in it goes?"

"Anything is possible when enough money is involved." Solar reels in his line and starts the boat.

We go around the island to the area where I spotted the outflow. It's a less developed section of the island, where mangroves and weeds hang over the seawall.

Solar checks his depth gauge. "Interesting. It's twenty feet here. That seems unusual."

"Not if it's been dredged." I point to a superyacht moored farther up the island. "They do that so you can park those things."

I strip off my T-shirt and jeans shorts, down to my bathing suit, and grab my fins and mask out of the gear bag I brought with me.

"Hold up there," says Solar. "What do you think you're going to do?"

"Have a look."

"I'm not sure if that's a smart idea." Solar glances back at Bonaventure's estate. "It looks a little suspicious . . ."

"Sloan McPherson 101: if you think something's there, get it before someone else does."

I dive into the water before he can protest or point out that my improvised adage makes absolutely no sense.

I make it halfway to the seawall, surface, and take a breath. Solar has his rod in hand and is pretending he's fishing again. I take a quick breath and go back under.

From thirty feet away, I see a dark rectangle about five feet below the low-water mark. It makes me think of the hangar bay on a spaceship.

When I get closer, I spot a metal grille covering the pitch-black tunnel. The bars are spaced fairly narrowly . . . but maybe wide enough for me to slip through.

I surface again, give Solar a thumbs-up, and dive back down before he can stop me.

Time to find out what's at the other end.

CHAPTER THIRTY-TWO

UNDERCURRENT

My chest, not exactly a buoyancy device but not exactly a plank, causes me more trouble than I expect as I try to slide through the bars. The rusted metal squeezes me and scrapes my back as I try to suck in my upper torso without losing any air—which is basically impossible.

I manage to get myself through and realize how ill prepared I am for this adventure. No tanks. No buoyancy compensator. Just my fins and a mask; this isn't one of my better-planned dives.

Am I showing off for Solar?

Obviously. That's been a trait of mine since before I could talk. I was always looking to show the men around me that I was every bit as capable. Which would be fine if I had stopped at some point and told myself mission accomplished. Although I'm the youngest, I'm the alpha wolf around my brothers. Dad certainly gives me room, and Run . . . well, he treats me more like an equal than any other woman he's known.

Yet, here I am, sliding into a dark tunnel, trying to show Dirty Harry that Sloan can play rough like the best of them.

Problem is, it's gonna get real rough if I can't get back out and drown inside.

I slide my hips past the grate and turn around to examine how it's attached—something I should have done before squeezing through.

Thick metal hinges run along the top, bolted into the concrete. At the base there's a bolt with a thick, waterproof padlock.

Okay, this *is* looking suspicious—that and the fact that this underwater channel seems wide enough for Winston's brainchild to fit through.

I've been diving in Florida waters all my life, including a few sewers, and I've never seen anything like this. Although I haven't exactly been looking. For all I know, this could be a new storm-drain construction technique.

Enough with the theories. I don't need to nearly drown twice in two days. I push off from the gate and swim deeper into the tunnel, keeping my arms in front of me.

Running into a wall at top speed could knock me unconscious—which would be fatal underwater. Although I have no idea what's in here, I can cross a few hazards off the list.

Sharks would hate it in here. An alligator wouldn't like the salt water. A crocodile would find it too confining—I hope. Large sport fish would avoid this too.

That leaves barracuda, eels, octopuses, groupers, and a dozen other things I can't think of right now. I really, really should have brought a flashlight.

My hand touches a wall, and I realize that I've gone sideways, or the tunnel curves. I'm not sure which. I've been busy counting my kicks. Five so far, which means about twenty feet.

I glance back at the opening and spot a blue rectangle of light. Twenty feet sounds about right. There's still enough light for me to see the bottom.

Something orange lies below me. I reach down and pick it up. It's a lead diving weight. *Interesting.*

I'm not sure why someone would dump that here. It might have been ballast for the sub. The craft would come in buoyant if empty and need to be weighted down. You'd need a lot more than one weight, but it's a possibility.

I drop the weight and continue kicking, keeping track of how far I can go before I have to turn back. Unlike the last time I dived, I was able to get a full breath. I'm good for a few more minutes if I don't exert too much.

I kick another ten strokes and find myself in complete darkness. I still feel calm, though, so I keep going.

My body keeps floating upward, so I use my hands to skim the top of the passage.

Ack. Something just slipped past my leg.

It's called a fish, Sloan. The ocean is full of them.

There's practically nothing here that could kill me. Maybe some flesh-eating bacteria they have no cure for, but nothing imminently dangerous, I think.

FUCK! What is that*?*

My fingers touched something . . .

Breathe, Sloan.

Um, bad advice, self. Stay calm.

Touch it again.

Wet denim. Kind of squishy.

Dead body.

Damn.

I can't pull it out of here. I need to go back and tell Solar. Let's just do a quick check to be sure.

Yep. That's an ankle and a shoe.

Ugh. Normally I wear gloves when I do this.

All right, time to turn around . . . Wait. Is that a light ahead?

Snap-judgment time. It's a hundred feet back to the grille, and there's a light ten feet ahead. What do you do?

The smart thing is to go back to the boat and have Solar call the police.

Then why am I swimming toward the light?

Dumb girl. Dumb, dumb girl.

The passage's ceiling has changed from concrete to metal. It feels like corrugated aluminum.

I slide under the gap in the ceiling from which the light is emanating. It's from a bulb overhead, which I can see through a grated cover.

This *is* some kind of underground loading dock.

I push against the metal grate. It gives only a little. Through a gap on one side, I see a chain crossing the hatch. They lock this from above.

What the hell are they afraid of? The Creature from the Black Lagoon sneaking inside?

I push again. It barely moves.

My lungs are screaming. I really need to start carrying around an emergency oxygen tank strapped to my leg—or move to the desert.

Okay, think. It's about 120 feet from here to the opening—which I have to squeeze through. Past a bloated corpse.

I just gagged and lost a mouthful of air. No time to think. *Do something.*

This tunnel is, what? Five feet tall?

I push against the roof and extend my legs to the bottom. Yep. Five feet.

Plant your feet, spread your hands. *Push, bitch! Push!*

My thighs explode as I try to move the heavens and earth at the same time.

I'm beginning to gag. My reptile brain is telling me to open my mouth.

PUSH!

Crack.

The metal door gives way and flies upward as the chain breaks.

My head surfaces, and I grab a mouthful of air, then the metal door slams back down on my head, knocking me back underwater.

Fucking gravity.

Stars.

Pain.

Get out.

I push the door up again and drag myself out of the tunnel, flopping onto the opened door . . . and feel something slice into my leg. I gasp for air, trying not to black ou—

CHAPTER THIRTY-THREE

KEEL

My head hits the trapdoor as I roll onto it, and salt water sloshes into my mouth. I taste my own blood.

I glance down at my leg—there's a narrow red gash where the edge of the grate sliced into it. It's not too deep, just long.

I'm in the bottom of a concrete pit that rises at least four feet above me. I could easily climb out if I wasn't feeling so woozy, but I have enough trouble pushing myself upright.

Something cold and metal touches my back, and I'm jolted with adrenaline. I turn around and find a chain hanging from an overhead lift.

I grasp it and start to pull myself out of the pit. After a few seconds of climbing and wincing, I roll onto the cold concrete floor of the bay.

At least I'm not going to drown. I start to stand, and my foot slips in my own blood. If I don't fix that, I'll bleed out.

The bay above the pit is spartan and about the size of a one-car garage.

This is where Bonaventure keeps his cargo before loading it into the Kraken . . .

This is where I'm going to die if I don't fix my leg.

At the far end, next to the stairs leading out of here, there's a row of metal shelves. I stumble over, look through a cardboard box, and find a white T-shirt.

It takes me a couple of attempts to tear the hem, but I manage to rip it open and use the fabric as an impromptu bandage on my gash.

The bleeding slows to a trickle, and I feel comfortable enough to walk and find out what's at the top of the stairs.

While I'm afraid it might lead directly to Bonaventure's guards, there's no way in hell I'm going back the way I came. My best chance of survival is to make a run for the nearest exit.

Hopefully they're watching for people sneaking in, not escaping.

As I'm about to go up, I notice an odd panel on the wall. I slide it open and find a foot-wide tunnel of plastic pipe that extends up and down out of my sight. No time to inspect that. I have to keep moving.

Thankful for handrails, I take the steps slowly. There's no light in the corridor, only the glow from the overhead light in the bay. At the top of the stairs I see a faint line at what seems to be the bottom of a door.

I reach the last step and put my ear to the door. *Silence.* Maybe there's a chance after all?

If I make it to the street, there's no way Bonaventure's guards are going to risk getting caught on camera dragging me back here. At least that's what I tell myself.

The question foremost in my mind is how the hell did the feds miss an entire submarine bay under the man's house? You'd think they might notice something like this.

I turn the knob slowly and pull the door toward me after realizing that it doesn't push.

Inside is another dark room. This one is the size of a closet and has a giant water heater in the middle, blocking the way out.

All right . . . ?

There's no way I can squeeze my body around it. What's going on?

Let's think this through . . . Bonaventure doesn't want people looking for the bathroom accidentally stumbling into his secret submarine lair. You'd put something in front of it—like a giant water heater. That means it probably moves . . .

I wrap my arms around the base of the cylinder and lift, twisting as I strain. Some kind of release lever clicks, and the whole contraption rises into the ceiling and stays there.

"Holy cow," I mumble, impressed by the engineering. This is some Batcave-level stuff here.

I don't have time to stop and admire the workmanship. If they didn't hear me coming in through the hatch, this had to make a noise or trigger an alarm.

I turn the knob on the next door and burst into an outer hallway. Empty. The floor is bare concrete, and the walls are unpainted drywall.

I turn and spot another staircase going up. Most of Turtle Isle is around thirty feet above sea level. I should be reaching the surface soon.

I go up the second set of stairs, prepared to find myself in another empty corridor smelling of concrete and dust.

Did I die back there? Is this how hell works?

I'm right, except this hall reveals sunlight ahead and to my right. I run down the hallway and enter a large room with blinds covering windows on either side.

There's nobody here.

I take a peek through the blinds and realize the source of my confusion. Bonaventure's house is down the street. This isn't even a separate building on his estate; I'm in an entirely different part of the neighborhood.

Clever bastard. That's why the police couldn't find anything. There wasn't anything to be found.

This house probably belongs to a separate owner completely unconnected to him. The feds wouldn't search here if they had no reason to.

Speaking of cops, Solar has to be worried sick about me. I run to the opposite side of the room and spot him still on the boat.

I try tapping, but he's too far away.

Think, Sloan.

I run upstairs and find a bedroom that faces the bay and walk out to the balcony.

I wave, but he doesn't see me. I run back into the unfinished bathroom and find a mirrored medicine cabinet lying atop a crude sink.

I can take it with me since it hasn't been mounted yet.

Back on the balcony, I use the cabinet mirror to reflect the sun back at George. It takes about three seconds before he catches the reflection and realizes it's me.

He makes some hand gestures, pointing to the street.

Does he want me to go there? Why doesn't he just pull the boat up? I furiously point to the seawall farther up the island from this house and run back down to the first floor.

I open a sliding glass door and run out on the patio. George hasn't moved the boat. He's just standing there with his fishing rod, watching.

What the hell, George? I'm about to point to where he should pick me up, but I check up when I hear the sound of boots stomping on grass.

"Freeze! Police!" shouts a hyperaggressive voice.

Before I'm tackled to the ground, I spot at least a half dozen armed officers in full body armor.

George continues to ignore me as I'm restrained and slapped into handcuffs.

CHAPTER THIRTY-FOUR

DREDGE

I'm scared. This interrogation room isn't in the federal building in Palm Beach, and it's not the FBI, DEA, or sheriff's office. I have no idea where I am.

After cuffing me on the lawn, the Palm Beach police, who arrested me, kept me down until a paramedic came and patched up my leg.

A green raincoat was thrown over my swimsuit, and I was shoved into the back of an SUV with blacked-out windows. A metal divider separated me from the driver, and another partition blocked the rear of the vehicle. The seat was the same hard plastic they use in the back of police cars.

It was a vehicle designed to transport suspects without letting them know where they're going. Nobody tugged a hood over my head, but it was the same result. After a thirty-minute drive, we pulled into a parking garage, and two armed guards wearing full body armor took me up a service elevator and down a hall into this room.

This room . . . with its black metal walls. It's like Darth Vader's bathroom—minus the toilet.

My best guess is that it's some spooky, federal-level detention center. Could these be the DIA contractors George mentioned? It's the kind of place you take suspected terrorists, Russian spies, or heads of cartels.

What worries me the most is that I have zero idea who's in charge. You hear about special CIA and FBI detention centers—and I know they even exist in our country. It's not always that sinister. Some suspects are extra risk. Sometimes you need to interrogate someone away from where their friends know they can be found.

And sometimes this kind of place can be the waystation to another, longer-term secret prison. That kind of thing used to be crazy—then September 11 happened.

Am I being paranoid and freaked out? Hell, yes.

Nobody has spoken a word to me since I was caught—technically I was never even arrested. I'm pretty sure it's not because they forgot.

The door opens, and two men enter. One is a white guy with short, prematurely graying hair. The other is black with a shaved head. Both appear to be in their early thirties and are wearing suits. Although they're dressed like stockbrokers, they move like they're ex-military.

"Sloan McPherson?" says the white guy. "I'm Chris." His tone is clinical. "This is Dr. Pierson."

I want to ask them questions, but I'm afraid if I start talking, I'll slip up. I keep my mouth shut.

"Are you Sloan McPherson?" asks Pierson.

"I want my lawyer."

"It's a simple question. Are you Sloan McPherson?"

I give him silence.

Chris turns to him. "Are you satisfied?"

Pierson pulls a sheet of paper from a folder and writes on it as he says, "Subject was found trespassing in a state of undress, is uncooperative or unable, and refuses to answer basic questions. Recommending psychiatric care until further notice."

"What the fuck? Are you Baker Acting me? You can't just do that!" They're declaring me crazy so they can hold me in a medical facility.

Pierson slides the sheet of paper over to Chris and leaves without saying anything else.

Chris reads it over, then lifts it so I can see the text clearly. "You understand what this is?"

"No judge will agree to that," I reply.

"We have one on the next floor. I'm pretty sure he won't have a problem."

This is some black-ops bullshit. When the Russian submarine, the *Kursk*, sank, I remember watching a video of the families of the sailors demanding answers from the Russian government and how one upset mother was tranquilized and dragged away by security people in white lab coats right on the spot. *Don't want to cooperate? This is how we handle you.* In China, they don't even bother with the lab coats.

So, a doctor signed a slip of paper declaring me crazy so they can hold me. Next they'll be injecting me with something to make me so loopy I won't even remember what happened.

Why?

"Cooperation is advisable," says Chris. He places the sheet of paper back on the table and leaves me alone in the room.

It's cold enough to be uncomfortable, and I have no sense of time. My hands are secured behind me to the metal chair, so I can't get up.

I don't have a lockpick and wouldn't know how to get out of cuffs like these, anyway. Not to mention the fact that I'm in a locked room inside some government detention center.

Time passes. It could be an hour; it could be two. The bandage they gave me on the way has already soaked through, but the bleeding has stopped. I've gone from refusing to talk to wishing someone would come in here so I could tell them everything—which is nothing. I have to see Jackie. I also have to pee. I'm about five minutes from doing that right here.

The sound of the lock being turned fills the room. I watch the door as my next visitor arrives. I'd already given up hope of someone coming in and saying this was a mistake. I know it's not. It's part of their game.

The person who enters isn't Chris or Dr. Pierson—it's worse. It's the woman from the secret boatyard. The woman who shot at me—and I shot back at.

She drops a duffel bag on the ground, selects a chair across from me, and sits for a moment, watching me with a faint grin. There's something hard about her, like she's gone through horrible things and thinks that's normal—that everyone deserves her hard experience. She's pretty but almost angry about it.

"I had a feeling we'd be seeing each other again," she says at last.

I give her the same cold stare I gave the others.

She picks up the paper and scans it. "Scary? No? The really frightening part is what happens at the end of the three-day evaluation. The doctors could decide you need long-term treatment. If you were still uncooperative, they might determine there's something medically wrong with you. A diagnosis would be made. Treatment applied. Some cures can kill you if you don't actually have the disease they're meant for."

"This isn't legal," I say, breaking my silence.

"It isn't? Which part? You studied the law. At what point did we break it? Maybe we use physicians and psychologists who are prone to saying what we want them to, but that's not exactly a crime—not a provable one."

"I'm allowed to have my own psychiatrist examine me," I say, grasping for hope but knowing it's futile.

"If this were a criminal detention. But it's not. According to this, you're not mentally fit to make demands, much less have them answered."

I'm in a no-win situation. She's got me in a legal box intended for terrorists and other enemies of the state. There'll be no trial, because I'm not being charged with a crime.

I'm most worried about Jackie now. I can't have her put through this—either never seeing me again or thinking I'm insane.

"You win," I reply. "I'll cooperate."

She laughs. "You'll cooperate? What do you think we think you know? If I suspected for a moment that you had any clue how to get what we're after, you'd have already told us by now. I don't want anything from you."

"What's with all this bullshit? Why take me to a DIA black site to scare me?"

"It looks like someone learned a new word."

I don't dare utter "K-Group." Saying "DIA" may have been tipping my hand too much already.

"You are correct," she says. "We're concerned that Mr. Bonaventure has been funneling resources to terrorists, and we're very anxious to recover any evidence relating to that. Do you have any information that might be of interest?"

It takes me a long, awkward moment to say, "No."

She didn't ask what she wanted to know. All I could think of was Winston Miller's transceiver, anyway, but it seems rather unimportant now.

"Well, there could be a reward for any evidence of significance relating to the matter. Anything?"

"No," I reply, still wondering what she wants from me. Maybe this is simply another kind of torture.

She stands. "I'll give you some time to think that over." She knocks on the door, and it's opened from the outside. "Please escort our guest to level S."

❧

After she leaves, two guards enter the room, uncuff me from the chair, and lead me down the hallway. We go down a different corridor than we entered from, and they shepherd me down a stairwell.

We travel down four flights. I no longer have the handcuffs on and think about making a run for the door at the next landing. Would it be an office? Or more of the black site?

Like it matters . . . They no doubt know how to handle a situation like this; it's not even worth attempting.

We reach the lowest level, a subbasement, I assume, and the guards use a key card to enter a dark corridor. This area has only one light, and the walls are painted black. The floor is dirty with broken tiles that hurt my feet when I step on them.

My mind races through the possibilities, each more terrifying than the last. The woman had a sense of cruelty about her. I probably killed one of her men. No way she'd take that lightly.

The pressure is too much. "I have a daughter. She needs to know I'm okay."

The guards ignore me and keep pushing me along the corridor.

My breath starts to go short at the thought of never seeing Jackie again.

Stay strong. Don't let them see you cry.

We reach the end of the hallway. There's a large metal door in front of me. The fear of what's on the other side has me panting.

Rumors about black-site prisons flood through me: waterboarding, solitary cells, electroshock . . . even rape rooms.

If someone places a hand where they shouldn't, I'm going to fight. Lock me up. Make threats. But try to take my dignity, and I will make you pay.

One of the guards places a hand on my shoulder, and I wince.

"Relax," he growls.

The other pushes the door open.

They shove me through.

CHAPTER THIRTY-FIVE

Reef

I go blind from the light. The corridor was so dark, and it's so very, very bright . . .

Outside?

I'm in an alley. I see cars passing at one end.

I'm *outside.*

The door slams behind me. I turn around, and my escorts are gone.

Someone with a dark sense of humor has placed a sticker on the door asking visitors to please leave a review on Yelp.

This has all been a mindfuck.

They released me.

The woman . . . I'll call her DIA Jane . . . must've let me go because I'm useless to her. After all, if I'd been working with Winston or Bonaventure, I wouldn't have nearly killed myself trying to sneak into the submarine tunnel.

She's pegged me for a clumsy idiot who stumbled into something bigger than herself.

She's exactly right.

And now I know how high the stakes really are. She could have disappeared me with a snap of her fingers, but she didn't. I wasn't worth the paperwork. It was easier to dump me in an alley barefoot, wearing little more than a raincoat.

I hurry out to the sidewalk in case Jane changes her mind. She's a crazy bitch—who knows what goes through that head?

I look around to get a sense of where I am. The building I was in looks to be an eight-story, black-glass structure. There're no markings on the exterior. Only a faceless building in a city filled with similarly faceless buildings.

I spot a lobby entrance but decide to go in the opposite direction. I can figure out the cover they use for their offices some other day. Right now, I need to get off the streets and get some clothes.

The raincoat could be covering a short work dress; the bare feet are harder to hide. I keep moving and get a few stares but don't attract that much attention.

I find an open restaurant and go up to the hostess stand. A teenage girl is there. She's got a warm smile but looks confused when she sees my bare feet.

"Are you okay?" she asks with concern.

"Yeah. Mostly. Can I use your phone?"

She takes a mobile phone from her pocket and hands it to me. "Are you sure you're okay? Need me to call the police?"

"It's okay. It's not that big of an emergency. I just got stranded. That's all."

I stare at the device, trying to think who I should call. I draw a bigger blank when I realize I can't even remember any of my contacts' phone numbers.

I take a wild guess and use her phone to send a message to what I assume is Cynthia Trenton's newspaper email account.

Forty-five minutes later, she pulls up in front of Reilly's Restaurant. Before stepping out, I give my new friend Ophelia a big hug and thank her for the assist.

❧

"You okay?" asks Cynthia when I get in her car.

"Give me a moment to process things."

Cynthia glances down at my swimsuit, visible through my open raincoat. "Did anyone ever teach you how to dress?"

I have to laugh, because a swimsuit was the family uniform for half my life. "You really haven't seen me at my best yet."

"I hope not. I called Georgie. I told him you were okay. He was scared out of his mind."

"George, scared? How can you tell? Is it a more concerned grunt?"

"Ha. Don't underestimate. He's more sensitive than he looks." She pauses. "And probably the most decent man you'll ever meet."

We drive on I-95 southbound for a while. I wrestle with whether to ask her the question that's been at the back of my mind since I saw her wall of newspaper clippings.

She seems blunt and to the point, qualities I pride in myself. "Can I ask you a question about George?"

"Maybe. What do you want to know?"

"Back at your house, the articles on the wall."

"He framed those. Not my idea," she replies.

"Yeah. But why the one about his arrest? That just seems weird."

Cynthia smiles. "We don't get too many guests. That article's from when we met. I covered the story."

"Okay. But it doesn't paint him in a flattering light. I get that he was young and maybe didn't do it. But still."

"George knew what he was doing," she replies. "You don't, apparently."

"Wait, what? If he knew what he was doing, why was he arrested for taking bribes?"

"When George joined that police department, he quickly found out that everyone, and I mean *everyone* in that unit, was on the take.

Not all of them wanted to, but they went along with it. He was given a pretty easy choice early on: quit or stay on and keep your mouth shut."

"So he took payoffs?"

"First he drove all the way to the FBI office in Tallahassee because he didn't know who he could trust. The last thing he needed was another South Florida police officer seeing him talking to the FBI down here and mentioning it to his bosses.

"The FBI put him undercover. Their plan was to use him as a secret informant, then force the others to turn on each other so George never had to testify and expose himself as the one who reported them.

"But he knew it wouldn't be enough. He told them they had to arrest him too. It was the only way it wouldn't look suspicious. If they didn't, he'd have a target on his back for the rest of his life." She pauses. "It hurt him to see some of those guys go to jail. They were friends. He went to their kids' birthday parties."

"So, George sacrificed his reputation . . . his career, for that?"

"Basically. The charges against him and a couple others were dropped because of insufficient evidence. He was able to get hired again after sitting out for a couple years. A private recommendation was made that he be hired, and he went back to doing what he loved best. What he was made for. Of course, not everyone trusted him. Good cops thought he was crooked. Bad cops thought there was something suspicious about him."

"And he never went public?"

"Nope." Cynthia smiles. "He's too goddamn stubborn. But I had him make me a promise. My last article, before I retire, is about a cop who spent his entire life letting people think he was a crook because he wanted to do the right thing."

Jesus wept. What was it like to walk into the police station every day and know that some of your closest colleagues were calling you a crook behind your back? What's it like to have every action scrutinized because there's this huge asterisk by your name?

What's it like to volunteer for that?

Who *does* that?

"You okay?" asks Cynthia.

"Yeah," I reply, wiping my nose. "It's been an emotional day."

CHAPTER THIRTY-SIX
BARGE

"Why is she looking at me like that?" George asks as we sit in Cynthia's living room and he redresses my leg wound.

She nods to the article wall. "I told Sloan about how we met."

"Oh, that story," he says, rolling his eyes. "I was young, idealistic, and too stupid to let them do it their way. That's the real story. The FBI was already onto what was going on. Cynthia loves to make it out like I'm some kind of tragic hero." He gets animated. "Want to know who the real villain is?" He points to her. "That woman right there! I'm twenty-two, in jail, afraid I'm going to get shivved when someone forgets to keep their mouth shut, and in walks this wet-behind-the-ears reporter telling me she wants the real story . . . or else.

"There was no *or else*. But I didn't know that. So I swear her to secrecy, being the dumb ass that I am, and tell her."

"And I didn't tell," says Cynthia.

"You've told everyone that sat on that couch!"

"But I didn't write about it," she fires back.

"Oh brother. So, she keeps coming back to the jail, asking me for details. Well, how long do you think a white cop can have a pretty black woman visit him in lockup before certain people start asking questions?"

"So, I dressed a little more . . . sexy."

"Like a stripper. And I told everyone she was my girlfriend."

"It worked."

"Hell, yes. Everyone assumed I was just another idiot cop who got himself an expensive stripper girlfriend—the whole reason I went on the take. Nobody questioned it after that."

"You did an excellent job of convincing everyone you were a dumb ass. Lord knows I still believe that after all these years."

"So, this is still a cover for the two of you?" I ask, half joking.

They look at each other and contemplate this. Cynthia asks George, "When did it start becoming real?"

"I knew it was real the moment I first saw you. But when you picked me up from jail with a bottle of champagne and said it was just for show, I suspected it was maybe more than that. If not, thanks for protecting my cover all these years."

"It's a journalist's job."

George glances over at me. "So, where did she pick you up from? I tried to bail you out of Palm Beach, but they said they never processed you. I called FBI, DEA, and everyone else I could think of. Nobody had an answer. The duty officer at Palm Beach hung up on me when I asked where you'd been taken. I was on my way to his house when Cindy told me you emailed her."

"To his *house*?" asks Cynthia. "What were you going to do? Beat it out of him?"

Solar responds gruffly, "I don't like to be hung up on." He turns to me. "So, what the hell happened?"

I fill him in on everything that happened after I jumped into the water. It seems like I left our rental boat a week ago. In reality, it's only been five hours. He stops me to ask a few questions but generally lets me tell it the way it comes to me.

At the end of it, he just sits there. I use my phone, which I'd left in the boat, to catch up on text messages with Jackie. She got a little panicked when I didn't respond after all this time. Although it caused her stress, it warms me a little to know I could be missed that much.

"So, the Kraken is real," says George. "And those DIA rejects . . . are neck-deep. I still can't believe they took you to an actual DIA site, though."

"Was it?" asks Cynthia. "How can you tell an official secret black-ops site from an unofficial one?"

"I guess it comes down to who pays the bills," he replies. "But if you're doing everything through contractors and subcontractors, who the hell knows? Jesus."

I notice a voice mail message from Chief Kate on my phone. I'm pretty sure I'm still on leave, so I'm not sure what it's about.

I play it, and a minute later, Cynthia and George are staring at me.

"You okay?" asks Cynthia.

"They fired me," I say flatly.

I'm still trying to make sense of what Chief Kate said. She'd always looked out for me.

"Just like that?" says Solar.

"She . . . my chief . . . says the city manager said they had to let me go because of budget issues." I stare at them, trying to find some sense of reason. "A week ago, everything was fine."

I think about my student loans and the share of Jackie's expenses I make it a point to pay for. Heck, she's on my health plan—which is now going away.

"How can she do this? Right now, of all times?" I ask aloud.

"Of course right now," says Solar. "This is how they play the game."

"What?"

"That Jane woman with K-Group. She did this," he explains.

"But Chief Kate is my friend."

"And she still is. The city manager probably got a call from some fed who said they couldn't pay them for some program like they promised and mentioned questions about you. Who knows how it really went down, but this is most definitely about our case."

"About what I did? Getting caught?"

"That, everything else."

"I like being a cop," I say from the gut. "How can they take that away from me?"

"Do you?" asks George.

"Of course." Maybe I didn't fully realize it until now. Maybe diving for the police started as a rebellious way to pay the bills, but I love what I do. I'm proud of it. I think it over for a moment. "I wanna take those assholes down. I don't want to sit on the sidelines."

"Do you really mean it?" asks George.

"Hell, yes."

"You want to keep going? You're not scared off?"

"One thousand percent."

"Do you want to take a trip across the state?"

"What?"

George checks his watch. "I'll explain on the way. We need to hurry. Cindy, I might be back kind of late."

"What else is new?"

After getting dressed, I follow George out the door and into his truck. "Where are we going?"

"I can't tell you yet."

"Enough mystery bullshit for today. Where are we going?" I demand.

"McPherson, I swear to you that I can't tell you yet. Trust me on that. Either get out or buckle up. Your choice if you trust me."

CHAPTER THIRTY-SEVEN

GULF

The sun is setting as we race toward the horizon down Alligator Alley. The Everglades, a vast sea of sawgrass, stretches into infinity on either side. This part of Florida has risen and fallen beneath the sea numerous times, reminding us that nothing stays the same. When it's back below water, none of what's going on right now will really matter. Small comfort when you measure your life in minutes, not interglacials.

George hasn't said anything about our destination. Since I suspect that this is a legit secret and not an "I'm going to surprise Sloan with a trip to the ice cream parlor" secret, I stop asking.

"So that house you broke into from the tunnel?" says George. "I did a little digging around while I was waiting to find out that you hadn't been taken to the county jail. It belongs to Heinrich Gustafson. He's an attaché to the Belgian ambassador or something like that. Anyway, he has diplomatic immunity. Which basically means you can't search his property without pulling a ton of strings—especially because the on-paper owner of the house is a Dutch company, making it even more difficult. Long story short, Heinrich owed some money a while back. He had to pay back a bribe or something. Guess who gives him a loan? His friendly neighbor Bonaventure. Through a shell company, of course. As far as I can tell, Heinrich has never even been to the place since the remodel."

"So, Bonaventure used that as his transfer point? Close, but not too close." I remember something I spotted in the underground bay. "Hey, I almost forgot, there was a narrow tunnel made of plastic piping hidden in a wall. It went on forever. Do you think it led to Bonaventure's estate?"

"Possibly. Did it look like a water pipe?"

"Yeah," I reply.

"He could have had that installed with his irrigation system. On surface sonar, it'd probably look like plumbing. Great way to get things to and from his house, like a bank tube."

There's a long stretch of silence as we go over what's in our heads. Finally, George says, "Tell me your working theory."

"My theory?" I reply.

"What do you think happened so far? Don't be afraid to fill in the blanks—just don't get too attached to any particular part of it. Tell me what happened."

I feel like this is a pop quiz. "Well . . ." I hate starting sentences with that word. I start over. "Right now, I believe that Bonaventure was using the Kraken to ship cash to and from his house. He may also have been using it to import drugs from a ship offshore. Maybe go all the way to South America and back."

George interrupts me. "That far?"

"Dad would know the range better than me. But a small gasoline generator and a snorkel would let it recharge the batteries for silent mode when it was safe to sail near the surface."

"Interesting. I hadn't thought about that. That could mean there are more than one of them?"

"Possibly. I don't know. It's just a thought. Anyway, Bonaventure finds out the feds, not DIA, are about to raid him. So he empties everything that's incriminating into the Kraken along with whatever he has on K-Group and sends it somewhere."

"And where would that be?" asks George.

"I don't know. It could have been some other secret location. But I don't think it made it there."

George glances over, seemingly surprised by this observation. "Go on . . ."

"I think it malfunctioned and sank with his blackmail material and drug-cartel money on board. Otherwise, if he had already moved the money, wouldn't he have fled the country? I know K-Group could get him anywhere, but they might not want to if he was already gone and under threat of being arrested. But since he didn't have the money, he needed to stick around."

"And maybe make sure the money goes to who it's supposed to—the Mendez cartel. They're the ones K-Group propped up and Bonaventure was laundering money for. DIA might not care if Bonaventure is out of the country and out of reach, but the Mendezes want their money. They're probably also not too thrilled about Bonaventure having their books."

"So, we really could have a sunken submarine with a half billion somewhere in South Florida," I say out loud. "Back on Dad's boat, it sounded like another crazy rumor. Now? I get why everyone's acting all nuts."

"Our Kraken," says George. "But where is it?"

"Somewhere between Bonaventure's estate and . . . well, anywhere. I'd like to search the bay we were just in."

"You think it could be there?"

"It's a place to start."

"I don't know. K-Group knew about the sub. I'm sure the first thing they did was search around Turtle Isle," George replies.

"Yeah, but they didn't use the best living treasure hunter in the business to look for it. I'd like to at least take a pass."

"We could also send you back for the body."

"The body?" I convulse at the memory of the corpse, the rough fabric of its jeans. "I almost forgot about that."

"And you didn't tell DIA?"

"Hell, no. We should have called it in, though."

"We will. After."

"After?"

"After you go back in there and retrieve the body and we get a look at it."

I stare at him in silence for a moment. "I know you live for this vigilante bullshit, but I got arrested back there and threatened with a lifetime sentence in a secret government loony bin where they execute you with medical malpractice once they're sick of you. I'm not going back there."

"And I'm not asking you to do anything illegal or without some kind of legal protection."

"How does that work?"

"We'll figure something out. Worst-case scenario, I go back in for it."

"No way. I'm not letting you do that."

"We have to get to it before anyone else does."

I watch the sun set in the distance and the sky turn from orange to purple then black. I try to imagine the wildlife on either side of the highway living out its own life-and-death struggles.

Somewhere, alligators are fighting pythons, owls searching for lizards, and mama panthers hunting to feed their babies.

Sometimes you don't get to choose your struggles—they choose you.

CHAPTER THIRTY-EIGHT

PRIVATEERS

We arrive at a Hilton hotel across the state in Naples, and George tells me to wait in the car. I make a sarcastic comment about him needing a nap, but he's in too much of a hurry to respond.

I text with Jackie while I wait and examine the cars in the parking lot. There seem to be more SUVs than I'd expect, and I spot two police cars parked in the far corner. The drivers have their windows down as they talk to each other.

I'm watching the police as Jackie sends me a disturbing text.

I had to go to the principals office today.

Then, There were some police people in the other room. They asked me some questions. They said it was a routine work thing. A background check?

My heart skips a beat and I furiously type, What? What did they ask you?

Nothing big. How we got along. If we were planning any trips.

What did you say? I type, panic and rage competing to overwhelm me.

I said you beat me all the time and lock me in the anchor well. HaHa

A pause, then:

I said you were the best mom.

Thank you. And I only put you in there when you changed the wifi password to momjeans.

:)

I said we talked about Australia.

I don't know who talked to her. Possibly the real feds. Or local cops. Or it could have been cartel. Maybe DIA. Whoever they are, they now think I'm planning to leave the country. Not a good look.

Worse, they went to my daughter's *school.*

Damn. Damn. Damn.

I call Run.

"What's up?"

"Some people talked to Jackie at school today."

"Yeah. Gunther checked them out. They were DEA."

"I don't care who they were—they can't question Jackie without me there."

"Gunther says legally they can if the parent isn't present."

I hold back my temper. "The principal is the acting parent. Tell what's her face that if she lets anyone talk to her without you or me there, I'll sue her ass."

Run doesn't argue with me. There's nothing he could have done to prevent it, but he also understands a mother's anger. "Understood. I'll call her tomorrow."

"No. Go down there and tell her in person!" I take a breath. "I'm sorry. You handle it however you see fit."

"No. You're right. I also need to talk to Gunther about this. Remind him that not everyone with a badge is our friend. Present company excluded."

"I don't have a badge anymore. Not technically."

Saying it hurts.

"What happened?"

"I don't know. It's this thing. It's . . . it's messed up. There are people in law enforcement who have a lot to lose. Others too. I don't know. I don't know what to do."

"Australia," he replies.

"That would only make things worse. I have to see this through."

"What does that mean?"

"I wish I knew. Right now, I'm with Solar in Naples at a hotel."

"Well, that's a development," Run says wryly.

"Shut up. He's in there talking to someone. Or taking a nap." I glance back at the police cars and SUVs. "It might be some kind of operational thing—another group investigating this. I have no idea why they'd be on this side of the state," I reply.

"He didn't tell you?"

"He has trust issues."

George emerges from the lobby entrance and walks toward me. He waves at me to come.

"Gotta go. Keep looking after our daughter."

I ring off with Run and meet George in front of the hotel. "What's going on? It looks like a command center out here."

"Basically, it is," he says as he opens the door. "But nothing to do with our situation. Just keep your mouth shut. If you hear me stretch the truth, don't correct me. If you're asked a direct question, answer it briefly. Got it?"

"Yep."

We walk past two men in suits standing by an elevator at the back of the lobby. George nods to them, and they press the button for us.

We step inside the elevator, and I keep my questions to myself all the way to the top floor. When we exit, we're greeted by two other guards in suits, one a man, the other a woman, standing by the door to a suite. They recognize George and open the door for us.

A man in a collared shirt and an older redheaded woman in a blouse and skirt are sitting at a table covered with folders and takeout containers.

The woman I don't recognize, but the man I do. He's the governor of Florida.

"Is this her?" asks the woman.

"Yes. Sloan McPherson, this is Irene Isaacs, and I believe you recognize the governor."

I shake hands with both and sit in a chair pulled out for me by the governor. George takes the seat to my right. I try not to look confused and remember his warning about keeping my mouth shut.

"George told us a bit about you. I think I met your father. You have an interesting family," says the governor.

George is on a first-name basis with the governor? Still heeding his advice, I don't say anything.

"Does she talk?" asks Isaacs.

"She understands discretion."

The governor nods. "That's a good quality. All right, George. You have ten minutes. Make your case."

"Do I have your permission to talk about Operation Marlin?"

"If you trust her."

"Uh . . . I think she's worthy of trust. If that helps?"

"Remember who you're talking to," says Irene.

"Right. Sure. Go ahead," the governor tells him.

"It's about the Bonaventure situation. This connects to Operation Marlin."

"How is that?" asks Irene.

"Operation Marlin was our attempt to shut down corruption within drug enforcement and the judiciary. We had a problem with cops, attorneys, and judges taking bribes. We only got a few indictments before more senior judges and officials put pressure on us to stop."

"I think the term they used was *overreach*," says the governor.

"I think the term is *covering their asses*. We had judges getting sweetheart loans from bankers connected to drug money and some of the worst cops I know put in charge of investigations that went nowhere. Hell, we had Florida senators on tape accepting bribes. We should have pushed this further."

"We did what we could," replies the governor.

George sighs, like he's holding something in. "You had a reelection coming up and knew it would fuck things up, not to mention most of these judges were in communities that didn't support you."

"Easy there, George," says Irene.

"No. He's right," says the governor. "I'm not going to deny that politics is constant triage. Every day, you decide what can be saved and what can't." He shrugs. "All right, George. I chose winning an election over the risk of letting it go further. But to be fair, I was getting all kinds of heat and even thinly veiled threats from intelligence agencies."

"Which is all the more reason to take those assholes down," says George.

"Unfortunately, not all of us have your courage."

George points to me. "She does. They tried to kill her. They threatened her family. They even took her badge away. But that hasn't stopped her. Earlier today, that DIA offshoot I told you about illegally detained her in a black site in West Palm Beach. Yet she's still here."

The governor stares at me for a moment, then asks, "What do you want out of all this?"

"I want my daughter to be safe. I want these people to go to jail for the lives they've ruined."

"And how do you plan to go about this, George?"

George turns to Irene. "Do you have it?"

"Right here." She slides a sheet of paper over to the governor, who reads it over.

"Why do I feel like I'm being railroaded?"

"There's nothing wrong with being railroaded if it's going the way you want," replies George.

"Okay. What about funding? I've got enough problems already."

"It'll be self-funding."

"Through seizure?" asks the governor.

"Yes."

"Legally tricky."

"Then try this on for size," says George. "Right now, there's as much as a half a billion dollars sitting on the bottom of a canal somewhere in Florida."

"That would have to go through the Federal Asset Forfeiture Program," replies the governor. "Lately, they've been playing tricks with those funds."

"True. But if DEA or the FBI get it without formal assistance from the state, then you'll get nothing. If the bad guys get it, we'll get less than nothing. But if *we* find it, you get it all."

"How is that possible?" asks the governor.

"Because if there are no narcotics present, we can claim it as salvage. That would be one hell of a budget surplus."

"Tricky, George. Tricky. The feds will still take us to court."

"If we settle on the right percentage for them, they'll drop it," says Irene.

"Especially if the trial is going to involve a lot of depositions from federal agencies that may not want to reveal the extent of their involvement," I blurt out.

"Fair point," Irene replies. "She's too smart to be hanging around you, George."

The governor scans the document again. "I can tell you two were planning this. What's this about *rewards*?"

"Because we're using maritime salvage law, we need a reward structure based on the percentage of the value. The percentage we're using is minuscule," says George. "Enough for a small budget for the task force and compensation for salvage contractors."

"Small? It's millions of dollars," says the governor, then sighs. "Fine. The courts may say something else. But how do I get this past the Florida Department of Law Enforcement? I'm going to have every law enforcement agency in Florida screaming jurisdictional encroachment."

"We restrict it to waterways," says Irene. "Remember how the EPA asserted jurisdiction of everything from swimming pools to aqueducts? You can create a special task force solely for crimes relating to water."

The governor thinks it over. "Okay . . . but I'm not sure if the legislature will pass this in the long run."

"They don't have to," says Irene. "Not as long as it's self-funded."

"You have all the angles worked out, don't you?"

She smirks at George. "Of course."

The governor picks up a pen. "Fine. It's only my career in politics if this goes south."

"Small loss," says George.

The governor lowers his pen and looks at me. "Can you teach him when to keep *his* mouth shut?" He slides the paper back to Irene. "Here you go."

"One more thing," says George with a nod at me. "We need to make her legal."

"Oh right," replies the governor. "Sloan McPherson, raise your right hand. Do you swear to uphold the laws of the state of Florida and the United States Constitution?"

What's going on here? "Um, yes?"

"Close enough. Then as governor of the state of Florida, I deputize you to enforce said laws and have whatever responsibilities are, um, set forth in that document. Irene? Make it legal."

"Will do," she replies.

"Okay. Don't come back unless you have a lot of money," says the governor.

George quickly ushers me into the hallway. I don't say anything until we're in the parking lot.

"What the hell was that about?"

"You're a cop again. Basically, an untouchable cop. The only person who can fire you is the governor."

"An unpaid cop," I say.

"Not if we find Bonaventure's money. You still have your severance from Lauderdale Shores, and I'm sure Irene will figure something else out."

"You trust her?"

"She was the district attorney I worked with back when I was arrested. We have history."

I climb into the passenger seat, still thinking things over. A realization hits me. "So, the governor just gave us a charter to seize assets in Florida waters?"

"Criminal ones," replies George. "That's kind of an important detail."

"Right. Right. But do you know what this makes us?"

"Cops?"

"Not quite. That document he signed is basically a letter of marque."

"What's that?"

"It makes us privateers—we're state-licensed pirates."

"Pirates, huh? I hadn't thought about it that way. Maybe we use some other name for our unit?"

"Fair point. Um, how about Underwater Investigation Unit?"

"UIU? That works."

This is still the worst day of my life, but strangely, I feel somewhat better now. I don't have to be Sloan McPherson, victim. I get to be Sloan McPherson, pirate cop.

CHAPTER THIRTY-NINE

SALVAGE

Dad has an anxious look on his face as I suit up in my dive gear. I wrestled with whether we should ask for his help. Despite his outburst at me and distaste for Solar, there's nobody I could rely on more in a situation like this. Sure, Dad might have put me in harm's way in the past by choosing risky dive locations, but once there, he was a master at understanding difficult conditions and handling emergencies. Also, *Fortune's Fool* is the best-equipped boat in our little fleet for this kind of venture.

When I suggested it to Solar, he saw the logic and took my word that Dad would keep his mouth shut about what we were up to. As long as the two aren't perpetually at each other's throats, I think we'll be fine.

The diving part doesn't have me concerned this time. I'll be using air and a set of bolt cutters to get inside the grate. It should be pretty straightforward. I've bagged dozens of bodies underwater. It's old hat for me.

What has me worried is the idea of getting apprehended again. Technically I won't be going onto the property of ambassador what's his face, but it doesn't matter. DIA Jane could nab me in a shopping mall.

If she let me go because she didn't think I was a threat, I'm not stupid enough to believe she'll make that mistake again.

I blast air out of my regulator and make sure the body pouch is sealed tight inside the dive bag. Solar is watching Turtle Isle with night-vision goggles.

"You sure we don't look too conspicuous?" I ask.

"We're officers of the law doing our job. Stop acting like you're sneaking into the neighbor's pool on spring break."

"Yeah . . . it's just that DIA Jane doesn't seem to have too much respect for laws or the Constitution."

He senses I'm more scared than I've been letting on. "Irene's keeping an eye on things. If either one of us disappears, there'll be hell to pay."

I'm worried that George and Irene are underestimating what we're up against. Jane's people are used to operating in countries where the rules don't apply to them.

I step onto the dive platform. "Okay." There's no point in arguing with him. Either I do what I set out to do or I run away. I'm tired of being the one running from things.

"Hey, remember, we're the good guys," says George.

"Well, that's a first," Dad replies from the captain's chair.

"Present company excluded," George answers back.

I jump into the water before the conversation goes any further. It's even odds that when I come back, they'll either be drinking beers together or knife fighting.

"Is this thing working?" George asks over the underwater radio.

I click the transmit button on my glove. "Affirmative."

We anchored far enough away from Turtle Isle to not look suspicious but close enough for me to swim there easily.

I've carried enough equipment underwater to know what's practical and what's not. This swim shouldn't be a problem, even though I'm carrying extra weights to keep the corpse underwater while transporting it back to the boat.

Right now it's low tide, which means there's only eight feet of water over my head. Closer to the tunnel, it'll get a bit deeper. My biggest concern is my usual one: staying deep enough that I don't get prop-chopped by a random speedboat.

The bottom has poor visibility because of all the sediment. My flashlight cuts about ten feet and disappears in the brackish dark.

Tufts of seagrass stick out from the floor. A school of minnows swims off to my right, and a grouper makes a quick exit when he spots me.

Night is my favorite time to dive. There are just as many fish down here—it's not like they have any other place to go—and your flashlight carves out your own little world. You forget about the surface and the sky above. The sea *is* your world on a night dive.

I keep track of my progress by counting my kicks and referring to my compass, more out of habit than anything else.

When I reach the dredged-out area, I spot more than the usual fish hanging out in the deep recession. They give me room to pass but don't display any sense of urgency.

I make my way through, and my light catches the entrance to the tunnel. The grille is still in place. When I get closer and shine my light inside, the body is visible.

"At the entrance. Body's still here," I report.

"Good news," George replies.

Either K-Group doesn't know the body's there or it doesn't care. The latter seems unlikely. The former is promising—it implies that this person might have been killed by Bonaventure. My suspicion is that it's Raul Tiago.

I use my marine bolt cutters to cut the lock. It snaps open on the second attempt. If that hadn't worked, we have a special tool back on the boat that's basically a car jack used to pry locks open. It's heavy and takes forever, so I opted for regular cutters.

"I cut the lock."

"Okay. There's some boat traffic. We'll keep you posted."

If that didn't work, I'd have had to slip off the tank and try to squeeze my body through the bars. That option didn't excite me. It was a narrow fit the first time. Who knows what kind of damage it could do to a corpse?

I once had a coroner call me up and yell at me for a postmortem bruise inflicted by a rope used to drag a body out of the water. I bit my tongue and told her that she was welcome to retrieve the bodies herself next time and, furthermore, the bruise came from her own lab techs, who told me they could take it from there and proceeded to lasso the corpse over the edge of the canal.

Folks, this ain't as easy as it looks.

I lift the grille and realize I have no idea how they dealt with it when the sub came and went. Did they send a diver down the tunnel?

A bar drops down on the side and props the gate open, answering my question.

I give my fins a kick and glide down the tunnel toward the body.

The corpse appears bloated from gases and is now clinging to the ceiling of the tunnel like a birthday balloon. There's enough of a current that no cloud of blood or fluids surrounds the body, an odd phenomenon I've witnessed in still environments. It also appears that serious decomposition hasn't yet begun.

In another day or two, when the body settled to the bottom, the scavengers would start gnawing on it. Crabs might have trouble getting up into the tunnel opening, but they'd figure it out eventually.

I pull my camera from its cord and snap a few photos of the face, hands, and clothing. I then put it into video mode and take a movie of the body and everything else around.

I learned to use this video technique long before I became a police diver. Sometimes the most important items aren't the ones you decided to photograph. We once found a couple of silver coins at a picked-over wreck because we watched a video of our dive afterward and noticed a funny-looking rock that gleamed from a certain angle.

One of the biggest treasure finds on land was made not too far from here, when a geologist stopped to examine a large rock on a public beach. Everyone who'd been to that beach had seen the odd, dark-black rock and just thought it was a curiosity. He recognized that it was actually corroded metal—several hundred pounds of silver coins that had been welded together by corrosion and washed ashore. You never know what's right in front of you.

I gently turn the body so I can see the face and get a good photo. It looks like Raul but could be a lot of people, given the puffiness of the features and paling skin.

After I get my photos and search the floor for anything that could have fallen out of his pockets, I unfurl the body pouch and pull it over his head and down to his feet.

I use my extra weight belt to make him less buoyant, and he settles down to the bottom of the tunnel.

"I have the body. Returning now."

"Okay. Standing by. Let us know if you want the boat closer."

"I'm good."

I pull the body back out of the tunnel and lower the gate. I can't do anything about the lock, but at least the grille should keep alligators from swimming into the secret basement.

I kick toward *Fortune's Fool* and try to compensate in my kick count for the load I'm carrying. Worst-case scenario and I get lost, which would be embarrassing, I can always surface and look for the boat. But the plan is to avoid being spotted crossing the bay dragging a body bag. That could lead to more questions than we want to answer. We do plan on turning the body over to the medical examiner in a few hours—but only after we've had a chance to examine it.

I spot the green glow of the light stick we tied to the anchor, but something is wrong. There's also light coming from above; I make out the shadows of at least two other boats besides ours.

"I'm at the anchor."

My dad gets on the radio. "Honey. We have a little situation here. How much air do you have?"

I used a smaller tank because I didn't think it would take that long. "I've got ten minutes. What's up?"

"Solar's arguing with the police."

"Which police? Palm Beach? FBI? DEA?"

"All of them."

Damn it. I'm running out of air and have a body they'll seize the moment I surface. I can try weighting him down to the sea bottom—but if we get towed in, that would be very, very bad.

Think fast, Sloan. You may be about to lose the most important piece of evidence yet.

Damn it. I know what I have to do.

I slide my weight off my waist and wrap it around the ankles of the body. It sinks to the seafloor in an upright position. I then pull back the body bag, exposing the corpse.

I use my knife to cut open his shirt.

This is sloppy, Sloan. Real sloppy. But it's now or never.

Autopsies should never be conducted underwater.

CHAPTER FORTY

DROWNED

The boats are only a few feet over my head. Propellers churn the water while their flood lamps cast a dark-green glow all around me. If someone were to look closely, they might spot me, so I pull Raul—I'm sure it's him—into the shadow of the *Fortune's Fool*.

I pull my camera out and take photos of the neck. There's no deep gash like the ones on Stacey and her father, but from the expression on his face, he clearly died in pain.

When I feel around the back of his skull, fractured bones shift under my fingers. I check for an entry wound and find a hole the size of my finger.

He was killed execution-style, but that wasn't the only injury he suffered. There's a dark contusion on his right cheek, like someone hit him. When I touch that area, I can feel chipped bones. Blunt-force trauma from something like a hammer—or maybe the diving weight I found at the bottom of the tunnel.

His chest shows numerous bruises, and the ribs feel fractured. There are also small red-and-black burns, the kind you'd get from cigarettes pressed into your skin.

When I take photos of his right fingers, I notice they're twisted at odd angles. They've been broken.

Good lord, Raul was tortured . . . extensively.

When I check the left hand, I notice that a pinkie and middle finger have been severed entirely.

This is cartel-level evil, torture methods you use when you want someone to talk. Cutting off the tongue and gouging out the eyes are what you do when you simply want to hurt a person before you kill them.

This wasn't a message or anything personal. It was simply business. They wanted what Raul knew.

When they were done, they put a bullet in his head and dropped him in the tunnel to handle later, probably because moving a corpse under police surveillance would be a challenge. The tide dragged him to the locked gate, where he remained until I found him.

I search his pockets. There's no wallet, no phone, no keys. They picked him clean.

If I were on land and had a kit, I'd try to get scrapings from under the fingernails. I'll have to leave some open questions for the other investigators. My goal is to make sure we don't miss anything big that they might not tell us about. I assume that whoever inherits Raul's body won't tell us what they found until they've chased down any leads it points them to—which means I need to be extremely thorough now.

I stare into his vacant eyes and tell myself this is not a person. It's just a meat puppet—a moist robot. The person is gone.

I double-check the mouth. The tongue is intact, but a tooth is missing. Jesus wept. These people didn't miss a trick.

"Sloan?" calls Dad over the radio.

"Here."

"How much air?"

"Three minutes."

"Why don't you come up now?"

I glance up at the silhouettes of the boats. "Is it clear?"

"Not really. But Solar just gave me the signal. And you can't breathe underwater."

"What about the . . . package?"

"They have their own divers coming. They're going to do their own search. Solar's been stalling them, but they know something's up."

Damn.

Okay, what do we know?

Raul was tortured for information. But what? By whom?

Is there anything else on the body I'm missing?

I give him a final pat down. When my hand hits his left pocket, I feel a small bulge I didn't notice before.

I pull the pocket inside out, and a small blue ball of what seems like plastic or rubber starts to float upward.

Damn it!

I chase after the ball and shove it in a pocket inside my vest.

Since all my weights are on Raul, I have to swim extra hard to avoid rising to the surface. My suit is too buoyant for this shallow a depth.

I grab the edge of the body bag, which is floating behind Raul's head, and pull myself back to eye level.

Anything more?

I contemplate trying to get the bullet out of his head, but using a dive knife to do that would be a little too barbaric.

Okay, what else?

One minute of air.

The missing tooth . . . something about that . . .

The angle of the bullet . . .

I open his mouth again and feel around inside, but the gloves are too thick.

Do it.

I take off my right glove and stick my bare fingers into his mouth, probing the hard and soft palate.

There's an exit wound . . .

I reach under the tongue.

Bingo.

There's the bullet.

I hold it up to my measuring stick attached to my vest and take a photo. The bullet is small. Not quite as small as a .22. There's something odd about it.

I wrestle with keeping it but decide that might be asking for trouble. Their forensics people will be able to tell somebody took it.

I place it back by the tongue and close the jaw. The slug lost so much momentum after it shattered the tooth, it's plausible that it landed where I put it. I guess.

I check my gauge. I'm effectively out of air. Time to surface.

I zip Raul back up, remove the weight belts from his body, and place them back on me. I use my remaining air to inflate my vest and drift back up the surface.

The moment I emerge, a spotlight shines in my face, and a voice shouts over a bullhorn, "Hands up!"

George shouts back. "Oh, fuck yourselves. She's trying to swim. Don't put your hands up, Sloan."

I ignore the men with the pistols aimed at me and swim toward the dive platform. Dad and George take the body onto the landing and then help me aboard.

After I remove my tank, I look out at the mini flotilla that's surrounded us. There're two Palm Beach sheriff's office boats, a US customs craft, and a small coast guard ship.

"We're towing you in," says a man in a DEA jacket on the nearest PBSO boat.

"Like hell, you are," says George. "You have no jurisdiction over us. Besides, we're bigger than you."

"Who the hell are you?" asks the DEA agent.

"I already told you, UIU."

"Never heard of it."

"Call the Florida attorney general." Under his breath, George murmurs to me, "I hope Irene called her."

The man lowers his megaphone and resorts to simply shouting. "Well, we don't have her on speed dial. Why don't we go into the harbor and straighten it out?"

"It is straightened out," says George. "If you want, you can follow us back to our HQ and sort things out there."

There's a heated discussion on board the PBSO boat. A deputy sheriff calls over to us. "Are you George Solar?"

"That's Captain George Solar of the UIU, as appointed by the governor of Florida."

I hear someone groan, "Fucking Solar."

More heated discussion takes place, and the PBSO boat pilot gets on the radio. A few minutes later, the DEA agent gets back on his megaphone.

"You can go, but you have to leave the body with us. Jurisdiction of that is very clear. It goes to the county medical examiner."

"Fine," George replies and kicks Raul's body bag off the dive platform. "Come get it." He turns to my father and says, "Take us home."

"Jesus," I whisper under my breath.

The whole thing is a pompous act, but it served its purpose. Once we're out of range of the other boats, Solar says, "I hope I didn't screw that up too much. Find anything?"

CHAPTER FORTY-ONE

CHART HOUSE

I scroll through the photos I took underwater on the television in the galley. Dad went to the grocery store to let us do our "cop stuff." I think he mostly needed a break from the drama he has no control over.

George has the small blue wad I retrieved from Raul's body in a plastic container and is using tweezers from a tackle box of forensic tools he keeps in his truck to unfold it. The scene reminds me of when I was a kid and we'd pull things up from wrecks, set them in tanks of water, and use toothpicks to carefully separate the dirt from the artifacts.

Our process wasn't as thorough as my professor's lab, but we were pretty good. Most of what we found were mundane objects like food tins, tools, and occasionally belt buckles and buttons. To my young eyes, they were every bit as cool as any emerald or ruby.

Probably the biggest disagreement I had with my grandfather and father was the fact that I was far more interested in where the treasures came from. I wanted to know about the people the gold was taken from.

I remember once looking at a crudely forged gold ingot my father found that still had Incan symbols on it. This was royal treasure that had been seized by the Spaniards and hastily melted down to be sent back to Europe, only to sink to the bottom of the sea, where it would be found hundreds of years later by other fortune hunters who didn't care where it came from as much as where it could take them.

Of course, I didn't complain too much when those questionable artifacts were used to buy me new school clothes or iPods.

"What's that?" asks George as I stop on the image of the bullet.

"Check it out." I show him the photo I took of the base of the bullet next to my measuring stick.

"That looks like an unusual size. Twenty-five?"

"Yep."

"That's the kind of thing a hooker would keep in her purse."

"Or a spy," I reply.

George thinks it over for a moment. "Interesting. Not your typical gangbanger gun. That's for sure. Also not the kind of gun you have your security team use. More than a few dozen yards away, it wouldn't be effective."

I show him the photographic evidence of Raul's torture and let him draw his own conclusions. For some reason, the images look more powerful now than when I was face-to-face with his corpse. That might be because my attention was focused on other things.

"Clearly they wanted to know something from him," George says after reaching the last photo.

"But did he tell them?"

"Yes," he replies, as if it's the stupidest question in the world.

"Why are you so sure?"

"Because they killed him. If he hadn't talked, they would have gone even further. I've seen much worse." There's a distant look in his eyes.

"So, who did this?"

He gives me the stupid look again. "Isn't it obvious?"

"Uh . . ." I try to think this one through. "Bonaventure?"

"Or one of his partners. Maybe a cartel enforcer they sent to find out what happened to their money. It's probable that Bonaventure had Raul brought in to be questioned."

"And they killed him right there in that house?" I ask. "That seems stupid on Bonaventure's part. Especially leaving him in there."

"It may not have been his choice. Imagine he loses his sub with the Mendezes' money. What's the smartest thing he can do?"

"Run," I reply.

"Okay, second smartest thing. Call them as soon as it happened and tell them he needs help. The longer he waits, the more suspicious he looks. So they send him someone good at asking questions. Probably an ex–intelligence agent from Colombia or Bolivia."

"What about Winston? Did they kill him too?"

"I didn't get a good look, but he didn't appear to have been tortured. I think at that point they knew what they wanted. He didn't have it."

"Or Stacey," I add. "So, what is it they want?"

George holds up the unfolded rubber wad. It's a latex glove. He swabs it with a Q-tip, then dabs the end with an eyedropper.

The swab changes to a dull orange. He places it next to a small chart.

Police departments use residue kits like this to see if someone recently fired a gun. They're also similar to the swabs the TSA uses on luggage at the airport.

"Gunpowder?"

"Tri-acetone tri-peroxide. TATP."

"Like plastic explosive?" I ask.

"A do-it-yourself kind. Terrorists love it—if it doesn't blow up in their faces. You found this glove in his pocket?"

"Yeah. Deep down. Like he balled it up and shoved it in there in a hurry."

"Curious." George taps his fingers on the counter as he stares into space. "Why did Raul have to handle explosives?"

"Maybe they were shipping them somewhere?"

"I don't see Bonaventure screwing around with that. Besides, that's not the kind of thing you make to export out of the country. We try to keep that kind of thing from getting in.

"Let's figure out the org chart here. At the top we have K-Group making introductions, providing cover and guidance. Below we have the Mendez cartel and Bonaventure. The Mendezes supply the cocaine, and Bonaventure launders the money. He may also help them get it into the country. He's working both ends.

"To facilitate his little pipeline, he hires Winston to build him a stealth narco sub. Winston works with Raul.

"Bonaventure, being the paranoiac he is, wants to keep the circle tight. This means that he might also use Raul to help him load the sub."

"He'd also need someone to do maintenance, check the batteries, that kind of thing," I add.

"Good point. He needs either Raul or Winston there when the sub comes and goes. Probably Raul, because he doesn't want to be seen with Winston. Or at least not have a rumored drug-runner handyman seen in his neighborhood. Does this track for you?"

"Absolutely." I don't think I would have put it together like George, but it makes sense. He's also had decades of experience dealing with operations like this.

"So," says George, "what was Raul up to with explosives?"

I was expecting him to lay it out for me. He wants *me* to explain what Raul was up to. Okay . . . um . . . why *did* he have explosives?

"Did Raul know Bonaventure was in trouble?" I ask.

"Everyone did."

"All right, but he kept showing up for work. Why? Was Bonaventure paying him that well?"

"Or was he paying him that poorly?" George replies.

"Wait? What? Oh shit." It hits me. Damn, I'm slow. "Raul made a bomb. A small one."

"Why?"

"To sabotage the Kraken. He wanted to sink it so he could recover the money." Winston's assistant had a half-billion reasons to sabotage it.

"Okay. You know boat stuff better than me. Why didn't Raul just reprogram the thing or hijack the controls?"

I shake my head. "Winston didn't trust anyone. Maybe he put all the controls inside sealed compartments and never let Raul near any of the frequencies. Bonaventure probably had him watched closely. Maybe even videotaped the whole procedure. Interesting . . ."

"Might be why the Mendezes left him alive," George replies.

"Maybe it was the proof Bonaventure showed the cartel? Maybe they watched the tape and saw Raul acting suspiciously?"

"Could be. So, Raul puts an explosive on board. Timed or remote-controlled?"

"My bet is timer. Radio control would be dodgy underwater. They probably had a timetable for the delivery. Raul could have put a timer on it to go off at a certain point so he'd know where the sub sank."

"Why didn't he tell them under duress?" asks George.

"Maybe he did and got the math wrong?" I pull out my phone and look up the weather for a few days ago. "We had more rainfall last week. That meant the currents were stronger on the canals. I think they did an Everglades release too. That could screw up a small wreck's location by several miles. He may have told them exactly where to find it, but it wasn't there." I open up a cupboard and start pulling charts out and setting them on the table.

"What are you doing?" asks George.

"Trying to figure out where it is."

"It could be anywhere. You don't even know where it was heading."

"South?"

"The Intracoastal goes all the way to New York. Or the thing could have gone out to sea, right?"

"Maybe . . ."

"How many wrecks are there within a twenty-mile radius of here?" he asks.

"Thousands," I reply.

"And you want to set sail and try to find it? Is this how your family plans all your expeditions?"

"More or less," says Dad from the sliding doors to the deck.

CHAPTER FORTY-TWO
RIPTIDE

Dad takes a beer out of the fridge and goes down the steps into his cabin. I think he's already resigned himself to the fact that I'm going to be my own McPherson. He's already watched two sons take jobs on land. It's only a matter of time before the seagoing renegade tradition of the McPhersons comes to an end—unless he can convince Jackie to become a Somali pirate.

I turn my attention back to the map of Florida on the table. Little red marks with numbers indicate potential wreck sites—ones you won't find in books. These are places where Granddad, Dad, and Uncle Karl thought we might find the remains of lost ships.

The problem with searching for wrecks is that the ocean has a habit of spreading things. The seafloor, far from being a fixed object, is a constantly shifting landscape. Dunes form and fall like the shifting sands of the desert.

One of the best times to go look for something is right after a hurricane. That's when you go to known wreck sites and see what's been unearthed after thousands of tons of sand have been swept away.

Fortunately, we don't need a hurricane. The Kraken is probably still sitting on the floor in the open. If it's in a canal, it could be in less than ten feet of water. If it's in an inlet or the ocean close to shore, the depth still wouldn't be that great. It would be an easy dive—if we knew where to look.

I draw an *X* on the part of Turtle Isle where the Kraken docked. I then place another *X* on the location of the secret shipyard.

"Our only two known locations," observes George.

"So where to now? It could be anywhere between here and Colombia."

"I don't think he was sending it there. Maybe he was doing the money handoff, but if he put incriminating info about K-Group inside the sub, he might have planned on fleeing," he replies.

"And you're sure his ship has been under surveillance?"

"Constantly. In fact, I suspect he used the *Good Fortune* as a distraction while using the Kraken. If he sent it to the Bahamas, DEA and coast guard would shadow it."

"So where was the Kraken going? Another location?" I ask.

"You're Bonaventure. Where would your safe house be?"

"My safe house is my boat—when it's safe. Is the *Good Fortune* his only ship?"

"That we know about. If he's using another vessel for running money and drugs, he's got it under another name."

I think about where we found the Kraken hangar. "If he used that Belgian guy for the house above the sub tunnel, then he could have a boat under a different name."

George nods, encouraging me on.

I think about how we took to the sea after Uncle Karl's trial. "Well, *if* I could use a boat, I'd do it. You don't have to deal with TSA or immigration like with air travel. Customs or coast guard might board you, but it's a hell of a lot easier to slip through—or hide on a big boat if they're looking for you."

George considers this for a moment. "So you think Bonaventure has a second boat."

"I think it's a possibility."

"We could search records and look for connections, but if K-Group doesn't know about it, then you can bet he's hidden it well." George leans back and stares at the ceiling. "Okay, McPherson, how do we find Bonaventure's other boat? Assuming he has one."

"I don't know." I glance around the interior of the *Fool*, trying to pick out what this boat has in common with all of Dad's previous ships.

There's the DVD player with his stack of movies. Some are new, and some he's watched over and over again, like *Last of the Mohicans*.

On the bookshelf, the predictable Dad library of Tom Clancy and Brad Thor thrillers.

What else? The cupboards have photos stuck to them. A few are faded, but I can still make out my big teeth as I grin at the camera, wedged between my brothers on a float when I was ten.

Visible through the open door of the cabinet is Dad's jar of Red Vines and chocolate chip cookies—the soft kind. Bringing any other type aboard is grounds for getting thrown overboard. In the refrigerator will be his favorite Jamaican beer.

"What are you thinking?" asks George.

"Dad always keeps the same foods on board. I'm sure I do the same. I don't think that's much help unless we can hack Amazon and see what's been delivered."

"In a perfect world. Although . . . interesting." George thinks something over. "You know, we once had a fugitive and no idea where he went to. He'd fled with a few hundred thousand dollars and could afford to lie low for a long time. His one problem was that he had tons of allergies and needed prescription medications. We tried to subpoena pharmacy records, but that came up empty. Then I decided to follow his mother one day. I watched her go to a pharmacy, then to a mailing store. I went in after her and was able to get a look at a mailing label. It wasn't on a package yet, so it wasn't an invasion of privacy . . . whatever.

Anyway, the meds were going to a small town in Georgia. I drove up there myself and busted him at a motel."

"But finding Bonaventure isn't the problem. At least not right now," I point out.

"Fair point. Is there anything else he'd need to have on the boat?"

"I don't know . . ." I take out my phone and connect it to the television. "Let's take a look." I do a search for Bonaventure and pull up his Instagram account.

"I've been through there," says George. "Maybe another pair of eyes is a good idea. He only posts a couple of times a year. He's also careful to turn the location off."

Most of the photos are of his dogs at his estate, views from the back porch, and a couple of party scenes.

I scroll farther down and find some images on board a yacht and get excited.

"That's the *Good Fortune*. I checked," George says.

I flip through a few other photos on the boat. Some have attractive women sunbathing or smiling next to Bonaventure.

"What about them?"

"Models from South Beach. Party girls."

"Yacht girls."

"I don't think they work on the boat," George replies.

"Oh, they *work* the boat. Don't you know what yacht girls are?"

"I've lived a sheltered life."

"That's a lie. Yacht girls are models and actresses—aspiring, some professional—that spend part of the season working on boats as . . . well, hanging out in bikinis."

"You mean hookers," George says bluntly.

"Not necessarily. Usually the arrangement is that they're paid to be aboard while the boat's in the Caribbean, Cannes, Ibiza, wherever. If they hook up with someone, that's extra work. Some do it. Some don't.

I had a friend who did that. She swears she just sunbathed and danced. Anyway, these women look like yacht girls."

"And do they get repeat customers?"

"I assume so," I reply.

"Interesting. I can't see Bonaventure letting them take photos on the other boat. Or do anything that leads back to him."

"True. But that might help us. We could talk to some of these women and find out if they've ever been on another boat with him where security was extra tight."

"Okay . . . but how do we find them?"

I roll my eyes like Jackie does when I say something stupid. "You are a caveman." I scroll up on the photo of the girl. "She tagged herself in the image." When I click on the photo, her Instagram page loads.

> XCatalinaCarolinaX. Available for shoots, fashion & film. #MiamiNewStarsModeling

Miami New Stars Modeling has its own page with an email address.

"Is that her agency?" asks George.

"That's her pimp."

"Ugh. Let me guess who'll have to contact them about hiring her for, um, a . . . session."

"Relax," I say. "I'll do it."

CHAPTER FORTY-THREE

Mast

Cat, aka XCatalinaCarolinaX, is twenty minutes late to meet me at Rico's Café on Lincoln Avenue. She greets me with a sincere smile and takes a seat across the booth in the back of the restaurant.

It's a slow Wednesday afternoon, and we're the only people here except for two German men sitting at a table near the street.

Cat's wearing a pale-blue cotton dress under a wide floppy hat, probably intended to keep more freckles from appearing on her tan skin.

She's pretty but a few years past the point where a modeling career's likely to break for her. I've known a few other women who persist, despite the fact that culture has made us an expendable commodity with a tiny shelf life.

"It's nice to meet you, Amanda," she says, using the fake name I gave her via email.

I told her that I worked for a client who was looking to do a photo shoot on his yacht in Bermuda. After talking to one of Run's friends, this seemed like the most innocuous way to go about meeting her.

Writing the email was easy—sitting across the table from a woman close to my age who is probably hoping that I'm going to help pay her rent is hard.

What somebody wants to do with their body is no business of mine. However, when I get the sense they'd rather be doing something else, I feel bad. I have friends who have married guys because of their paychecks—and guys that used money to attract women seeking stability. This game is the same; it's only the terms that are different.

I don't bullshit around about the photo shoot. "My friend is looking to hire some girls to spend two weeks on his yacht."

"You're to the point," Cat replies. "I don't do that kind of work. I'm a straight-up model."

Okay. Then why did she meet with me?

She hastily adds, "But if he's looking for someone to help him with his social media, I can do that. Some guys want photos with hot girls because it helps them meet others."

Social media consulting? All right, this is the game. I suspect it's designed to prop up her sense of self-worth as much as to make sure I'm not a cop.

Let's see where this goes. "My client prefers to avoid the media. Social or otherwise."

Cat thinks this over. "What can you tell me about him? Is he a banker? Middle Eastern?"

I notice a bit of apprehension about the last part. "He's more the banker type. Actually, an internet guy. You may have used his technology."

This gets her attention. I must have accidentally used the code word for *ex-husband material.*

"Oh really? What can you tell me?"

Hooked. "I can't. He doesn't actually know I'm here. He's very, very shy. One of his investors asked me to set this up. Make it easy for him to have a little fun. He thinks we're inviting a bunch of model friends."

"You'll be there?"

"Of course."

Now she's thinking this might be a fun cruise with some other young people and not a bunch of old rapey dudes. I feel worse than horrible.

"This could be cool."

"Here's the thing. His company is about to go public, and nobody can know what he's doing or up to. Partying on a yacht could impact the stock."

"I get discretion. Trust me." She looks off to the side for a moment.

"Yeah, Jason said so."

"Jason?" she asks.

"Jason Bonaventure. He mentioned you when I asked him about this sort of thing."

"Really?" She seems surprised.

"Yeah. Is everything fine between you and him? I don't know him that well. He's a friend of a friend."

"Yeah, he's cool," she says flatly. "I've hung out with him on his yacht a couple of times."

"Which one?"

"*Good Fortune.* Does he have another?"

"I thought he did. I remember going aboard one in Bimini . . . the . . ." I fake searching my memory.

"The *Morning Sun*?" She shakes her head. "That's Gustav's. I've been on it a couple times. Nice. Actually, Jason was there both times. Weird, though. Gustav's a control freak. We had to leave our phones in the safe. I guess he's married, and he's terrified his wife will find out."

I resist the urge to text *Morning Sun* to George right now. The mysterious Gustav sounds exactly like a Bonaventure shill.

"Your friend? How well does he know Bonaventure?" There's a bit of worry in her voice.

"I don't think he does. Why?"

"Okay. It's . . . it's . . . I got a call a week ago about the *Morning Sun*. I couldn't do it. They only needed one girl, and it sounded . . . well. I don't do anything in Miami. Anyway, I haven't heard from her."

This could have been around the time the Kraken went missing. Damn. If the Mendezes were asking questions, I'm not sure Bonaventure would want a yacht girl back in Miami talking about a pleasure cruise that suddenly got canceled.

I lean in and lower my voice. "I've heard some scary things too. That's why I had to check you out."

She sits still for a moment and reads my face, then replies, "This is all bullshit. Isn't it? There's no fucking client. What are you, a cop?"

She gets up to leave. I grab her wrist. "Sit the fuck down."

Her demeanor changes, and she slides back into the booth. "I'm not what you think I am," she says.

I ease my grip on her wrist. "I'm not here to arrest you. I'm not here to get you into trouble. Actually, the opposite. If I were you, I'd stay clear of South Florida. Hell, if some rich, horny asshole wants to take you around the Med and chase your ass around his yacht, I'd do that instead of sticking around here."

I pat her wrist and let go. "Your friend is probably dead. Sooner or later, someone's going to make the same connection that I did. Only they're not going to give you a dumb lie. They'll hurt you for everything you know, and then they'll kill you."

I recall the sensation of the hole in the back of Raul's skull. "They'll want you dead for what you know or what you can tell someone else."

"Fuck." She shakes her head. "Damn it. I knew something awful happened to Yvonne. Goddamn it. Okay. I got a friend in France. Am I safe there?"

"I don't know. It's better than here."

"I'll do that."

"Sooner is better. Fly somewhere else in the US if you have to. Just make yourself hard to find."

"Yeah. Yeah. I wonder if Wilmer did it."

"Wilmer? Who's he?"

"Some guy Jason knew. Met him on the boat. Scary as fuck. One of the girls said he worked for the cartels as a killer. Not a thug. A smooth guy. I stayed clear. Other girls dug it."

"Was he on the *Morning Sun*?"

"Never. You know, Jason seemed even more worried about us mentioning that boat. He said he had a jealous girlfriend or something. But, no, Wilmer wasn't on that ship. We met up with him in Bimini. He sailed with us all the way to Aruba."

Aruba? Interesting. "Did you ever see anything weird on board?"

"Like messed-up sex stuff?" she asks.

"No. Just something that happened that didn't on other boats," I reply.

"No. They were super strict about their crew drills, though. When they had one, you had to stay in your cabin. I got caught in the hallway one time, and Jason went ballistic. I couldn't figure out why he was out. Anyway, that's it."

"Were these drills during the day or at night?"

"Night. Always night." She starts to look around the place nervously.

"One more thing: Did Jason ever board the *Morning Sun* in Miami?"

"No. Never. He always caught up with us in Bimini or sometimes out at sea."

"Did the night drills happen only after he boarded?"

"Uh, yeah. I think so."

Now we know how and when the Kraken was loaded and unloaded. We just have to figure out where the *Morning Sun* was the night the Kraken went missing.

CHAPTER FORTY-FOUR

Harbor

I snap a photograph of a young, tanned, blond man wearing white shorts and a maroon polo shirt as he walks down the gangplank of the *Morning Sun* and onto the pier of Sea Isle Marina. According to the harbormaster, the boat is owned by Klein Holdings, an investment firm based in the Caymans.

The ship itself is a custom-built, 190-foot, sleek, black vessel with an extra-long rear deck. Below that deck is a "toy locker," a recent development in yachts. Basically, a garagelike cavity that opens to the sea so you can store Zodiacs and Jet Skis.

The locker's also the perfect size for the Kraken. Conceivably, you could use the submarine to take whatever contraband you wanted to and from the yacht by loading it inside the locker.

George and I have been staked out at the Miami Marriott in Biscayne Bay, overlooking the marina, watching who comes and goes from the vessel.

We count a total crew of eight, which feels light for a boat this size but still manageable. God knows Dad operated boats almost as large with child labor when hired help fled over wage disputes.

I tell George, "I think that's Himmler."

He makes a note on a large piece of white paper stuck to the television cabinet. We've given each of the crew made-up names, because we haven't figured out their actual ones.

Since we started watching the boat last night, only crew have come and gone. Seven of them returned to the boat at eleven p.m. sharp, suggesting that they had a curfew.

They mostly have fair features, and all appear to be Northern European or Scandinavian. I offered to go chat one of them up in town, but George pointed out that they've likely been trained to smell anything suspicious. If you're willing to pay, there are highly dedicated former Russian sailors for hire—ones with experience working on Russian oligarch yachts.

I set the camera down and drop on the twin bed closest to the window. "Now what? That's got to be the boat? Right?"

"I'd say that's a fair assessment. We need to know where it was when the Kraken missed its rendezvous. You know boats better than me; how can we find out?"

"The logs aren't going to be much help. Lord knows *we* didn't log places we anchored when we didn't want anyone to know about it. Although . . ." I pick up the camera and zoom the telephoto onto the mast. It has radar and other communications equipment attached to it. "I'm sure there's some kind of electronic record aboard. They might wipe their computers when they get to port, but even that could tell us something."

"Are those systems networked?" asks George.

"Probably. Know anybody who could hack them?"

"No. You?"

"Hardly. I mean, I know how the systems work. Generally. But nothing about accessing it remotely. I could probably get the data if I could put my hands on their positioning system."

"What if I could get you aboard?" asks George.

"Do you mean like inside a birthday cake?"

"No. Maybe we could create an excuse . . ." He takes a seat by the window. "How hard would it be to start a fire?"

"Don't even go there. That's two hundred million dollars of boat right there."

"I'm just brainstorming," he replies. "What if something malfunctioned? Like their radar up there? They'd need to call a repair crew."

"What are you thinking?"

"I don't know. A rifle?" he says quietly.

"Are you serious?"

"I'm not sure sometimes."

"Let's put your grassy-knoll idea on hold," I reply. "What's the smarter way to do it?"

"Sometimes I just flash my badge and barge in."

"Ever been shot at doing that?" I ask.

"Yep," he sighs.

I immediately regret the question. "Okay, let's use our limited brainpower. They're a boat, so they're used to inspections in port. Coast guard, customs, immigration. Maybe even DEA. It's not that uncommon. The problem is they probably know who their local feds are. If we show up pretending to be some agency, they could call our bluff."

"McPherson, you're forgetting something."

"What's that?"

"We're not pretending to be an agency. We *are* an agency—or at least a division."

"Yeah, but not a federal one. Not one who can just show up and inspect a boat for no reason," I reply. "I mean, we have laws."

"Correct. But sometimes nobody knows what the law is until we push it. Give me a reason we could search the boat."

"Like with a search warrant?" I ask.

"Of course not. We'll never get one. I mean a good reason for us to show up and ask to search the boat and have them let us aboard."

"It can't be too accusatory. If we say we're doing a drug search, they'll call their attorneys. What if we said there was a runaway in the harbor and we're looking for her?"

"No. They'll insist on searching the boat themselves because they know it better. What else do you have?"

"Why is this on me?"

"Solar 101: don't use your own brain if there's a perfectly good fresh one to pick."

What *is* a reason they'd voluntarily let us aboard? Who boarded us when I was a kid?

"I got it!" I blurt out. "Dad once talked Winston into installing a naval-grade sonar system we could use out at sea. This thing was a monster. We'd been in port maybe two hours in San Diego when two naval officers showed up at our dock with some fancy gear. It turns out their listening posts were picking us up all the way into the harbor and flagged us as a Russian spy trawler. I also saw the FCC show up once when someone was using an old Chinese transmitter that interfered with local radio stations."

George raises his eyebrows and lets me go on.

"So, what if we tell them we want to check their radar because it might be interfering with government systems?"

"Make it more innocuous," says George.

"Okay, hmm, how about we say there's been some interference with weather radar? There's a big radar ball visible from the harbor."

He smiles. "And they do have the tallest mast."

CHAPTER FORTY-FIVE

Sextant

A Finnish first mate named Irro greets us at the bottom of the gangplank after I press the button on the intercom built into the railing. He's in his late twenties and has short, close-cropped hair on a round skull.

We waited until the captain and the rest of the crew left for their nightly adventure. It turns out Irro pulled the first watch.

"Alo?" he says when he greets George and me on the pier.

"Hello," George replies in his least threatening tone—which is still pretty intimidating. "I'm Mr. George and this is Ms. Sloan." He holds up a State of Florida employee ID card—but no badge. "We're with UIU. We're trying to track down a signal interfering with the long-range radar. It's a bit of an emergency."

I show the guard the radio scanner we picked up at a surveillance supply store and point the antenna at their communications mast. "We need to check out your array to make sure it's not the source of the interference."

"What's your full name?" asks George as he pulls a clipboard from under his arm.

"My full name?" asks the confused man.

"You're in charge of the ship right now? Correct?"

He looks back and forth between us, trying to understand how serious this matter is. "Yes. The captain is ashore."

"Okay. Then the fine has to be made out to you. I'm sure the owners will reimburse you. I'll make sure you have a copy."

"Fine?"

"Yes, it's a thousand dollars an hour as long as the antenna's causing interference."

Irro is getting nervous. Our goal is to get him to let us aboard without calling the captain. I'm fairly certain his response would be to call in their attorney or whoever Bonaventure uses to maintain security.

"We've had everything checked. I'm sure it's not it," he says.

George stabs a finger at the radar mast. "Do you see anything else here that tall? Whatever. We'll write the fine, you have your electrician check the radar, and then you can show up in court in a week and get it cleared up."

"It's not our radar causing the problem," Irro insists.

"It could be an echo from a building," I say to George.

"Are you trying to tell me my job?" he snaps at me.

"I'm just saying that if we make a physical inspection and it's not it, then we can move on."

"Or I can just write this up now. What was your last name? Also, I'll need to see your passport."

I push his clipboard down and put the scanner to my ear. "I'm not sure that it's coming from up there. I can't tell from here, though."

"Would getting closer help?" asks Irro.

"It's only going to tell me what I already know," George growls.

"Sorry, Irro. If I can check the signal strength from the bridge, that might settle this. Otherwise, we have to fine you and call the captain down."

"Fine," George acquiesces, as if the choice is his. "Lead the way."

Irro undoes the chain blocking the gangway and takes us up to the boat, relieved to avoid involving the captain.

I make a show of checking my scanner, which is actually set to a channel that will blip if the radar antenna points in its direction. George studies the boat while trying not to look too interested.

The surfaces are spotless. Not even any water spots. The deck is free of scuff marks, and from what's visible through the windows, the interior is equally well kept.

We go up a flight of stairs, and Irro takes us onto the bridge. Large flat-screen displays show everything from a map of the vessel's current position to weather to a hundred other details.

I go over to the navigation and check out the system. It's a KVVM positioning system that uses GPS and the European Galileo satellites not only to tell them where they are, but also to steer the boat. A box on the screen is asking for a password. That'll be tricky. George notices this and gives me a slightly raised eyebrow.

Next to the KVVM is a screen showing several views of the harbor with colored rectangles around other boats and the dock. I've never seen that before.

"What's this?" I ask.

"OceanEye," responds Irro. "Vision-based automatic navigation. It can pilot the boat in the harbor."

"Hmm. Can you operate the radar?"

"Which one? Weather? Short range?" he replies.

"Weather."

Irro sits down at a console across from the KVVM and types in a password. The screen changes to a map of South Florida, and a line begins to sweep around, illuminating pixels of storm clouds in the area.

I turn my scanner up, and it makes a *blip* sound every time the antenna points in its direction. "We'll need to try this from the deck."

Irro gets up and heads to the door. "This way."

I step after him, then stop. "I'm being stupid. I need to get a GPS fix. George, did you get one?"

"I left the unit at the office."

"Oh, I can help," Irro offers. He quickly types a password into the keyboard on the KVVM.

I don't catch it, but I notice out of the corner of my eye that George is recording it with his phone. What a tricky dog.

Irro reads out the numbers on the screen. "Latitude: 25° 47′ 27.18″ North. Longitude: -80° 11′ 5.20″ West."

George types that into his phone. "I'll send that to you."

A moment later I get a text message. Password = mermaid.

A bit obvious. I guess they weren't too worried about people hacking them from the bridge.

"Can you take us to the aft deck?" asks George. "That'll give us the best line of sight."

"Certainly."

Irro begins to lead us down the steps. When we're halfway there, I stop. "I forgot the scanner." I conveniently left it on a chair when Irro wasn't watching.

"I'll get it," he replies.

George grabs him gently by the elbow. "Actually, can you show me where the bathroom is?"

Irro seems torn. He's faced with two people roaming the ship. One going back to the bridge, the other wandering the interior.

"Go ahead and show him. I'll meet you right here."

George starts walking toward a sliding door. Irro chases after him.

I hightail it up the steps and back into the bridge. The KVVM is back to requiring a password, since Irro logged out.

I enter it and go straight to the dropdown menu and find a tab for historical data. There's an option that says, Past 30 days.

A list of GPS data flies across the screen, and I start to panic. I'd been hoping for a map with a dotted line. This is raw data.

While it'd make sense for criminals to wipe their GPS history every chance they get, coast guard and customs require that they keep records going back several months.

I'm sure they have a wipe switch in case they thought they were being investigated for smuggling; otherwise they'd keep only the current data or remove data for specific trips.

I shove the thumb drive on my key chain into the port and download the raw data file. It takes two seconds to transfer, but closing the window trips me up.

I hear footsteps on the deck outside and the sound of men talking in another language.

Damn. Earlier this afternoon, news broke about a tropical storm forming in the Atlantic. The crew could be coming back early to prep the ship.

I check the screen again, trying to find a "Close" button. Nothing.

They're climbing the stairs.

Think . . .

I reach behind the KVVM and find the power switch.

Screw it.

I flip it off, then on again.

The screen displays a boot-up sequence.

Ugh. It'll have to do.

I grab my scanner from the chair, flip it back on, and stare at it, ignoring the captain and a crew member as they enter.

"Alo?" says the captain.

I hold up a finger, asking him to wait a moment, and hold the radio scanner to my ear. I figure it's better to pretend I own the place than act afraid.

Another set of footsteps, these running to the bridge. Irro bursts in with George behind him.

Irro exchanges rapid-fire Finnish with the captain, who looks at George and me suspiciously.

George returns the stony gaze with a "you're in serious shit" expression. He's playing the part of bad cop extremely well.

"We've had our radar checked extensively," says the captain. "I insist that we call in our own technician if you're going to persist in this matter."

I covertly turn the dial of the scanner, and the beeping stops. "Is your radar still on?"

The captain walks over to the console and stares at the screen. "Yes."

"Huh," I reply. "Mr. George, I think it must be something else."

"Let me see that?" He grabs the scanner and makes a dramatic show of changing the frequencies, with no effect, then thrusts the device back at me. "Fine." He pushes past a crewman as he heads toward the door.

"Captain, I'm sorry for the inconvenience. We'll get this matter sorted out."

I follow George down the steps and gangplank. The sound of the captain yelling at Irro reaches us all the way to the dock. I'd feel bad, but he knows who he works for.

George points to dark clouds in the distance. "That doesn't look good. Get what you need?"

"I hope so."

CHAPTER FORTY-SIX

LOGBOOK

"It looks like they spent about nine hours offshore near Hobe Sound," Dad says over the speakerphone.

George and I are in the hotel room overlooking the *Morning Sun*. We don't want to leave until we're sure we have the data that we came for. Sending it to Dad seemed the best way to make sense of it, and he didn't let me down.

"Can you give me the coordinates?" I ask.

Dad calls them out, and I put an *X* in the location, then draw a line from it to the submarine tunnel on Turtle Isle.

George turns from the hotel-room window. "Does that help?"

"It's twenty-one miles from Turtle Isle to there. So . . . um, there's that," I reply.

"How about if we use sonar and retrace the route? Could we pick up the sub?" asks George.

Dad makes a snorting sound on the other end of the line. It's the same problem I face doing a dive search—I'm limited by how far I can see and how fast I can swim.

I explain the problem to George. "Assuming only a one-mile drift on either side of the route—and that the Kraken followed a straight line—the sonar on the *Fortune's Fool* can only cover a band about five hundred feet wide. And the *Fool* has the best sonar you'll find on any vessel of that size anywhere," I hastily add, because Dad is listening.

"That's twenty passes to search a two-mile-wide corridor," George says after doing the math. "And a twenty-mile route means four hundred miles to cover."

"Assuming no false positives," my dad says over the speakerphone. "You're looking at a six-day job. And that's assuming it followed a straight line. Which it didn't, it being the ocean and all and not space or whatever. Without looking at tide tables and currents for the time, I'd call it a six-mile-wide corridor, which means twelve hundred miles of seafloor to search. So basically it's like finding something between here and New York City."

"I get it," says George. "So, what do you suggest we do?"

"Figure out where Raul wanted to sink it," I reply.

"I'm sure he told Bonaventure before they killed him."

"And I'm sure he only had a rough estimate of the spot."

"That's the part I don't understand," Dad interjects. "How was Raul going to find the submarine after he sank it?"

"Good question," George replies, then turns to me.

"Maybe a short-range transmitter beacon? Something only good for a couple of miles?"

"Underwater?" asks Dad. "That has to be some transmitter."

"I guess. But first we need to know the area where the sub went down. We don't even have that."

"Maybe you do," says Dad.

"You onto something?" asks George.

"Me? No. But maybe you should talk to somebody who understands the currents and area better than anyone else I know. He could probably tell you the best place to try to sink and recover the sub—also where it might have drifted to."

"And where do we find this person?" George asks.

"The FCI in Miami," I tell him. "He's talking about Uncle Karl."

George makes a loud groan. "Something tells me you shouldn't go in there and tell him you've partnered up with me."

"You think?"

"He'll help Sloan out," says Dad. "Or he'd never hear the end of it from me."

"I don't know." George is shaking his head. "I'm not sure if we can give him this data."

"You told *me*," replies Dad.

"I know where you live. And you're not serving time with a bunch of other undesirables who would kill to know this."

George raises his binoculars to the window.

"I think I can trust him."

"No good," says George.

I'm about to disagree when I realize he's watching something in the marina. I stand up to look over his shoulder.

"Shit," I say when I see DIA Jane strutting down the dock away from the boat, flanked by three men wearing jackets in warm Florida weather.

I spot a flash of black gun metal inside one of their jackets. "Are those . . . ?"

"Probably MPX machine pistols. That's a hit squad."

"Which way . . ." My words freeze in my mouth as DIA Jane glances at the hotel where we're staying.

"We've been made. Time to go," says George.

"Later, Dad!" I grab my phone and throw everything from the table into a duffel bag.

George is already at the door. He holds it open for me. I start running to the stairs.

"Negative," he replies. "The first thing they'll do is put someone there. We take the elevator to the floor below, then take a different one down."

I trust his judgment over mine. The elevator doors open, and we rush inside. Mentally I'm counting how far away DIA Jane and her crew were from the hotel. They're probably entering the lobby now.

We switch on the next floor and take the adjacent one down. Our elevator is almost at the lobby, and my anxiety is building. "What are we going to do? Your truck's in the parking garage across the street."

"We're going to walk out of here," he replies. "They're not stupid enough to do anything in the lobby. But I am . . ."

Before I can ask him what he means, the doors open, and George steps out, raises his weapon in one hand and his badge in the other, and shouts, "Freeze, UIU!"

DIA Jane is in the middle of the lobby with her hired guns. She looks confused, and the goons don't know what to do. One of them brings a hand to his jacket, but Jane pushes it back.

"Hands up," says George as he approaches them.

He gets within five feet, and Jane finally responds, "Come any closer, and we drop you."

"Doubtful," George replies, but he doesn't come any closer. "McPherson." He nods to the front door.

I chase after him as he heads out of the lobby. The guests are still in shock, trying to figure out what just happened. So am I.

I check over my shoulder, but we're not being followed. When we reach the parking garage, I finally break my silence. "What was that?"

"A distraction. They were coming to talk to us. I don't know what they would have done if they got us in the hotel room. I didn't want to find out. I also didn't want them to try to arrest us in the lobby. We were outgunned."

"So you threatened to arrest *them*?" I reply.

"It was worth a shot. Let's go talk to your uncle. Chances are they know what we do about the *Morning Sun*, and we're running short on time."

CHAPTER FORTY-SEVEN
Bait Well

Karl's eyes narrow as he enters the room and he sees George Solar sitting next to me at the table. When I contacted Karl, he told me flat out that Solar had to ask him himself. Somehow, through the prison grapevine, Karl had already found out that the two of us were working together, and he wouldn't see me without him.

Having lost my patience for family drama, I told him fine. I was lucky enough to be able to get him on the phone in the first place, let alone arrange a meeting. George had to pull some strings, because someone high up had been putting pressure on limiting access to inmates who had information about Bonaventure or the current situation.

Most likely the Department of Justice was trying to gain an information advantage. George was so paranoid he swept the marshal's office in the prison for bugs with a scanner.

"McPherson," George says, greeting my uncle.

"Solar," he replies, taking his seat. He glances over at me. "Sloan. So, let's have it. What's the offer?"

"Offer?" I repeat.

He taps the charts on the table. "Isn't that how it works? I help you. You offer to take time off my sentence."

I've never heard him sound this cold. "I'm asking you for help."

"Are you? Last time you said that and pleaded for me to help you for Jackie's sake. When, actually, I was talking to a cop using whatever angle she could."

I grab the charts. "This is bullshit." I stand up and turn to George. "I can talk to Zhang over at FIU. He knows these currents too."

"Sit down, Sloan. Please," says George. "Your uncle is right. We're asking him for something without offering him anything in exchange. What would you do in his situation?"

"This is ridiculous. I'd help family," I reply.

"That doesn't mean much when you're in here, does it, Karl?" says George. "The problem is, we're not in much of a position to offer anything."

"That's not what I heard. I heard you have a direct line to the governor."

"In a manner of speaking," replies George. "Do you think I can call and ask him to pardon a narco trafficker with multiple parole violations and a high risk of recidivism? How will that go over? A DA might ask a judge to reduce your sentence, but I'm not friendly with many of them. The problem is, I don't have a lot of friends in general. I can't pull that kind of weight."

Karl searches my face for an explanation. I don't have one. He shakes his head. "So why the hell are you here?"

"Because your brother said you could make sense of this data."

"My brother. Right. It's a family affair," Karl grumbles.

"So? Can we have your help too?"

"Did you not hear yourself speak? No." His eyes drift toward me. "No."

This is his revenge. All that pent-up frustration and anger are now directed at me. The man who protected me from bullies and taught me how to throw a punch. The man who a few days ago told me he thought of me as his daughter . . . now he's treating me like dirt because his hatred for George Solar is so intense.

I dab at the corner of my eye. "Let's just go."

"Fuck this guy," Karl growls. "Fuck you, Solar, and your manipulative bullshit. I'm not letting you do this."

"I'm sure I don't know what you're talking about," George says mildly.

"It's all fucking head games with you. Goddamn it." He turns to me. "And now he's got you playing along too."

"What are you talking about?" I'm experiencing emotional whiplash right now.

"Just give me the damn charts and tell me what you know."

I lay them back out, and Karl studies the tables and data in the folder. After a long silence, Karl sets down the paper and glowers at George. "If anything happens to her, I'm holding you responsible."

"Now you're worried about my well-being?" I reply, exasperated.

"It takes a while to process things."

"Have you considered talking to a psychologist?" I ask.

"The ones in here will make you even more batty," Karl says. He points to a spot on the map three miles from the location of the *Morning Sun* around the time when the Kraken went missing. "Here. This is where I'd try to sink it. Assuming the sub was going about seven miles an hour—which, from Winston's original specs, is what I'd estimate if it were fully laden—and I rounded the time to the nearest minute, then this would be the spot. It's about eighty feet and fairly calm. I've been there. It's kind of a dead zone."

"So, look here?" I ask.

"I didn't say that. That's where I'd try to sink it, but there was a big rain runoff and an easterly current. I doubt this Raul character is much of an oceanographer. The sub probably went farther out before it hit sand and then drifted."

Karl traces his finger down the map to an area 110 feet deep. "It probably got dragged into this basin. Remember when they tried to make a reef out of tires, and they had a tropical storm? A few hundred ended up here. It's a couple miles to search, but that would be the best bet."

"Thank you." I start to gather up the maps.

"There's one more thing. One of the guys here had a visit from his brother—a former SEAL, like the actual go-in-the-water kind, not a desert rat. He said that his brother was working on some kind of secret search-and-recovery operation. Sound familiar?"

"We'll be careful," I reply.

"You don't understand, Sloan. This guy's brother's been working privately for several years doing security for some shady people. He's a killer." Karl glares at George. "I'll say it again: I'm holding you accountable for what happens to her. I know you don't think that's much of a threat from a guy stuck in here, but she's the only thing that matters to me in this world. The only thing."

"I understand. She's pretty special."

"And if I find out you two have been screwing," he growls, "I'm gonna throw up, then hang myself."

CHAPTER FORTY-EIGHT

TANKER

The seas are choppy as Tropical Storm Baker begins to churn off the coast of South America, sending currents in our direction. Rain slicks the deck, and winds buffet the *Fortune's Fool* as Dad keeps the boat steadily slicing through the waves. I stare at the ocean behind us through binoculars. A small black dot is visible near the horizon.

"Still back there?" asks George.

"Affirmative."

Six hours ago, after we left Fort Lauderdale, an eighty-foot black cruiser with a massive radar array started following us from a distance.

At first we thought it was an unmarked DEA boat, but George couldn't find any reference to it, and nobody we know had seen it docked in South Florida.

That's the thing about this state—while it's huge, people recognize boats, because there are only so many marinas and places to dock. A boat like this should have attracted attention. At least if it were familiar.

We've come to the conclusion that it's probably K-Group's. George has long suspected that one of the services they provide is countersurveillance. A boat like this would be ideal for keeping track of coast guard cutters and customs ships, as well as for spotting aircraft.

Right now, it seems fixated on us. There's no way the *Fortune's Fool* could outrun it, and chances are the other ship—the *Vader*, as we've been calling it—is armed.

"Coming up on the basin," says Dad. "Do we have a decision?"

If we stop in the spot where we think the Kraken sank, then we're basically telling the *Vader* where to look. Chances are, even with as much effort as Dad has put into the *Fortune's Fool*, the *Vader* will have even better sonar and god knows what else to find the sub. Not to mention the fact that Karl's renegade SEALs may be aboard.

"If I dive right here, they'll probably hold back for a while."

"And then swoop in when they think we found something. God knows what they'll do then," replies George.

"Do we just keep going and then loop back?" asks Dad.

"What would you do if you were them?" George asks.

Dad thinks this over for a moment. "I'd keep my position farther back. They probably have as much fuel as we do. Maybe more. If they're patient, all they have to do is wait us out."

"And we run the risk of them finding the Kraken in the meantime," I reply.

Dad points to the sonar. The bottom of the ocean is unusually elevated for this far out. The sea bottom mostly runs three hundred to four hundred feet deep in this zone.

The sonar scan shows a number of irregular-shaped objects from the size of microwaves to ones bigger than the boat. Some of them are rocks and coral, and others are probably man-made—parts of hulls, shipping containers, and other debris that ended up in the basin.

The Kraken could be anywhere in this mess. The only way to know is to go down and look.

"What if we bring the boat about broadside to them and I go over the other side?" I suggest.

"And leave you out here?" asks Dad. "No goddamn way."

"I'll have my vest and radio. You can take a GPS of my position."

He points to the choppy seas. "No way." He turns to George. "Don't even let her think about something like that."

"Do we just turn back?" I reply. "Is that it?"

"Better than losing you."

George takes off his hat and squeezes water out of it. "I agree. If that's the only plan, then it's a dumb one. We can't leave you without a boat."

"Okay . . . what if I have one? There's a Zodiac raft in the locker along with a motor. I could use that."

"What? Just set you adrift out here with them watching?" says Dad. "How suspicious would that look?"

"We do it later. Right now you stay on course, go a few more miles, preferably north, and then I take the raft back here. With the current the way it is, I can make good time. I can use a light anchor to keep it in position. That way I have a raft and everything I need."

"You mean a night dive?" asks Dad.

"Yeah. That's the point. You keep heading north. I drop off with the raft and wait awhile until you're out of sight, then start up the motor and double back here. If they stop you, you have nothing to hide."

"That's a horrible idea," replies Dad.

"You have a better one that doesn't involve surrendering?"

"I'm not leaving you alone out there."

"What if I go with her?" asks George.

"When was the last time you went diving? What happens if she gets in trouble? No way."

"Dad, we've done more dangerous dives."

"Just because I was careless doesn't mean I should repeat that. Solar can't actually *watch* you, and I'm not letting you out there alone." He takes a long pause. "I'll go with you if Solar promises not to wreck my house."

George nods. "I'll treat it like my own."

"Treat it better. This is everything I own." Dad sighs. "All right, Sloan, let's get my gear out of storage. Solar, you're the pilot now."

CHAPTER FORTY-NINE

RUNABOUT

Solar peers back through his night-vision goggles as the *Fortune's Fool* steams ahead in a straight line. "They're directly west of us. About three miles."

Dad and I each take an end of the Zodiac raft and set it in the water on the far side of the boat. It bounces around and knocks into the hull, but the inflatable raft doesn't hurt it. We took the extra precaution of strapping everything down.

"Think they can see us?" asks Dad.

"I'm sure they can. The question is whether they're paying attention at this moment. I imagine they're watching us on thermal. Hopefully your little trick helps with that."

Dad added some extra oil to the gas mixture so we'd be leaving a warmer exhaust trail behind the *Fortune's Fool.* The goal was to allow us to drift away in the heat cloud and only start our motor after we were far enough away.

I sit on the edge of the boat and prepare to jump into the raft, praying that I don't get bounced straight into the ocean.

"Time to go."

Dad stands next to me while Solar grabs the release to the raft. "All set?"

I hop into the Zodiac, and Dad jumps after. George doesn't even wait for the thumbs-up; he just yanks the rope, and we're set free.

The raft slides down a large wave, then gets bumped into the air. I lie flat next to Dad with our tanks wedged in on either side.

"Just like the Vikings did it," says Dad as we're rocked around.

We stay put, riding the waves for a half hour as Solar chugs away on the *Fortune's Fool*. Finally, Dad says, "I hope you trust that guy."

"I don't trust anyone," I reply.

"Fair enough."

I peer over the edge. The *Fortune's Fool* is now only a tiny light on the sea. I can't see the *Vader*.

The satellite phone tucked into a plastic pouch chirps, and a message appears on the display.

Still following me.

This is George's signal to us. We know better than to use the terrestrial radios. The *Vader* will almost surely be listening in on radio traffic. Even an innocuous one-way message from George might sound suspicious—especially if it's his voice. We might be a little paranoid, but the men on the other boat have guns and bad intentions.

"Start her up?" I ask.

"I think so," says Dad. He takes out the GPS unit and checks our location. "About forty-five minutes south-southwest."

I press the ignition, and the engine roars to life, drowned out almost completely by the crashing of the heavy seas.

"What's the weather report?" I shout over the noise.

Dad refers to a small computer that gets updates. "Baker is kind of lingering, but another depression may change that. We're good for a few hours, I think."

I steer the boat up and over the rising waves and make gradual progress. It's like driving over hills that sometimes go forward and other times backward.

This is seriously not good weather to be out in a raft, let alone scuba diving. Fortunately, Dad and I have plenty of experience with rough seas. Some intentional. Some accidental.

Sitting midboat, Dad watches the horizon and refers to the GPS often. He glances back at me, pats me on the knee, and grins.

He's loving this. Whatever disagreements we had a day ago about my career choice, he's in his element now. This is high adventure, and not the first he's taken part in.

When Dad was a kid, Granddad took him on rough-and-tumble expeditions to places where piracy was still rampant and sharks followed boats in the hopes of someone falling overboard. He regaled us kids for hours with stories that seemed better fit for a novel.

"We're about over it, Sloan," he shouts over the roar of the sea.

I give him the okay sign, then cut the motor. We're bounced around as the waves play catch with our tiny craft.

Dad, unperturbed, unfastens the anchor from its strap and heaves it into the water. The narrow cord slides through his gloved hands as the anchor plummets toward the seafloor.

In weather like this, we'll have to try to hook it on something—a rock, a wreck, anything to keep the raft from drifting away.

The cord stops sliding, and Dad gives it a tug. We probably drifted twenty feet since he let it loose. The anchor appears to have caught on to something.

Dad gives it a few more tugs to make sure it doesn't slide free. We'll use the line as a guide on our way to the bottom so we don't accidentally lose the boat.

"Ready to gear up?"

I nod and help him slide into his vest, double-check everything, then pat him on the shoulder. He does the same for me. We turn on the flashlights attached to our vests, and I give my pockets a final pat.

"Ladies first," he says.

I roll into the water and give him the okay sign before descending below the waves.

As soon as he plunges in, I swim to the anchor line and attach a glow stick.

Dad, the designated divemaster, points down, and we begin to descend into the blackness below.

Strangely, despite the approaching storm, the death squad nearby, and whatever's down here, I feel calm for the first time in days.

CHAPTER FIFTY

The Deep

I once chaperoned Jackie and her class on a field trip to the Miami Space Transit Planetarium and had my mind blown. We watched a presentation about exploring our solar system, including images of one of the moons of Jupiter, Europa.

At first, I was like, okay, a big rock. That's nice. Then they explained that it was actually ice, and under that ice was an ocean twice as large as the one on Earth.

We watched as computer-generated alien squids and other life-forms swam around while scientists speculated about what could be down there. Jackie whispered to me that she wanted to be a "space aquanaut." I decided that sounded like a pretty cool idea too.

When you dive at night in water this deep, you feel a lot like an astronaut drifting through the cosmos—only it's a cosmos without stars. When you're on the seafloor, it's like landing on an alien planet, but above, in deep water, you have little sense of up or down. Divers get killed swimming the wrong direction when they lose their way.

Dad and I keep our hands on the rope as we descend. Even though we're excellent divers, it's possible to get caught up in a current and pushed away before your dive partner realizes you're gone.

Your only choice then is to surface and hope that you can find each other.

Dad is ten feet below me. I keep my light aimed away from his head so that when he looks up to check on me, he doesn't get blinded. Our lights are so powerful you can't use them out of the water for long because they'll overheat.

At the bottom we're going to need them. While it's considerably calmer down here than on the surface, the ocean is still moving and churning up sediment, decreasing visibility.

We'd hoped it wouldn't be this bad, but no such luck. This will seriously limit the area we can search.

Dad's light bounces off the seafloor and the corral of rocks the anchor drifted into. I let go of the line and hover off to the side as Dad makes sure the boat isn't going anywhere.

"You good?" he asks over the radio.

I give him the okay sign.

Down here, we don't have to worry about the *Vader* picking up our transmissions. If they could do that, they'd have better things to do with their time than search for a puny half-billion dollars. The navy would pay ten times that for the ability to pick up transmissions that way. The current state of the art is ELF—extremely low-frequency radio—that requires antennae miles long.

I tie another glow stick to the anchor line so we can find it at the bottom. I also affix a strobe light so we can find it from even farther out if we get lost. Diving is all about redundancies.

Dad makes the signal for us to check our air supplies. We're both good for at least forty minutes with our large tanks. That's not going to be nearly enough to search the area. We'll have to surface and use the other tanks after letting our bodies recover from the depth. We won't be following the official dive-safety tables, but we won't be cutting any dangerous corners either.

Dad grabs some sediment, drops it, and gauges the direction of the current. He points upstream. We'll travel against the current in our outward search, then use it to swim back when we're tired.

I take the lead and swim over a low rise of rocks and soft yellow coral that stick out of the ground like clusters of antlers. Small fish dart in and out of the rocks, going about their business, and I catch a school of silver minnows in my light as they swim away.

I keep my eyes ahead while Dad watches around us for potential threats. Tiger, bull, hammerhead, and other large sharks frequent these seas. Divers generally aren't much concern to them, unless you happen to be spearfishing and you're carrying a bag of recently killed fish at your side.

In some areas, sharks have learned to recognize the sound of a speargun and will actually speed toward it in hopes of reaching the kill before the diver.

Fatal human-shark interactions are extremely rare, even in those situations, but it's always wise to be cautious. In a zone like this, with few nocturnal human visitors, you're sure to catch the attention of nearby sharks, who have the curiosity of a five-year-old. They want to know about everything around them that makes unusual noises.

Besides sharks, there are also barracuda, sea snakes, and a hundred smaller things that can be fatal if you accidentally touch them. It's generally not a good idea to touch anything you don't have to while underwater.

"On your left," Dad calls out over the radio.

The rusted pilot house of a tugboat is sticking out of the ground with part of its hull visible. Coral has formed around it, slowly claiming the boat as its own.

"Beverly M?" I ask.

"That's closer to shore. Probably insurance fraud."

Florida waters are littered with unmarked wrecks that went down in completely different places from where their owners claimed they sank.

Sometimes this is because of bad records; other times it's intentional because they scuttled the ship for insurance money and wanted to make sure investigators couldn't recover evidence of fraud.

I sweep my light back and forth for anything else unusual but only find more rocks and scattered coral formations.

Eventually we come to a steep rise that ends abruptly and drops off. If the Kraken got caught on anything before going over the edge and off the shelf, it would have been here. The problem is, this area stretches for several miles in either direction.

"Left or right?" I ask.

"Right," he replies.

We go right another ten minutes along the rise, spotting more rocks, rusted debris, and corals trying hard to extend the Florida Barrier Reef northward.

"Time to turn back," he calls over the radio.

I check my air gauge and don't question him. He gave us just enough margin to be safe. There's no point in pressing it.

We swim back toward the raft, scanning the floor for our submarine, but only manage to see more of the same.

Halfway back, Dad taps me on the leg. I follow his hand to my left and see an eight-foot bull shark swimming twenty-five feet away.

It's not in hunting mode; it's just investigating the racket we're making. We keep swimming, and it drifts off and out of sight.

I don't have to look to know that Dad has his knife drawn and is checking our vulnerable angles to ensure we don't get sneak attacked.

I spot the blinking strobe on the anchor before the glow stick. I'm disappointed by our lack of results, but at least we have another set of tanks. After slowly ascending, taking our safety stop, and decompressing on the raft, we can try again.

Getting on the raft in rough seas is like the world's worst amusement-park ride. Fortunately, Dad thought ahead and attached two rope ladders on either side. This allows us to climb up and enter the Zodiac at the same time, keeping the raft's balance and making the whole process safer. It's a tricky feat, but one we've had plenty of practice doing.

After removing our vests and tanks, we lie back on the soaking floor of the boat to catch our breath. It stopped raining, but the waves are every bit as high as before.

I roll over and check the satellite phone. There's a message from George:

Lost sight of the Vader. I don't know where it is.

CHAPTER FIFTY-ONE

Whirlpool

I'm toweling off my hair while Dad uses George's night-vision goggles to scan the horizon for the *Vader*. We're both still in our dive suits, and the Zodiac is tied behind *Fortune's Fool*.

I didn't want to leave the dive site, but I knew it was stupid to stay out there with the *Vader* roaming around. I also didn't exactly love our chances of finding the Kraken in the next dive. What we really need is the *Fool*'s sonar.

"The *Vader* vanished about an hour ago," says George. "Not too long after you guys went in the water. That made me a little nervous."

"We didn't see them on the way back. Maybe they returned to port?" Dad says.

"Or maybe they have a better idea where to look than we do. I think we need to take the *Fool* back there and do a sweep," I say.

"Then we run the risk of the *Vader* seeing where we are. It could even be a trick, if they think we went too far out for the Kraken. Otherwise they might've pulled back to see where we go next," Dad theorizes.

"I agree with your father. These people aren't dumb. And to be honest, they probably have more experience with this kind of thing than us."

"Maybe," Dad allows. "But I agree with your larger point."

"So, we take the raft back," I say. "If the *Vader*'s waiting to see what the *Fortune's Fool* does, then we keep it anchored here and go back in the Zodiac."

"I think we're missing something," says George. "If two of the smartest treasure hunters around can't find the Kraken, what chance did Raul have? Much less doing it by himself?"

"He wasn't," I reply. "He had Stacey, remember? They probably were going to use their own boat to go out there, and he'd do the dive." Something dawns on me. "Hold on . . . wait . . ." I get a sinking feeling in my stomach.

"What is it?" asks Dad.

I sit on the bench. "What if Stacey wasn't trying to get hold of me because I was a cop?"

"What if she wanted to recruit you to salvage the Kraken?" asks George. "She and Raul decided they needed help, but didn't know who to trust?"

"Yeah. Maybe. Either way, they had their own salvage operation planned."

"And their own boat, I agree," says George. "If it's traceable, I'm sure K-Group already did that. But the question of how they planned to *find* the Kraken still isn't answered." He turns to Dad. "If you could set it up from the start, how would you do it?"

Dad doesn't hesitate. "Transmitter. I'd hide it on the Kraken and have it set to beep every minute or so. It wouldn't transmit more than a mile underwater, but that would be enough if I knew the area."

George produces the electronic component we found on Winston. "Like this? Can we plug this into something?"

Dad shakes his head. "That's probably for just surface communications. We're looking for something else. A whole device tuned to a specific frequency. You could modify a standard radio if you knew what frequency you were looking for."

A buzzing rises in the back of my mind.

Wait . . . What did I miss?

"Shit!" I leap up from the bench and run for the cabin where I stowed my gear.

George and Dad chase after me, crowd into the passage, and watch as I open my duffel bag and dump the contents onto the floor.

"The day I found Stacey, someone had been in my truck."

"They took your driver's license," says Dad.

"Yes. Her killer. He probably didn't know my connection to her and was just being cautious. But I forgot about this." I reach into the pile of gear on the floor and pull out a police radio. "I found this in my bag the day after, on a different dive. I assumed someone loaned it to me at some point and I forgot to return it. Some police departments issue you their own communication gear to use. Sometimes I'm too focused on the dive to pay attention to what goes in my bag. Now I'm wondering, did *Stacey* put this in here?"

Dad takes the radio from me and inspects it. "Interesting." He shows us the bottom of the radio, on which a number has been handwritten in permanent ink. "Want to make a bet as to what that frequency's for?"

"No way." I feel so stupid for ignoring the radio all this time. "I can't believe I didn't even notice that. Some cop I am."

"Well, it's useless anywhere but right over the site, but I'm glad you brought it with you."

"Assuming that's where the radio came from," says George. "My gut says it is."

"So, let's take the *Fool* back there and have a look," says Dad.

"We can't," I say. "Not with the *Vader* out there. They could be just beyond our line of sight, waiting for us to do exactly that."

"And I can't have you two diving while the *Vader*'s stalking you," George says. "They might be waiting for that too."

"I go down," I reply. "Dad stays in the Zodiac and keeps an eye out for the *Vader* and watches the satellite radio in case you see it first."

"I'm not letting you dive alone," says Dad.

"I won't be. We'll still be on our radios. They'll reach far enough for us to be in touch. I'll keep you updated, and you'll do the same if George sees the other ship."

"And if something happens?"

"I surface."

"If you can't? Then what?" He sees that we're about to get into a McPherson stubborn match. "We'll take turns."

"Agreed," I say. "George, you still good keeping an eye on the *Fool*?"

"I'd rather be here than in your little dinghy. I'll be ready to come to you if there's a problem. Which right now may be more weather related than K-Group. Baker's getting nastier. Could be a coastal evacuation. I'm not sure how much longer we can stay out here."

"That depends on who's at the helm," says Dad.

"Tell that to the *White Dolphin*," I murmur. That was a ship that sank on Dad before I was born.

"The *Dolphin* was already a wreck before she went down." He eyes the interior of the *Fool* as we ride over a wave. "But be careful, George. The moment the storm starts hitting hard, let us know. We may need you."

CHAPTER FIFTY-TWO

MONSOON

The last thing I remember is Dad telling me to slow down. As soon as we were out of sight of the *Fortune's Fool*, I gunned the outboard motor, the raft jumped across waves, and we were airborne as much as we were touching water.

There's an optimum speed for crossing waves. That wasn't it.

Right before Dad's slow-down warning, a black wave twice as tall as the others crashed into the front of the boat and flipped us over. My head hit a tank, and everything went black.

"Sloan!" A hand slaps me across the cheek.

The cold air snaps me to attention. "Ouch!" I try to sit up in the rough seas, and my own dizziness knocks me back down.

The Zodiac is upright. Dad must have managed to flip it while I was out. No small feat, but he's had plenty of experience.

His hands touch the back of my skull. "Ouch!" I shout as he hits a sore spot.

"Shut up. Hold on. Nothing fractured." He studies his fingers for blood. "Not even a cut. I'm not surprised, with that thick head of yours."

"Sorry?" I grab a strap to keep from getting rolled to the side in the crashing waves.

"We need to turn back," he says.

"Back? I'm fine."

He gives me a dumb look. "You probably have a concussion. You can't dive."

"I'm fine," I insist.

"You're an idiot. We're going back to the *Fool*."

"I'm fine, Dad. I mean, yeah, I got a knock, but I'm okay." I force myself upright, fighting gravity and nausea. "Just give me a minute."

I'm so busy arguing with him that I don't understand why he's staring at the dive pouch in the raft.

For a moment I think *he's* the one with the concussion, and then I hear a beep.

Dad takes the receiver from the pouch and holds it to his ear. Twenty seconds later, there's another beep.

"That's it!" I shout. "We can't go back now. The *Vader* could be anywhere out there."

"That's *why* we should go back," Dad replies.

"No. I swear, if you turn this boat around, I'll jump overboard."

Dad taps the tanks strapped by his feet. "Without air?"

"I'll free dive it," I reply.

"A hundred feet?"

"I did it before."

"Once, and you nearly drowned."

"Then let me use the gear," I insist.

"No . . ." Dad is thinking this over. Another beep cuts through the roaring wind. "I'll go."

I'm not exactly in a position to argue with him right now. He's clearly in better condition to dive than I am. "Fine."

"First we need to triangulate." He hands me the radio. "I'll drive, and you listen."

I don't protest. Clearly, I'm on driving probation for the foreseeable future.

Dad takes the raft on a due-south heading. Figuring out exactly where the Kraken went down is tricky. We could be a half mile away and search in the wrong direction if we don't try to pinpoint the signal.

After a minute, the beep fades. "Losing it," I call to Dad, who aims us due west.

The beep grows louder, and Dad steers the boat toward the point where we first heard it. I get the loudest ping yet. Dad cuts the motor and drops anchor.

By triangulating the point of origin, we've narrowed the area from a square mile to a football field.

I help Dad strap on his tank and check his equipment. It's a little past midnight, and the moon has already set. Clouds are thickening overhead, and the light drizzle is beginning to come down heavier.

"Watch for lightning," he says as he slides into the water.

"Watch for Kraken," I tell him over the radio.

"Always do."

A few minutes go by as he descends, following the anchor line.

"Here," he says over the radio.

"Kraken?" I reply excitedly.

"No. I'm at the bottom."

I don't radio my disappointment.

"Heading south for three minutes," he says.

This is so I can keep track of him underwater if we lose contact. By giving me a time and a direction, he's enabling me to retrace his path.

While I wait, I write down the GPS location of the signal and text it to George on the sat phone.

A minute later he responds:

No sign of our friends. Be careful.

"Nothing this way. Saw our tugboat. Starting due west for three minutes," radios Dad. His voice is breaking up, and I have trouble making his words out.

"Affirmative," I reply.

A rogue wave splashes over the Zodiac, and I turn on the little electric pump to bail out the water. I check the weather computer to see how Baker is doing.

Not good. The storm is starting to head up the Florida coast. In a few hours, we'll have to bring the *Fool* into port or else sail somewhere safe and try to ride it out.

We've outrun storms before, going up the coast. Sometimes that backfires when the storm keeps going and you realize that there's no place left to go except Nova Scotia.

"Going due north," says Dad.

"Affirmative."

This will put him three minutes west of the Zodiac. I'd use starboard or port, but I'm being flung around so much my only point of reference is the distant glow of the coastal cities to the west.

The satellite phone starts to ring.

"Hello?"

"It may be nothing, but I thought I saw the *Vader* again," says George.

"Damn it."

"That's not all. I have your dad's scanner set to search, looking for anyone talking out here. I picked up a half second of chatter."

"You mean like another boat?" I reply.

"Yeah. I think the *Vader* was talking to someone."

I look around the Zodiac, straining to see over the waves.

"Where does your dad keep the weapons?"

I tell him where to find the shotgun. George already had his pistol on board, but an extra gun isn't a bad idea. I look around the raft and wish I'd brought one as well. I didn't even pack a speargun.

I get ready to call down to Dad to tell him we need to go, only to be interrupted by him calling to me.

"Found it."

CHAPTER FIFTY-THREE

Bulkhead

"It's bigger than the blueprints. Longer. More hydrodynamic," Dad says over the underwater radio, his voice barely audible.

"We have a problem. George says he may have seen the *Vader*, and he thinks there's another boat out here. And the storm is getting worse," I explain.

"Of course. Stand by. Let me check this out."

Several tense minutes go by as I wait for Dad to check back in. I hear a couple of bursts of static and respond to him to repeat that. All I hear are the same unintelligible words.

As long as Dad's saying something, I assume he's okay.

It's a dangerous assumption, but I have little choice. I'm ready to dive in and get him if the need arises. My tank is already set up and by my feet.

I'm at the end of my patience when he speaks again.

"Coming up."

A few minutes later, Dad bubbles up from the churning sea. It's a struggle to get him over the edge of the Zodiac, and we almost flip in the process.

After he's caught his breath, he stows his mask in a pouch and shakes his head. "Unbelievable."

"What? Was the cargo in there? What did you find?"

"How's George?"

"I'm still waiting for an update. What about the Kraken?" I demand.

"Winston was a damn genius. It's sleek and camouflaged. I almost missed it. It's more gray than black and has smooth lines, not that angular crap he and I had planned. Of course, we weren't trying to build a stealth boat. The skin is something interesting too. I think it's designed to reflect back a smaller target, maybe look like a fish. We'd have to see what the *Fool*'s sonar says."

"What about the cargo? Could you see inside?" I ask.

"Barely. Raul was smart. He blew a small hole in the starboard saddle tank. That sent it to the bottom. The damn thing's nose is buried under several feet of sediment. It hit it like a missile, but it's otherwise undamaged."

"Maybe he was planning to repair it and drive it out of here?"

"Maybe. I couldn't get inside. The thing is sealed shut with hex bolts. But I was able to get a look through a porthole on the front—about as big as a sand dollar. There are rows of Pelican cases on either side and a small corridor down the middle. Big enough for a person."

I start searching the gear bags in the Zodiac for tools. We brought a basic kit with a hacksaw, bolt cutters, and a torch.

"What are you doing?" asks Dad.

"We have to get that cargo out. We need to find his files."

"Sloan, there're fifty cases in there. The files could be in any one of those." He gestures to the storm. "We can't exactly open them up out here. What if it's a hard drive or something that'll corrode? Not to mention the money."

"We can't leave them," I reply.

"I know. But we need the *Fool* to get them. There's also the fact that I can't get in there without a hex set. Unless you want to cut it open.

Even then, that leaves the problem of what to do about the cases," Dad explains.

"Damn it." I stare back toward where we left the *Fool*.

"Call George. Tell him to bring the *Fool* to us. We'll work quick."

I pick up the sat phone and dial George. The phone makes a connecting tone but doesn't ring. "I think the storm is interfering with the phone."

"Let me see that." Dad takes the phone from my hands and tries to dial. After a moment of frustration, he starts clicking through menus. "I can't even get a satellite lock."

I stare up at the sky. "Can a storm do that?"

"No." He gives the phone back and grabs the GPS unit. "Look." He turns the screen toward me.

The display says it can't acquire a signal.

"What the hell?"

"We're being jammed," Dad says.

"How do you jam a satellite phone or a GPS?" I ask.

"They're not directional. Just blast a more powerful signal." He reaches over the edge of the raft and yanks at the anchor cord, releasing us from the bottom.

"What are you doing?"

"Changing our position." Dad starts the motor up and begins to steer us toward the last location of the *Fool*. "Check your watch. I've got it at half throttle."

I call out every ten seconds. Dad stops us after we're eighty seconds distant from the Kraken and lowers anchor again.

"What was that about?" I ask.

"If they find us before George does, we don't want to make it easy for them. If they look down and see the Kraken, they're not going to need us around."

Damn. He's right. These people play for keeps. If they catch up with us *and* have the submarine, they'll kill us. They already have their own divers.

Dad grabs the transceiver we used to find the Kraken and smashes it with the bolt cutters, then chucks it overboard. "Can't let them have that either."

"Okay. So, what's our plan?" I ask.

"Besides prayer? Hope George finds us fast and we can get the *Fool* loaded before they get to us."

"We're not going to be able to outrun them."

Our raft rolls to the side, and I almost lose my balance. The winds are picking up, and the waves are getting more violent.

"No. But we might be able to lose them."

"They have radar and thermal imaging. Hell, they may even have airplanes spotting for 'em."

"Not in this weather. And they've never had to deal with a McPherson in their natural element," Dad replies.

I try to make myself believe his bluster, but I know it's just his way of keeping his spirits up. I'm glad he's trying.

Dad looks at something over my shoulder, and his expression goes slack.

I spin around. "What is it?"

"I saw something."

I turn around. "The *Fool*?"

He starts digging through the gear packs until he finds a flare gun. "This one didn't have any running lights. Put your tank on and go in."

"What?"

"Just go down a few feet under the chop." He throws a line over. "If it's them, I don't want you in the boat."

"Dad . . ."

"Do it!"

CHAPTER FIFTY-FOUR

BALLAST

I stay on the surface and bob like a cork but keep my distance from the Zodiac until Dad gives me the signal to dive.

I let the air out of my vest and drop down fifteen feet, where I get handled a little more gently by the waves and am in less danger of getting chopped up by a propeller. My lights are off, and I feel extremely vulnerable.

The sound of the waves hitting the raft is what attracts sharks. While I'm just as much of a target going up or down the anchor line, I feel better when I'm moving. I also have my light, but right now it's off. We can't risk someone on the surface seeing a strange glow if I'm supposed to be hidden.

Although it's dark, it's not pitch-black looking up at the surface. The outline of the Zodiac is clear, and I can see it bobbing up and down in the waves.

I hear the other boat approaching before I can see the shadow of its hull about thirty feet away from Dad. My heart races as I wait for him to give me the signal.

One flash for danger. Two for the all clear.

One flash . . .

Two flashes . . .

I kick upward and pop out of the water as George throws a line to Dad from the stern of the *Fool*. He's turned out all the lights and is trying to keep himself from falling over as the waves knock both vessels around.

Dad reaches down and grabs my hand to steady me, then escorts me around the raft and to the dive ladder on the back of the *Fool*. George grabs the back of my tank and lightens my weight as I climb. We pull Dad into the boat and tie off the Zodiac.

Dad turns his eyes to the clouds. "This is getting bad."

"And they're jamming us," adds George.

"How far away are they?" I ask.

He shrugs. "I thought I saw something a couple miles out. I turned off the lights, hoping the weather would make it harder to see the ship. I don't know if it worked. I think we should make a run for it."

"We can't," I reply. "Dad found the Kraken."

"What? Here?"

"About a thousand feet that way," Dad explains from memory, pointing south. "We moved the raft in case they got to us first."

"Can we get the cargo?" asks George.

"I need my tools," Dad replies, trying not to fall as a wave tilts us.

When his sea legs start to give, it's time to worry.

"I can open the hatch and start bringing up the cases. There could be as many as fifty of them. We don't know which have the files," he says. "I suppose we want the ones with the money too."

"You think?"

Dad goes into the boat to gather his tools. I climb up to the bridge and use the night-vision goggles to scan the horizon. George climbs up after me.

Far to the west, I spot a tiny light. "Is that what you saw?"

George takes the goggles from me and looks through them in the same direction. "That's it. I can't see it with the naked eye. So

I'm assuming it's someone with infrared goggles like us, only their illuminator is on."

"As long as they're out there, I'm okay with it," I reply. "We'll have to figure out how to get past them."

"I was thinking about that. I have a crappy plan," he explains. "We find which case has the plans and load them into your little raft with me. You head to port, and I wait a few hours and then head straight into Hobe Sound and beach it."

"That's a horrible plan. We're not going to *last* a few more hours out here. And that Zodiac will be a death trap. Especially . . ." I don't point out that he doesn't have as much ocean experience as Dad or me.

"We could try getting out of range and calling for help," George says. "The problem is, the DEA agents we want to avoid probably have someone on every coast guard boat out here."

"They can't all be bad," I reply.

"No. But I'm sure at this point they've been told you and I have pledged eternal allegiance to ISIS and should be arrested on sight."

"Damn it. Who do we trust?"

"Nobody out here. I have people. Unfortunately, they're not out in this crap."

Dad climbs up to the bridge. "I've got a tool kit ready. I need you to lower me down an extra air cylinder."

"What are you trying?" I ask.

"I've got the salvage balloons. I want to try to raise the nose a bit. Winston may have put a hatch underneath. The saddle tank was ruptured, but the interior was pressurized and still has some air."

"Did you see anyone inside?" asks George.

Dad shakes his head. "There's barely enough room. But air is a good sign."

"To breathe?" asks George.

"It'll make it easier for me to float the thing. Trying to transport fifty cases from down there to here is going to be a challenge," he replies.

"What if we rope them all together?" I ask.

"The current will drag them away. If I can't get the whole thing to float, we'll drag them up one by one."

I do the math in my head. Assuming two minutes per case at best, we'd need a hundred minutes. That's longer than Dad should be down there after the other dive.

"All right. Let's hope that works." I'd insist on going down myself, but Dad knows how Winston's boats work better than I do.

I pilot the *Fool* back to our spot, and George helps Dad into the water. He returns to the bridge once Dad's beneath the waves.

"Your dad is one brave man," says George.

"I think it's equal parts stupid. It runs in the family."

I go back down to the stern and check the anchor line we set for him. A hundred feet below, the crazy bastard is trying to rescue one of the largest sunken treasures ever, even though none of it is his.

I feel like an ass for calling him a pirate and questioning his ethics. I should have known all along what his real priority was—his idiot daughter, who may yet get him killed.

George comes running down the ladder and peers over the port side of the boat. "You see something?"

"What? No." I look around the horizon as the waves slap into us, trying to see into the dark.

George turns from the sea and whispers, "I heard a weird knock."

"Probably driftwood . . ." My words freeze in my mouth as I see a red dot light up on his forehead.

I know it's a laser sight from a gun, but I can't understand how someone could keep it this steady in rough water . . . until I realize it's because they're already on our boat.

CHAPTER FIFTY-FIVE

Tow Rope

I turn and follow George's eyes to the space just above the bridge where the sniper is crouched. All we can see is his dark silhouette against the night sky. It would seem the renegade SEALs found us.

The boat rocks as more waves slap into the side. A gruff voice shouts from behind us, "Take your sidearm out and throw it into the water."

Shit. I catch a glimpse behind me; two more frogmen have climbed up the dive platform. Christ, they're good.

Both are wearing face masks with compact rebreathers and all-black dive suits. Their chests and legs are covered in pouches and tools.

George doesn't move. His hands stay at his side. "Get the fuck off our boat."

Damn, even under pressure he still acts the alpha.

The diver directly behind him pushes a Sig Sauer P226 into the back of his skull. "Drop the gun."

"You can shove that all the way to my tonsils, but I'm not giving up my weapon."

The red dot moves from his forehead to mine. "Mario up there is going to count to three," says the diver behind George.

A wave hits the boat, and George and I stumble while the ex-SEALs don't move. They must have some special deck shoes, or amazing balance.

The pitch of the boat sends a weight belt gliding across the deck to stop a foot away from me. I look to George.

"Fine," says George. He takes the gun from his hip, grasps it by the muzzle, and tosses it starboard while staring straight ahead.

I realize the gun is heading for our raft and decide to distract them. "This is ridiculous. We're all on the same side." I step forward as I say this, raising my hands.

A powerful hand grabs me by the back of my neck, and a gun muzzle pokes behind my ear. "One more inch and I shoot."

"I don't think they're on our side," says George.

"No shit," mutters the diver behind him.

The *Fortune's Fool* is rocked by a massive wave, and George and I are thrown to starboard. The divers behind us even have to brace themselves against the rail to keep from falling.

The lead diver keeps his compact rifle on us. "*Sit down!* Link, cuff 'em."

George and I follow his order—partially because it's easier than standing. The other diver, Link, pulls plastic zip cuffs from a pouch and binds our wrists.

"Anybody inside the boat?" asks the third diver as he aims his gun into the cabin.

"No," I reply.

"You got 'em covered?" he asks the leader.

As if in response, the red dot bounces from my chest to George's, and the divers enter the cabin and start sweeping for people. It's not a large boat and only takes a minute—although I can think of four hidden compartments they almost surely missed.

"What did you find down there?" the leader asks.

"Nothing," I reply. I'm still wearing my dive suit, so there's no point insisting that I wasn't down there. Right now, my main concern is Dad. He could come back to the surface at any moment.

Mario, the original sniper and team leader, drops down onto the deck from the bridge with the grace of a gymnast. He can't be more than five and a half feet tall.

"Hey, Sonic," he says to the third SEAL, "I saw a glow stick on the bowline."

Sonic? Mario? Christ. We've been taken hostage by a group of psychopath gamers.

"Do you still have a diver in the water?" the leader asks me.

"No."

"Nice try," says a diver.

"Take out their VHF," Mario tells Sonic.

Sonic turns and fires at the radio on the helm. Although the sound is suppressed, the noise still hurts my ears, and I instinctively duck. My gaze lands on a fish knife Dad keeps tucked under the railing.

I glance at George and let my eyes dart back to the knife, letting him know something's there. He twitches, signaling he understands. I think.

Mario puts his gun to my head. "Sit up and tell me who's down there."

I refuse to answer.

Smack! I see stars as he slaps the side of my face, hard. George bolts upright but gets a solid kick in the shoulder from Link. He falls back, making a loud groan.

"Next time you do that, I put a bullet in her," says Mario. The barrel of his gun goes back to my head. "Who and what is down there?"

"We sent two Broward County deputies down there," says George. "Someone gave us this GPS coordinate; it's the fifth one we checked. So far, it's bullshit. We got had."

"Sonic, watch them," says Mario. "Link, you're with me."

The two of them step to the edge of the dive platform and jump into the ocean. They vanish beneath the waves, and Sonic takes a seat in the captain's chair with his gun trained on us.

George whispers to me, "These men are killers."

I know. And right now, they're on their way to get my father. When they see the Kraken, they'll have no use for us.

My dive gear's in a locker by Sonic's feet. There's no way I can get him to move an inch, much less get the upper hand.

We hit a wave from the port side, and George and I roll to the side. I can hear him groan as his aching shoulder strikes the hull.

Sonic braces himself against the impact, and his gun points away from us for a moment.

Sometimes it's all about instinct. It's the only way you survive situations like this. George knows this too.

"We can't stay here like this," he whispers, putting his body between Sonic and me. "They only need to keep one of us alive until they find it."

A huge wave rocks us.

Now, Sloan.

I fall toward the bait knife, pull it from its sheath, and stick a toe in the weight belt, sliding it toward me.

Sonic fires his gun, and the bullet hits the deck in front of me.

"Don't hit the fuel tank, asshole!" George screams.

I try to distract the SEAL to give George a chance. I bounce to my feet, grab the weight belt, and run along the gunwale for the bow of the boat.

Sonic fires behind me, and I hear the windshield break. I don't look back. Hopefully this will give George enough of a distraction to do something if he can. Right now, my main concern is one hundred feet below me.

My hands are still bound, and I don't have my scuba tanks. I don't have my fins. I don't even have my mask.

All I have is a knife, thirty pounds of weight, and one breath of air . . .

I jump anyway.

CHAPTER FIFTY-SIX

Amphibian

My earliest memory is the water. It was actually my mom calling me to step into the ocean. She stood there in her blue bikini, a sleek giant, the surf surging past her ankles as she beckoned me closer.

It wasn't the water that scared me. It was the way the wet sand shifted beneath my feet. The ground had been so sturdy until then; now it couldn't be trusted. Under the onslaught of a wave, it literally slipped away beneath your feet.

"Sloan . . . come on, sweetheart," she called to me.

But it wasn't her soothing voice that made me step in.

It was the giggling of my brothers as Dad tossed one of them into the water, farther out, much farther.

They were out where the waves came rolling in as whitecaps, bounding around like sea creatures playing in the surf.

"Come on, Sloany, it's okay," Mom said.

Robbie jumped up on Dad's back and wrapped his arms around his neck. It was just play, but I didn't know that at the time.

I was two.

Dad was in trouble.

I ran.

I ran past Mom.

I dived into the waves.

I swam.

I couldn't see my mother, but I heard her calling to me. She was too stunned to chase after me. I must have seemed possessed.

I fought the current.

I tried to paddle through waves taller than me.

I swam as hard as my tiny body could.

Daddy needed me.

The current pushed me under. I kept swimming.

Mom's muffled cries sounded so far away.

I paddled. I kicked. When my head poked above the waves, I breathed.

They say that swimming is instinctual for humans—that it taps into some ancestral ability. I believe this.

I caught a glimpse of Dad staring in my direction, trying to understand why Mom was yelling. Part of me knew he was no longer in danger, but I kept swimming. My brain only understood one purpose.

The waves kept throwing me around, and at some point my arms tired.

Just when I was ready to cry for Mom, powerful hands lifted me out of the water. I saw the bright sun making a halo around Dad's head.

I giggled.

He laughed.

Mom waded her way over to us as Dad put me up on his shoulders. I didn't understand the look in her eyes then, but I understand it now—I was Daddy's little girl. I was a sea creature like him. I wasn't an interloper like Mom, who kept close to the shore. The water was my home.

It was where I belonged.

But it wasn't where I wanted to die.

And it's not where Dad is going to die either.

Not today.

The weight belt I'm grasping is pulling me down. The knife is in my right hand.

Ten feet.

I slide the blade between the plasticuffs and my wrist, nicking the skin slightly. I twist the handle and cut the thin binding.

My arms free as the weight belt pulls my left hand toward the bottom.

Twenty feet. I'm at two atmospheres and feel the pressure in my ears.

The bottom is a dark abyss. The divers lie somewhere below me.

Thirty feet. My lungs feel the crush of the ocean. You're never supposed to hold your breath when you scuba dive—but this is free diving, and the physics are different.

Forty feet. My ears are really hurting. I didn't equalize the pressure. I might blow out an eardrum.

Fifty feet. The sea is crushing my body like a can as the air in my lungs begins to compress.

It's only pain.

Sixty feet. I see the glimmer of a flashlight on the bottom.

Dad.

I'm coming.

A dark shape glides between the light and me.

At first I think it's a shark, but then I realize it's worse.

Seventy feet. The pressure at this depth is so intense my skull feels like it's about to implode.

I can see the outline of two divers.

They're spreading out so one can meet Dad from the front while the other sneaks up in the shadows from behind.

The one descending in the darkness has his knife drawn. He's going to kill my father.

Eighty feet. My joints hurt. My sinuses are about to collapse. I've never gone this deep this fast before.

Free divers spend years training their bodies for this kind of abuse. Their joints have cartilage and deposits built up over hundreds of dives and recoveries.

I had eight seconds to prepare for this.

Ninety feet. Everything aches.

The shadow diver's right below me.

He's wearing body armor and has a knife and gun.

All I have is speed and surprise.

Sometimes that's enough.

CHAPTER FIFTY-SEVEN

Cleat

The weight belt hits the back of the shadow diver's head. Not enough to knock him out, but enough to stun him.

He probably thinks he's been attacked by a shark.

I make him wish he had. A shark would take one bite and let him go. I'm taking him out of the picture.

I let go of the belt, grab the back of his pack, and start slashing at the hoses going to his regulator, then stab his vest, puncturing the thick rubber, making it impossible for him to inflate it and use it for an air supply.

My blade slides through his vest, and I accidentally stab him in the shoulder. Blood begins oozing from the wound. His knife hand swings back at me, and we roll in the water.

His gear is streamlined for combat, but I'm even sleeker.

I rip his mask from his face, which is instantly hidden behind a mass of bubbles.

He's trying to control the hoses, but it won't make a difference. I cut them all. They writhe around like an angry hydra as the air escapes.

I see the gun strapped to his chest breather and pull it free. His arm shoots through the water and grabs my wrist. His knife swipes at my wrist, almost catching it. Almost.

I kick his chest with both feet and slide away. My back hits the Kraken, and I roll over.

The other diver is coming at me, his knife pointed at my face.

BANG!

The gun I took from the other diver is loud underwater, and I feel the concussion in my chest.

The bullet hits his chest breather.

I fire again, and a jet of bubbles shoots out, blocking the second diver's face.

The knife arm comes at me, and I slip out of the way, but he turns fast. His gun is drawn now, and the muzzle's swinging toward my body.

BANG!

He fires and misses. I think.

I pull myself over the Kraken and under the far wing.

Before the diver can reach me, I move to the front of the submarine and catch a glimpse of the diver I cut swimming fast for the surface.

He's going to get the bends real bad. But he doesn't have a choice. It's that or dying.

I can no longer ignore the screaming in my lungs.

BANG! The other diver fires at me, and I shoot back.

I have no idea how effective these bullets are underwater, but I'm pretty sure at a yard or so they're not fun.

I swim farther out of range, my lungs ready to tear apart.

He's flattened out over the Kraken, taking aim at me, waiting for me to come closer.

Oh god. I'm about ready to pass out.

I either have to head for the surface or think of something fast.

Everything goes white as something incredibly bright lights up the seafloor like the sun.

I have to cover my eyes. The diver turns, and I hear something like a scream.

When I glance up a moment later, I see his body swimming for the surface, a cloud of blood billowing from his leg trailing behind.

Dad is hovering over the edge of the Kraken, turning off the underwater torch he used to burn the diver. From the amount of blood entering the ocean, the burn went deep. So deep it didn't cauterize.

Damn, that's harsh.

Dad swims over to me, and I start furiously making hand gestures in our underwater sign language.

He puts a finger to his mouth, signaling me to be quiet. All of a sudden, I'm thirteen, and we're hiding from an aggressive bull shark off Bimini.

Dad holds up his hand and removes his regulator from his mouth and pushes it toward me.

Breathe, Sloan. Breathe, he's telling me.

I take a deep breath and let my lungs fill up with air. He places his spare in his mouth, then takes a small underwater clipboard from his pouch and writes a question mark on it.

I take the board and the pen and draw a crude picture of the *Fool* with one man aiming a gun at another and two stick figures swimming to the surface.

I write "George" under the man at gunpoint.

Dad nods and looks up. He takes the board from me and erases the picture, then writes, "We have to save him."

I give Dad a thumbs-up, indicating we should surface. He shakes his head and points to the Kraken, then writes "Fixed" on the board.

I take another breath of air and swim over to the rear of the submarine, where Dad had been working. A small hatch, not much bigger than a large doggie door, hangs open underneath.

I stick my head inside and emerge in a tiny compartment filled with air. The interior area is no wider than my shoulders and lined with

Pelican cases. At the far end is the porthole Dad peered through. Below that is a small control stick and a display panel.

Dad swims underneath and pokes his head into the compartment.

"How much air?" I ask him, indicating the sub's interior. I hear a small hiss in the background.

He takes the regulator from his mouth. "Winston put in a rebreather. One oxygen cylinder is good for at least twelve hours. The other one seems to be defective." He points to the ceiling, where a small aluminum plate is riveted to the hull. "All I had to do was put that patch there and repressurize. Everything else is fine."

"Can we take it to the surface?" I ask.

"You can. Just do your safety stops. The depth gauge will tell you where you're at."

"We need to get back before they do something to George. The divers may be badly hurt, but the guy up there isn't."

"What do you need me to do?" asks Dad.

CHAPTER FIFTY-EIGHT

BREAKER

The Kraken glides more smoothly than I expected. I've used underwater vehicles before, but they all felt like slow-motion versions of land craft. This is different. Winston designed an extremely low profile that lets it cut through the water like a knife.

Wedged between the cases in a crouch with no seat doesn't make for the most comfortable ride, but it works well enough. Going full throttle dislodged the sub from the sand and shot the sub forward, almost hitting Dad, who was guiding me.

Now that I have it under control, I'm tilting the control stick to the side and spiraling up toward the surface.

Dad follows along, swimming up the center of my corkscrew. We want to hurry, but going too fast could lead to serious problems as air expands in our tissue.

I finally surface near the bow of *Fortune's Fool* and am immediately tossed to the side and battered in the heavy surf.

I pull myself backward through the confined space of my minivessel and open the bottom hatch. Water splashes in as the sub tilts and air escapes. The Kraken could sink again, but I'm not worried about that right now.

I dive into the water and swim for the bowline. My glow stick is still dangling where I left it. About twenty feet away, I catch the outline of a small craft. This must have been what the divers used to sneak up on us.

Now we'll see if I can play the boarding game as well.

I pop my head out of the water and spot a small ladder hanging over the bow of the *Fool*. It appears to have been attached to a cleat on our boat. That must be how Mario got the drop on us.

I grab the bottom rung and start to climb the ladder. It's a challenge in the waves. Half the time you're being tilted up into the air, the rest you're underwater.

I finally reach the top and slide myself onto the bow. The ocean tries to toss me back in, but I hold fast to handholds I improvise from the hatches and navigation lights.

When I pull myself up to the bridge, I can see through the cracked windshield.

Sonic has George flat on his stomach with the gun pointed at his head while his other hand uses the gaffing pole to help one of the divers, who's dragging the third.

Blood is trickling from George's head across the wet deck.

Damn it.

I slide onto the bridge, above and behind Sonic. I could shoot him from here, but for some reason, I can't bring myself to do that. My hand falls on the fire extinguisher behind the captain's chair.

I slip it from its mount and take the ladder down to the stern.

One of the injured divers sees me and calls to Sonic.

But not fast enough.

I smack the metal cylinder across his head so hard he falls backward and cracks it again on the railing.

Mario raises his gun at me. I fire the extinguisher at him, then hurl the heavy device in his direction.

When the cloud clears, Dad has a knife to the unconscious Sonic's throat and his gun in hand. I take it and toss his knife into the ocean.

George rolls over and sits up. There's a gash on his scalp and blood all over his shoulder.

I need to help my father. "Can you manage?"

"I'll hold."

I cut George's plasticuffs and hand him the gun I liberated from one of the SEALs on the sea bottom. "Keep your eye on him."

Signaling to my father, I run to the rope attached to our Zodiac and drag the raft alongside the boat. George's gun glints in the light on the bottom of the craft. I reach down and recover it.

Good thing I saw that. It could have been bad, considering what I have planned.

I pull the Zodiac alongside the *Fool* and toward Dad. "Tell them to get in!" I shout over the wind.

I yank the fuel line from the engine and toss it into the water.

Dad understands what I'm doing and pushes Mario and Link toward the raft.

He backs off and lets the slightly less injured Link climb over and help Mario aboard the Zodiac.

"This man needs medical attention!" Link shouts. "We both need oxygen!"

Pure oxygen is how you prevent decompression sickness. We have a cylinder aboard the *Fortune's Fool*, but they're not getting it.

Dad pulls himself over to the dive platform and pulls himself up. I motion to Sonic's slumped body. "Help me out."

We roll him over the edge and into the Zodiac. George has pulled himself up into a standing position and has the rifle aimed down at them. "What's your plan?"

I feed some line out, letting the current drag the Zodiac away, giving us some distance. "Keep them back there. Tow 'em in to shore."

George shakes his head. He goes over to the cleat where the line to the raft is fastened and unties the rope. "We can't have them back there. They'll kill us first chance."

I turn to Dad. He nods. "Rock and a hard place. Besides, they'll have a rescue beacon on them."

That makes me feel slightly better as I watch them vanish behind a wave. Just because they're cold-blooded killers doesn't mean I have to be one too.

Our boat shakes as something metallic hits the hull.

"What's that?" asks George.

"The Kraken. Damn." I run to the front of the boat and dive in with another line to stabilize the submarine before it does serious damage to both vessels.

CHAPTER FIFTY-NINE

JETTY

The Kraken gets pulled into an upswell and starts to list to starboard, raising the port winglet out of the water. A tall wave crashes down on the hull like a giant's fist, and I'm slammed into the Pelican cases, adding another bruise to my shoulder.

I've got to learn how to control this thing better. The trouble is, I'm trying to keep it far enough below the waves not to get tossed around in the surf while also trying to avoid hitting the bottom or, worse, getting trapped on a sandbar.

The storm is having its way with the ocean, sending wild waves back and forth and surging across the Florida coast. The last time we had something like this, they were using bulldozers for weeks to clean up the sand on A1A.

The stern camera view is only worth looking at when I'm above the waves. The last one tossed me high enough to get a glance behind me. The lights of the *Fortune's Fool* were barely visible at the outer edge. I pray our little gambit works.

While we cast our would-be murderers adrift, the *Vader* is still out there, lurking beyond our field of view.

They tried sending ex-SEALs to take over our vessel. Now they have to know it didn't work. With the *Fool* on the move, that leaves two options—rescue their men, who have undoubtedly signaled them, or chase the *Fool.*

Dad's strategy, based upon a lifetime at sea and reading Patrick O'Brian novels, was a ploy to get the Kraken safely away from K-Group while also avoiding another kill team.

As soon as I tied the Kraken to the stern and swam back up onto the dive platform, Dad told me I had to pilot into the harbor alone.

"They're going to board us," he explained. "If they find the Kraken, we're all dead."

"We could sink its payload," I replied.

"It'll take them two minutes to locate it with their instruments." He looked out into the distance where we'd sent the divers. "Even if they take the time to retrieve the cases, they could still beat us to shore. Especially if we're hauling the sub."

"I can't *leave* you here."

Stinging rain pelted our faces, and the *Fool* rocked so hard we had to brace ourselves on the rail.

"We have a plan," said George.

I was sure the two of them had talked this over while I was bringing the Kraken aft. I didn't like the idea of them making decisions without me—especially ones dedicated to putting my safety first . . . if piloting an untested undersea vehicle in a tropical gale could ever be called "safe."

"Once you're on the way, we're going to haul ass for shore and call the coast guard for help," George explained.

"But the *Vader*'s still jamming us," I replied.

"They'll have to turn it off closer to shore," Dad said. "Either way, we'll start sending up flares."

"What if they catch you?" I asked.

George answered, "As long as we don't have the money or the files, they won't risk killing us and losing any chance of recovering them. If we stay free, the coast guard will help us in to port and either impound us or let us go. What matters is you getting the Kraken somewhere safe."

Somewhere safe. We still hadn't figured out where that was. Dad told me I should go with my gut. Worse case, ride the surge across Fort Lauderdale beach and park it in front of the tourist bar that always stays open during storms.

I check my compass, the one instrument I can reasonably trust as I'm bounced above and below the waves, and make sure my heading remains steady.

My only goal at this point is to get out of range of the *Vader*'s jammer and close enough to shore to use my cell phone. If I can get a signal, I can call for help—that is, send help to Dad and George.

I steer the Kraken down and glide over the ocean floor, watching the depth gauge. It'll indicate my distance from the seafloor but won't warn me about anything in front of the craft. Winston added some kind of sonar to the craft that could help, but I'm not sure how to read the display. I'm left using the porthole to keep an eye out for anything about to slam into me.

The craft bounces, and I get a view of lights along the shore. That would be the city of Jupiter. Okay, where exactly could I go?

I know there's a big boat ramp a mile or so past the Intracoastal. There're also a bunch of nice hotels with marinas for luxury boats.

Those are viable, but they won't help me keep this submarine on the down low. I'd likely be swarmed by police and covert K-Group operatives in no time. While I could slip away without the Kraken, that would mean leaving Bonaventure's evidence behind.

Jupiter . . . *Keep thinking.* What else? Why is something buzzing in the back of my mind?

Blue Ocean Marina. It's near there . . . Why am I remembering that?

Oh snap. Run's buddy owns the place. They have a lift and a huge warehouse where they store boats. It would be ideal for hiding the Kraken.

I bring the nose of the sub up and breach the surface. The vessel's belly slams down into the water, and I bump my head into the porthole.

Pain can wait. I take out my phone and check for signal.

One bar.

Good enough.

I dial the only number I can think of.

"Hey! Are you okay? We're worried sick," Run answers in a near shout.

"I'm in a stealth submarine off Jupiter Beach. Dad's aboard *Fortune's Fool* and needs help right away before a team of rogue ex-SEALs kills him and George."

To Run's credit, he doesn't miss a beat.

"What can I do to help?"

CHAPTER SIXTY

GUNWALE

Tropical Storm Baker is raining billions of gallons of water into the Everglades and the streets of Jupiter, causing a massive current of water to flow through the inlet and out into the ocean, which makes navigating the Kraken underwater next to impossible.

The surge is so powerful the craft begins to get dragged backward and almost smashes into a seawall until I realize that piloting it close to the surface, limiting the amount of drag, is the only way I'm going to keep it going upstream.

The battery gauges are flashing, warning that the drain is too high and I'm going to be drifting soon. I already tried to start the engine that recharges the batteries but gave up when I couldn't figure out Winston's controls.

At the moment, I'm cruising through the inlet, exposed for anyone to see. Thankfully it's dark out, and no sensible person would be on the water right now.

I bring the Kraken around the next bend, trying to navigate from memory. When the tall metal warehouse for Blue Ocean Marina comes into view, I feel a wave of relief.

A smile spreads across my face when I see Run standing out in the rain by the ramp next to a boat trailer, his black polo shirt drenched and his tan legs poking out from equally soaked shorts.

There's something about the way he seems immune to the forces of nature that makes me feel at ease.

At first he doesn't see me, then an expression of bewilderment crosses his face. The Kraken is a strange sight. The best description I can think of is that it resembles a stubby stealth bomber about to sink.

His shock only lasts a second before he grabs a hook from the winch on his boat trailer and wades out into the rushing current.

I aim the Kraken at the ramp and gun the motors, afraid that the current will broadside me and send me downstream with dead batteries.

The craft lurches forward, and Run races to meet the nose. He peers in through the porthole and smiles when he sees my face.

The hook snaps shut, and Run hurries back to the winch to start the motor. My sub swings away from the ramp, then gets yanked back as the trailer pulls me in like a tractor beam.

As soon as it's on the skids, I pop the loading hatch on the top and slide down the winglet, taking a breath of fresh, albeit humid, air.

"Dad and George?" I ask.

"The radio said a coast guard boat caught up with them. They're being towed into Palm Beach." Run stares at the Kraken. "What the hell is this?"

"Narco sub. Right now there's a few hundred million inside here. We need to get it inside. Fast."

He shakes his head in disbelief. "Nothing is ever easy with you McPhersons."

I help him secure the Kraken to the boat trailer. Run hops in and pulls the truck through the open door of the warehouse. I stand to the side, guiding him, because the Kraken is so wide.

Once we're inside, Run bolts from the truck and presses the button that closes the door to the marina. We both stare out into the storm as it closes, making sure we weren't observed.

"Kevin sent everyone home," Run explains, "but the building should survive a category five. In theory."

Five-story metal racks holding almost a hundred boats line the walls. Most of them are in the twenty- to forty-foot range. A few sixty-footers rest on the floor around us.

An absurdly tall forklift is parked near the office, and a huge overhead crane dangles almost exactly over the Kraken.

Rain is pelting down hard on the metal roof, and the wind howls all around, yet the enormous space feels safe. For the first time in my life, I'm glad to be back on land.

"Mom!" Jackie's voice echoes across the interior as she comes running toward me from the front office.

Skinny arms embrace me, and I turn to Run with an accusing tone. "Why'd you bring her here?"

"What was I supposed to do? Gunther had to go. I couldn't leave her with my mother."

"There are people out to kill me." I squeeze Jackie's head into my chest. "They almost did."

"Tell me what to do," says Run.

I want to yell, *I've done all I can! You tell me what to do now.* But that's not how it works. I'm the one with the gun and the badge. It's my responsibility and my call.

"You did the right thing," I say. "How are you doing, Fish Face?"

Jackie has a worried look. "Who's trying to hurt you?"

"Renegade intelligence operatives who have taken over the illegal narcotics trade."

She stares at me, trying to decide if I'm joking or not. "Why are you wearing a wet suit?"

"I had to use it to get this." I point to the Kraken.

Jackie turns and for the first time notices something other than me. "Holy shit!"

I exchange glances with Run. We have bigger problems to deal with than our daughter's language.

"We may need a place to hide," I tell Jackie, then notice a ladder that leads to the second level of boats. "I want you to be super careful and go up there and see if there's a cabin we can hide in if we have to."

This will keep her occupied for a while and could be helpful if things get bad.

Jackie runs to the ladder and scampers up it like a monkey.

Run glides a hand along the Kraken. "What are we doing with this?"

"There are fifty Pelican cases in there with half a billion dollars. Inside one of them are files that Jason Bonaventure hid in case the shit hit the fan. Well, it's raining shit now, and we need to find those files before the people who are after me figure out we're here."

"And the half-billion dollars?" he asks.

"Not important right now. We need the files. They may be the only way we get out of here alive."

CHAPTER SIXTY-ONE

SKIFF

Four hours later the sun is out, though hidden behind storm clouds, and fifty Pelican cases are spread across the floor of the warehouse like split clams. The money, tightly wrapped hundreds in hundred-thousand-dollar bundles, is laid out in rows.

Jackie is watching us in wide-eyed wonder from above. Adults are mysterious enough in so many mundane ways; I can only imagine what she's thinking right now.

Run taps the inside of another case with the handle of a screwdriver. "Nothing here either."

We've searched all the obvious places and found zero documents. We're about to split apart the money packs and toss the cash into garbage bags.

"Nothing on the sub?" he asks again.

"This is everything," I reply.

The inside of the Kraken is pretty spartan. Other than the battery compartment and the motors, there's no sealed-off compartment that we can find. Winston made sure every square inch was utilized.

"Can I help?" asks Jackie.

"Stay up there, Sunfish," Run replies. "Go check the Sea Ray at the end. Okay?"

"I hate busywork," Jackie grumbles as she rises from her roost.

"Me too," says Run. "Me too."

"It has to be someplace convenient, right?" I ask.

"Your guess is as good as mine. Better, actually. Was Bonaventure always going to be on the receiving end?"

I pick up a stack of bills and flex them. "What do you mean?"

"Would he stick those files in the money if there was a chance it could get lost in the shuffle? I'd think he'd want them separate."

"Maybe. He was a launderer and a banker. I don't know how much planning he had time to do. When they served the warrant on his place, he had to act fast to get the money out and away."

"Why not just leave it at the dummy house?" asks Run.

"I think he was planning on fleeing the country. When the sabotaged Kraken didn't meet up with the *Morning Sun*, Bonaventure had to stick around."

BANG! BANG! BANG! I nearly jump out of my skin at the sound of someone hitting the metal door. Run picks up his shotgun from its resting place, and I draw my pistol from the fold of my wet suit at my waist. I motion for him to stand back as I approach the door.

Run ducks down behind the boat trailer, and I keep to the shadows as I walk to the side door where we heard the banging.

BANG! BANG! BANG!

I put my eye to a peephole in the door and see George and my father standing outside in the downpour.

"Took you long enough," says Dad as he steps inside and greets me with a hug.

George gives me a lopsided grin. His shirt is cut away, revealing a bandage that matches the one on his head. He has a hospital admission bracelet around his wrist.

"Did you just bust out?"

"People die in hospitals," he replies, then lets out a whistle when he sees the money. "Why didn't you two just take this and run?"

"I've been asking her the same thing," says Run, greeting them.

"Grandpa!" Jackie shouts from above.

"Hey, Princess," he calls up to her.

I point to the Pelican cases. "We've gone through everything. Tons of money but no sign of Bonaventure's files. I'm beginning to think he didn't actually have any."

"I'd say we ask him, but we can't. He was found floating down a canal an hour ago," George says.

"What? Not because of us? Is it?" My stomach twists at the thought.

"His days were numbered," says George. "He was not a nice man. I'm guessing K-Group decided the files weren't under his control and got rid of him."

"Damn it. And we're at a dead end here."

"Were you hoping for a box that said *secret files*?" asks George. "Think about it."

"Well, we can't find them. Maybe they're somewhere else."

"Do you know how many times I've been on busts and someone says, 'We've looked everywhere,' only to find a suspect hidden under a pile of laundry or a stash inside a used-diaper bin? It's here," George says flatly.

"Is that intuition?" asks Run.

"It's experience, son. Experience."

"Okay," I say. "What does your experience tell you now?"

Dad interrupts, "We need to disassemble the Kraken. Winston could have had a compartment inside there."

"We checked," Run replies. "But by all means, have a look."

"I knew Winston for twenty years. I know his tricks. I think." Dad picks up a tool belt from the floor and climbs into the sub.

A minute later we can hear the sound of parts falling and clanging on the sub's deck. Run sticks his head inside and starts pulling the loose components out and laying them on the ground.

George and I inspect the panels, pumps, displays, and other parts as Dad dismantles them and Run delivers them to us.

An hour later the insides of the Kraken are spilled across the floor like the entrails of a mechanical fish.

George and I are unscrewing and inspecting the insides of all the battery packs. Dad is checking the electronics in case the files are stored digitally.

Run crosses his arms and stares at the Kraken. "The problem is, they could literally be anywhere." He flicks a temperature gauge. "A microchip could fit under a washer, and we wouldn't know."

"Bonaventure would want hard copies of the most important stuff," says George. "Ledgers, cashed checks, that kind of thing."

"I don't see where he could fit all that," I reply.

The wind gets stronger, and the whole building shakes. I call up to Jackie, "What's the weather report, sweetheart?"

She's sitting on the stern of a Chris-Craft on the third level. "I don't know. I can't get any signal."

"Probably the storm," says Run.

George and I look at each other and pull out our phones. Mine shows full signal, but when I try to make a call, it doesn't even ring.

"You too?" I ask George.

He nods. "Hey, Jacobs," he says, using Run's last name. "You got a VHF radio?"

"There's one in the truck." Run leans inside and turns it on. A clicking sound fills the air. "What the hell is that?" he asks before turning it off.

"We're being jammed," I reply. "They know we're here."

George nods to Run. "You take the front. I'll take the back."

"We have a landline back there. You can try calling out."

"What should I do?" I ask.

George points to the pile of parts. "You and your dad find the files. *Fast.* We have to assume Bonaventure told them where to look."

Dad starts to tap the hull of the Kraken with a wrench, listening for hollow compartments. I run my hand along it, trying to feel anything abnormal.

We race around the submarine, desperately searching for something, finding nothing.

"See anything?" George shouts to Run, who's watching the front door.

"No. Wait. There's an SUV across the street with a funky antenna."

"That's them. They probably have a search team on their way. Shoot anyone that comes close."

I watch their exchange and almost scream when Jackie grabs my elbow.

"What can I do to help?"

"Go back up there and hide," I reply.

"Ugh." She kicks at a nut on the floor, and it ricochets off one of the sub's many oxygen cylinders.

Dad and I glance up.

"That son of a bitch," Dad whispers.

"What's going on?" asks Solar, still standing by the door.

Dad and I hurry to the oxygen tank. He hits it with his wrench. When a tank loses pressure, it changes its pitch when it's rung. The metal makes a "nearly empty" clang that you never want to hear when diving.

"We may have something . . ." My voice is interrupted by the hissing sound of Dad letting the air out of the tank.

It quickly dies, and Dad pulls a tank-valve tool from his key chain and unscrews the top. "Got a light?"

I aim my phone light into the tank, revealing something sealed in plastic inside.

Bingo.

"Someone's here," shouts Run.

"Someone?" George yells back. "What the hell does that mean?"

CHAPTER SIXTY-TWO
Lagoon

Dad uses a pair of pliers to pull a plastic bag from the cylinder. He hands it to me, then retrieves another. Inside is a sheaf of documents and a thumb drive.

He hands those to me as well, then points to the upper row of boats. "Go there, now."

I take Jackie by the hand. "Come on."

"What's going on with your guy?" George shouts to Run.

"He's at the property line. I think he's talking on a radio."

That sounds ominous. But there's no time to worry about that. I follow Jackie to what she described as her best hiding spot, a midsize boat with a large cabin and deck.

We climb inside, and I spread the documents across the galley table. Jackie takes a seat behind me on the windowsill and watches.

First I find pages of checks made out to different people for amounts ranging from a thousand dollars to tens of thousands. Different company names are shown as account holders on the checks, most sounding like investment firms but with slight differences. There's Vanguard Investments, Fidelity Funds, and a few others of that type.

"Who are those people?" Jackie whispers.

"I don't know . . ." I stop on one check and stare at the payee, Caldwell Thompson. I know that name. He's a drug-court judge.

Holy crap. I flip back through the pages of checks and recognize at least five other judges' names. Two of them are federal.

This is big. This isn't DEA agents taking bribes. Bonaventure owned *judges*. Federal judges. There's even a check to a circuit-court justice.

I flip past the checks and find copies of emails. They're to anonymous accounts, but Bonaventure has annotated them, pointing out who they were sent to. These seem to record transactions with high-level law enforcement officials.

It's not the number of names that stuns me, it's how high up they are. Bonaventure must've worked on these people for years.

A chill washes through me. This is scary. These are powerful people. Trying to bring one down could draw interference from others.

I start photographing the documents with my phone. "Hey, honey, you want to help Mommy?"

Jackie slides them across the table as I snap the photos. After a few seconds, I decide it's quicker simply to shoot a 4K video and make a movie of them all.

After I'm done, I call down to George. "Hey!"

He puts a finger to his lips then points outside.

Oops, they're listening.

"The man's walking to the door," yells Run. "What do I do?"

"Don't let him in, for crying out loud," Dad answers.

"Switch," George says as he runs to the front of the warehouse and Run races to the back.

I look back at the documents. They're practically nuclear. I have to get them out of here. It'd be nice if I could email or text or transfer the video file somewhere safe . . .

"Do you have any signal on your phone?" I ask Jackie.

She shakes her head. Mine is dead too.

I recall Run mentioning the landline in the warehouse office, and an idea straight out of the eighties hits me.

"I need you to stay here. Okay?"

"All right."

I shove the documents back in their bags and take them with me down to the warehouse floor. George is watching the front while Run keeps an eye on the back.

George catches me approaching out of the corner of his eye. He waves for me to stay out of the way of the window.

"Find anything?" he says loudly and meaningfully.

I raise the documents. "No. I don't think it's here," I lie in a loud voice.

K-Group or whoever probably has us bugged. In this day and age, that could be as easy as landing a drone with a microphone on the building.

He waves for me to stay back. I point to the office off to his right and mouth the words *fax machine*.

He nods.

I hurry into the office and set a sheaf of papers into the feeder, then try to think who the hell has a fax machine anymore.

"Our man's approaching," George announces.

BANG! BANG! BANG! The man's fist on the door sounds like gunshots and makes me wince.

George pokes his head in the office and whispers a number to me. I dial it in and get a fax tone. I cringe as the sound fills the air before I can hit the "Mute" button. The machine makes a humming sound and starts to scan the documents.

A voice calls from outside. "Mr. Solar, Ms. McPherson, I was hoping we could talk."

George remains silent. I don't even move, hyperconscious of the sound of the fax machine.

"My name is Owen Landsberg. I'm the deputy director of the Defense Intelligence Agency. I'm unarmed and just want to speak with you."

I hear the sound of George cracking the outer door open. "Care to explain why your people are trying to kill us?"

"First off, they're not ours. We've apprehended several people who have been acting illegally."

This just got interesting.

"Great. Well, have a good day." George shuts and locks the door. A moment later, he pokes his head in to check on me.

The documents are only half done. I point this out to him. He rolls his eyes.

"Mr. Solar, I can guarantee your safety if you cooperate," Landsberg calls from outside the door.

"That sounds like a threat," George tells the DIA man.

"If we wanted to breach the building, we'd be inside already."

Damn this machine. Then again, I'm not sure how faxing this information will get us out of here alive.

"That also sounds like a threat," says George.

"We're not here to threaten you, Ms. McPherson, or her daughter or father."

Jesus, that really sounds like a threat.

"Then why are you jamming our phones?" asks George.

"The storm took out a cell tower," replies Landsberg.

"And the VHF bands too? That's pretty amazing."

There's a long pause from outside, then Landsberg responds, "Certain precautions have to be taken."

The last page slides out of the fax machine. I push them all back into their bags but pocket the thumb drive. We need a way out of this.

I poke my head around the corner and nod to George. He makes a talking mouth with his hand, indicating that he plans to stall them.

"Mr. Solar, I just want to come inside there and see what you've retrieved. I'll be unarmed."

"That sounds like a trick," replies George.

I feel a surge of hopefulness when I realize there may be an easy way out of this stalemate. I wave at George and motion to my wrist: *Keep stalling.*

I run back to the Kraken, where Dad is crouched by the boat trailer with his shotgun. I put a finger to my lips and explain using hand gestures.

Three minutes later I run back to the front, where George is demanding to talk to a lawyer. I whisper into his ear, then hurry back to the Kraken.

Run is already up in the boat with Jackie, ready to shoot. Anything to protect our daughter.

"All right," says George. "You can check it out, but the salvage belongs to the state of Florida."

He lets Landsberg inside, and the man enters, soaking wet from the downpour. His eyes fall on the stacks of money, which Dad and I are counting.

I glance up at the unremarkable-looking man. He's a little shorter than average, late forties, and wearing a drenched raincoat.

"Wow," says Landsberg, eyeing the money. "That's impressive."

"How do we know this guy isn't another one of their assassins?" I ask.

"I assure you, I'm only a desk jockey," says Landsberg. "I'm here to fix a problem."

Although he appears to be impressed by the money, his attention's on the Kraken. He's studying all the parts on the floor.

"Mind if I look inside?" he asks.

"Be our guest," George replies. "But it's stripped clean."

Landsberg leans into the top hatch for a moment, then hops down. "Very interesting." A faint smile appears at the edge of his mouth.

"Here's the deal. I'm going to restore communications here and let local authorities sort out the jurisdictional matters regarding the seized money. We're going to have to impound this vessel, because it utilizes classified technology."

Dad stands. "I found this thing. Unless you have a title, it's mine."

I can tell he's bluffing his ass off, but Landsberg doesn't know that.

"Mr. McPherson, I'm sure we can see about some kind of salvage fee."

"We're not ready to turn this in," I reply. "We've already seized it on behalf of the UIU."

Landsberg pulls a letter from his pocket. "I have a signed warrant."

I bet I can make a good guess at the name of the judge on the warrant, but I keep my mouth shut.

"This is bullshit," says George, continuing our ruse. "We get to search it first."

Landsberg kicks a console on the floor. "It looks like you already did a pretty thorough search. Now, I need to ask you to leave the premises. My team is about to secure this building."

"This is bullshit!" George growls, so convincingly that I almost wonder if he understood what the hell I did.

I drop a stack of money. "George, we don't have a choice. Just call and make sure we're not going to get ambushed."

"I assure you that you're safe," says Landsberg. "Palm Beach Sheriff's Office is being called to the scene. Have a look."

George peers out the window. "I guess we're not getting ambushed . . . yet."

I wave to Jackie and Run to climb down from the boat racks. They join me at my side. Jackie's shaking, but Run has his hand on her shoulder. She reaches out and grabs my fingers.

"What's going on?" whispers Run.

"We're leaving," I tell him.

He turns around and stares at the money, the submarine, and all the pieces. "Just like that?"

"Just like that."

We exit the building and all climb into Run's Expedition. Black SUVs line the road outside the marina, and men in tactical gear stand in the rain watching us.

After we're a mile down the road and heading for I-95, George speaks up. "I think we're good. You get the fax off?"

"Yeah. Where did it go?"

"Governor's office. It may be too hot even for him. If so, Cindy can fix that."

"Why did they let us go?" asks Run.

"He was the cleanup guy," says George. "His job was to contain things. He thought they were contained."

"We sealed the documents back in the oxygen cylinder," I tell Run. "If Bonaventure gave up their location before K-Group killed him, then Landsberg knew exactly where to look. Hopefully he'll assume that if we didn't get into the oxygen tank, then we never found them."

"Right," says George. "He let us go because he thinks what he's looking for is still there."

"Jesus wept," says Dad. "What if he knew we found them?"

"Good question," says George. "Good question. All I know is that we should probably stay clear while this blows up. There are going to be a lot of angry people in South Florida."

"What about all that money?" asks Jackie.

"The state and the federal government will fight over it for years," he replies.

"And your little governor's task force, the UIU?" I ask.

"He has to keep it around now. It's the only way the state can make their claim stick."

"You planned that all along?" I reply.

"Maybe not this exact strategy."

"Just like that? It's over?" asks Dad.

"For us," says George. "Copies of those documents are with the governor now, so that's done. And K-Group has no reason to go after us. No practical reason," he adds, checking the rearview mirror. Then, after a long pause, he sighs and says, "But you never know."

CHAPTER SIXTY-THREE

Bridge

A cold breeze rolls down the street and chills me even as I gulp down my Cuban coffee. George makes a face but stops himself from saying anything. He's learned by now that I'm a stress eater—and drinker.

He offers thanks in perfect Spanish to the barista in the tiny Cuban coffee shop and takes the tiniest of sips from his cup. A furrow wrinkles his forehead, which I've come to learn is *his* sign of stress.

I glance at the stack of coffee-stained folders under his elbow at the counter, but don't ask. We already told the federal prosecutors everything we know. Bonaventure's files led to nearly two dozen indictments, including eight judges.

South Florida news has been all over the case for weeks as new names surface. Bonaventure used K-Group's money and resources to buy influence, divert investigations, and change court decisions with brilliant efficiency.

One of his best techniques was buying off the clerks that handled the procedural work for judges. We found numerous examples of major cases that were dismissed or postponed because a clerk lost evidence or changed filings, creating procedural errors.

All of that takes a back seat in my mind to K-Group—especially DIA Jane, or Katarina Alonzo, which we've come to believe is her real name.

She and her partners were apprehended by federal authorities shortly after we made our deal with the DIA director, but *which* federal authorities and the particulars of her apprehension weren't divulged to us.

The word on the street was that K-Group's activities were limited to a handful of contractors and two DIA supervisors who had gone rogue. Whether this word was spread by the DIA to limit their exposure is anyone's guess. Closed-door congressional hearings are being scheduled, and there's now talk on Capitol Hill about a special prosecutor.

But all of that is politics. We're waiting to find out if Alonzo will be tried for the murders of Winston and Stacey. Federal cases are all fine and dandy, but I want nothing less than to see Alonzo stand trial for homicide in South Florida and face *our* justice system.

"Here she comes," says George, indicating the stout red-haired woman walking toward us, sweating in her suit.

Claudine Bauer is clearly from up north and hasn't figured out how to dress for our climate. The Cincinnati native was given a special appointment to handle this case after it became apparent that an outside attorney might be required to handle it fairly, given the state of things.

"Can I get a real cup of coffee?" she says, giving George's drink a dismissive nod.

"Sure thing," George replies and gives the order to the man behind the counter.

The three-second wait is more than I can handle. "Well?"

"You don't beat around the bush, do you?"

"No," I reply flatly.

She takes a seat on a stool next to me. "I got good news and bad news."

"Damn."

Claudine looks to George. "Did she even hear the good news part?"

"It's never good news when it's phrased that way," I reply.

"Well, Alonzo and two of her colleagues are going to be tried in South Florida."

"Oh," I reply.

"But not for murdering the Millers. There's just not enough evidence right now for that," she explains.

"Are you serious?"

"That's not to say she won't be charged for the deaths . . . just not immediately."

"Then what?"

"Well, kidnapping, for starters."

"Who?"

"You. When she took you to that little DIA workspace, she did it without authorization—at least, the DIA is claiming that's the case."

"What a crock—"

She holds up her hand. "Hear me out. In Florida that can be up to thirty years." She continues quickly, sensing that I'm about to interrupt. "And . . . and Wilkinson, the other guy on your boat—the one you didn't fatally injure—we're charging him with attempted murder. Now between the two of them, one is going to want to make a deal. My bet is it will be him. In the meantime, they've also got the federal conspiracy case to deal with. They aren't going anywhere."

"Neither are Stacey or Winston," I reply.

Claudine takes a drink of her coffee, then sets it back down. "Yeah, I know. But that's the best I can do under the circumstances."

I want to say something, but I don't know what. The attorney's right. It's a convoluted case with many interested parties.

"Sometimes it takes decades. You know how it is, George," she says to him.

He gives her a grunt—which I've learned to interpret as Georgespeak for, "Whatever."

"It'll take us a couple of months to build that case and give her a chance to try to plead. In the meantime, go off with your kid and your boyfriend somewhere and have a vacation. You're going to be up to your ears in courts and deposition rooms soon enough."

I'm about to point out that Run is not my boyfriend and that we'll be staying in separate rooms while we're in Australia, then realize how childish that sounds. I shrug instead as Claudine leaves us.

George and I sit and watch cars passing by for a minute before I finally say, "This sucks."

"Yes, it does," he replies.

"How do you deal with it? You probably went through this dozens of times."

"Yep" is all he says.

After a few moments more of watching cars drive by, he slides his coffee-stained folders across the counter to me.

"What are these?"

"From my filing cabinet. Cold cases. Ones that got away."

"Is this supposed to make me feel better?"

George gives me a funny look. "No. I pulled the ones relating to water. Victims, abandoned vehicles, weapons, that sort of thing."

"You're an odd man." I pick up a folder. Inside are photos of some high school kids.

"They went missing eight years ago. A fisherman found one of their wallets in a canal."

"That's messed up. What happened?" I ask.

George shakes his head. "I don't know. I was thinking maybe we find out."

"We?" I ask.

"Yes, us."

Realization dawns on me. "Wait? Are you saying these are *our* cases? UIU? Is that even still a thing?"

"The governor hasn't shut us down. The state treasurer keeps sending us paychecks. It sounds to me like we're still in the game."

I flip through the other folders and see photos of cars with bullet holes, children's shoes covered in blood, and a dozen other dark images of crimes still seeking justice.

"This is how you deal with it," he replies. "Or at least how I do. You do the best you can, then you find something else that needs your attention. Every now and then, you make a difference. It's not often enough, but in the scheme of things, it tilts the balance a little more toward the good guys."

I weigh the stack of folders. "There's a lot here."

"Not to mention what else someone might throw our way—that is, if you're still in the fight."

I glare at him, letting him know that's a stupid question.

"Can I take these with me on the flight?"

About the Author

Andrew Mayne is the *Wall Street Journal* bestselling author of *The Naturalist*, *Looking Glass*, *Murder Theory*, *Dark Pattern*, and *Angel Killer*; an Edgar Award nominee for *Black Fall* in his Jessica Blackwood series; and the star of Discovery Channel's Shark Week special *Andrew Mayne: Ghost Diver* and A&E's *Don't Trust Andrew Mayne*. He is also a magician who started his first world tour as an illusionist when he was a teenager and went on to work behind the scenes for Penn & Teller, David Blaine, and David Copperfield. Ranked as the fifth bestselling independent author of the year by Amazon UK, Andrew currently hosts the *Weird Things* podcast. For more on him and his work, visit www.AndrewMayne.com.